Scotsman

'A cracking murder mystery'
The Times

'One of Donna Leon's best'
Spectator

Also by Donna Leon

DONNA LEON

A SEA OF TROUBLES

arrow books

Reissued by Arrow Books 2009

5 7 9 10 8 6 4

Copyright © Donna Leon and Diogenes Verlag AG Zurich, 2001

Donna Leon has asserted her right under the Copyright, Designs and Patents
Act, 1988, to be identified as the author of this work.

First published in Great Britain in 2001 by William Heinemann
First published in paperback in 2002 by Arrow Books

This edition published in 2009 by
Arrow Books
The Random House Group Limited
20 Vauxhall Bridge Road, London, SW1V 2SA

www.randomhouse.co.uk

Addresses for companies within The Random House Group Limited can be
found at: www.randomhouse.co.uk/offices.htm

The Random House Group Limited Reg. No. 954009

A CIP catalogue record for this book
is available from the British Library

ISBN 9780099536574

Typeset by SX Composing DTP, Rayleigh, Essex

The Random House Group Limited supports The Forest Stewardship
Council (FSC®), the leading international forest certification organisation.
Our books carrying the FSC label are printed on FSC® certified paper.
FSC is the only forest certification scheme endorsed by the leading
environmental organisations, including Greenpeace. Our
paper procurement policy can be found at
www.randomhouse.co.uk/environment

Printed and bound in Great Britain by Clays Ltd, St Ives PLC

for Rudolf C. Bettschart and Daniel Keel

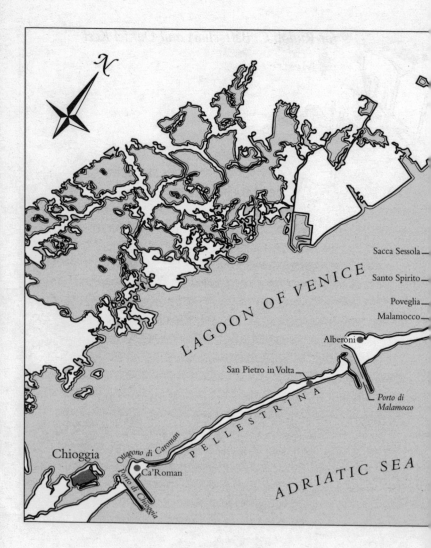

Sacca Sessola

Santo Spirito

Poveglia

Malamocco

LAGOON OF VENICE

Alberoni

San Pietro in Volta

Porto di
Malamocco

PELLESTRINA

Chioggia

Ottagono di Caroman

Ca'Roman

Porto di Chioggia

ADRIATIC SEA

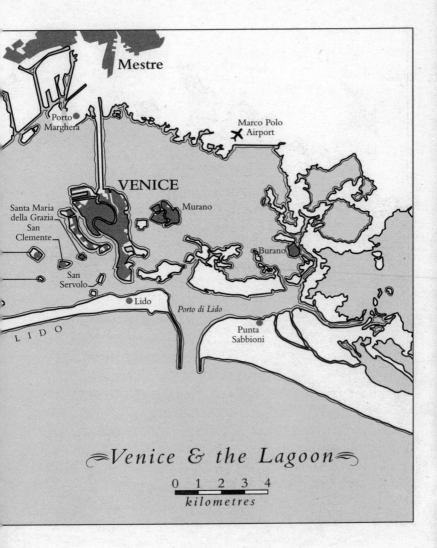

Mestre

Porto
Marghera

Marco Polo
Airport

VENICE

Murano

Santa Maria
della Grazia
San
Clemente

Burano

San
Servolo

Lido

Porto di Lido

L I D O

Punta
Sabbioni

Venice & the Lagoon

0 1 2 3 4
kilometres

Soave sia il vento
Tranquilla sia l'onda
Ed ogni elemento
Benigno risponda
Ai vostri desir.

Gentle be the breeze,
calm be the waves,
and every element
respond kindly
to your desires.

Così fan tutte
Mozart

1

Pellestrina is a long, narrow peninsula of sand that has, over the course of the centuries, been turned into habitable ground. Running north and south from San Pietro in Volta to Ca' Roman, Pellestrina is about ten kilometres long, but never more than a couple of hundred metres wide. To the east, it faces the Adriatic, a sea not known for the sweetness of its temper, but the west side rests in the Lagoon of Venice and is thus protected from wind, storm and wave. The earth is sandy and infertile, so the people of Pellestrina, though they sow, are able to reap little. This makes small difference to them; indeed, most of them would no doubt scoff at the very idea of earning a living, however rich, from the earth, for the people of

Pellestrina have always taken theirs from the sea.

Many stories are told about the men of Pellestrina, the endurance and strength that have been forced upon them in their attempt to wrest a living from the sea. Old people in Venice remember a time when the men of Pellestrina were said to spend the nights, winter or summer, sleeping on the dirt floors of their cottages instead of in their beds so as to more easily push themselves out into the early morning and make the tide that would carry them into the Adriatic and thus to the fish. Like most stories that are told about how much tougher people were in the olden days, this is probably apocryphal. What is true, however, is the fact that most people who hear it, if they are Venetian, believe it, just as they would believe any tale that spoke of the toughness of the men of Pellestrina or of their indifference to pain or suffering, their own or that of others.

During the summer Pellestrina comes alive, as tourists arrive from Venice and its Lido or across from Chioggia on the mainland to eat fresh seafood and drink the crisp white wine, just short of sparkling, that is served in the bars and restaurants. Instead of bread, they are served *bussolai*, hard oval pretzels whose name, perhaps, comes from the *bussola*, or compass, that has the same shape. Along with the *bussolai* there is fish, often so fresh it was still alive when the tourists set out to make the long and inconvenient trip to Pellestrina. As the tourists pulled themselves from their hotel beds, the gills of the *orate* still fought against the alien element, the air; as the tourists filed on to an early morning vaporetto at Rialto, the *sardelle* still thrashed in the nets; as they climbed down from the vaporetto and crossed Piazzale Santa Maria Elisabetta, looking for the bus that would take them to Malamocco and the Alberoni, the *cefalo* was just being hauled out of the sea. The tourists often leave the bus for a while at Malamocco or the Alberoni, have a coffee, then walk on the sandy beach for a while and look at the enormous jetties that stretch out into the waters of the Adriatic in an attempt to prevent the waters from sweeping into the *laguna*.

The fish are all dead by then, though the tourists could not be expected to know that, or much care, so they get back on the bus, sit in it for the short ferry ride across the narrow canal, then continue by bus or on foot down toward Pellestrina and their lunch.

In winter things are vastly different. Too often the wind tears across the Adriatic from the former Yugoslavia, carrying before it rain or light snow, biting into the bones of anyone who tries to stay out in it for any length of time. The crowded restaurants of the summer are closed and will remain that way until late spring, leaving the tourists to fend for and feed themselves.

What remain unchanged, lined up in long rows on the inner side of the thin peninsula, are scores of *vongolari*, the clam-fishing boats that

3

work all year, regardless of tourists, rain, cold and heat, regardless too of all the legends told about the noble, hard-working men of Pellestrina and their constant battle to win a living for their wives and children from the merciless sea. Their names sing out: *Concordia, Serena, Assunta*. They sit there, fat and high-nosed, looking very much like the boats painted in picture books for children. One longs, walking past in the bright summer sun, to reach up and pat them, stroke their noses, as it were, just as one would with a particularly winsome pony or an especially endearing Labrador.

To the unschooled eye the boats all look much the same, with their iron masts and the metal scoop at the prow that protrudes up into the air when the boat is docked. Rectangular and framed, these scoops all have the same grade of what looks like chicken wire strung across them, though it is far stronger than any chicken wire ever made, as it has to resist the pressure of rocks dug up on the seabed or chance encounters with the heavy and unforeseen obstacles that litter the bottom of the *laguna*. They also have, of course, to resist the seabed itself as they ram into and then under the nesting clams, dragging along the sea bottom and then to the surface kilos of shells, large and small, trapped within the rectangular tray, water and sand cascading out and back into the *laguna*.

The observable differences between the boats are insignificant: a clam scoop smaller or larger than that on the next boat; life buoys in need of paint or shining bright and smooth; decks so clean they gleam in the sunlight or stained with rust in the corners, where they touch the sides of the boat. The Pellestrina boats, during the day, ride in pleasant promiscuity one beside the next; their owners live in similar propinquity in the low houses that stretch from one side of the village to the other, from the *laguna* to the sea.

At about 3.30 on a morning in early May, a small fire broke out in the cabin of one of these boats, the *Squallus*, owned and captained by Giulio Bottin, resident at number 242 Via Santa Giustina. The men of Pellestrina are no longer solely dependent upon the power of the tides and winds and thus are no longer obliged to sail only when they are favourable, but the habits of centuries die hard, and so most fishermen rise and sail at dawn, as if the early morning breezes still made some difference to their speed. There remained two hours before the fishermen of Pellestrina – who now sleep in their homes and in their beds – had to get up, so they were at their deepest point of sleep when the fire broke out on the *Squallus*. The flames moved, at quite a leisurely pace, along the floor of the boat's cabin to the wooden sides and the teak control panel at the front. Teak, a hard wood, burns slowly, but it also burns at a higher temperature than softer woods, and so the fire that spread up the control panel and from it to the roof of the cabin and out on to the deck moved with frightening speed once it reached those softer woods. The fire burned a hole in the deck of the cabin, and burning pieces of wood fell below into the engine room where one fell on to a pile of oil-damp rags, which flared instantly into life and passed the fire gracefully towards the fuel line.

Slowly, the fire worked at the area around the narrow tube; slowly it burned away the surrounding wood and then, as the wood turned to ash and fell away, a small piece of solder melted, opening a gap that allowed the flame to enter the pipe and move with blinding speed down towards the engines and to the dual fuel tanks which supplied them.

None of the people sleeping in Pellestrina that night had any idea of the motion of the flames, but all of them were rocked awake when the fuel tanks on the *Squallus* exploded, filling the night air with a glaring burst of light and, seconds later, with a thud so loud that, the next day, people as far away as Chioggia claimed they heard it.

Fire is terrifying anywhere, but for some reason it seems more so at sea or, at least, on the water. The first people who looked out of their bedroom windows said later that they saw the boat shrouded in heavy, oily smoke that rose up as the fire was extinguished by the water. But by then the flames had had time to slip through the *Squallus* to the boats moored on either side of it and set them smouldering, and the exploding fuel had splashed in deadly arcs, not only to the decks of the boats moored beside it, but out on to the levee in front, where it set three wooden benches ablaze.

After the blast from the *Squallus*'s fuel tanks, there followed a moment of stunned silence, then Pellestrina exploded into noise and action. Doors flew open and men ran out into the night; some of them wore trousers pulled on over pyjamas, some wore only pyjamas, some had taken the time to dress, two were entirely naked, though no one paid any attention to that fact, so urgent was the need to save the boats. The owners of the boats moored alongside the *Squallus* jumped from the dock on to the decks at almost the same instant, though one had had to pull himself from the bed of his cousin's wife and had come twice as far as the other. Both of them yanked fire extinguishers from their stanchions on the deck and began to spray at the flames that had followed the burning oil.

The owners of boats moored further from the now empty space where the *Squallus* had once floated churned their engines to life and began frantically backing away from the burning boats. One of them, in his panic, forgot to cast off the mooring rope and yanked a metre-long strip of wood from the railing of his boat. But even as he looked back and saw the splintered wood floating where he had been moored, he didn't stop until his boat was a hundred metres from land and safe from the flames.

As he watched, those flames gradually lessened on the decks of the other boats. Two more men, each carrying a fire extinguisher, arrived from the nearby houses. Jumping on to the deck of one of the boats, they began spraying

7

the flames, which were quickly controlled and then finally quelled. At about the same time the owner of the other boat, which had not been as heavily sprayed with fuel, managed to get the flames under control and then extinguished them with the thick white froth. Long after there was no more sign of fire, he continued spraying back and forth, back and forth, until the froth was gone and he lowered the empty fire extinguisher to the deck.

By then, more than a hundred people were clustered along the levee, shouting to the men on the boats that had managed to back out into the harbour, to one another, and to the men who had conquered the flames on their boats. Expressions of shock and concern flew from every lip, anxious questions about what had been seen, what could have started the fire.

The first to ask the question that was to silence them all, the silence slowly rippling out from her like infection from a uncleaned wound, was Chiara Petulli, the next-door neighbour of Giulio Bottin. She was standing at the front of the crowd, not more than two metres from the large metal stanchion from which dangled the scorched cable that had once held the *Squallus* safely in place. She turned to the woman next to her, the widow of a fisherman who had died in an accident only the year before, and asked, 'Where's Giulio?'

The widow looked around. She repeated the question. The person next to her picked it up and passed it on until, in a matter of moments the question had been passed through the entire crowd, asked but not answered.

'And Marco?' Chiara Petulli added. This time everyone heard her question. Though his boat lay in the shallow waters, its scorched masts just breaking the surface, Giulio Bottin was not there, nor was his son Marco, eighteen years old and already part owner of the *Squallus*, which lay burnt and dead at the bottom of the harbour of Pellestrina on this suddenly chill springtime morning.

2

The whispers started then, as people tried to remember when they had last seen Giulio or Marco. Giulio usually played cards in the bar after dinner; had anyone seen him last night? Marco had a girlfriend down in S. Pietro in Volta, but the girl's brother was in the crowd and said she'd gone to the movies on the Lido with her sisters. No one could think of a woman who would be with Giulio Bottin. Someone thought to look in the courtyard beside the Bottin house; both their cars were there, though the house was dark.

A curious reluctance, a kind of delicacy in the face of possibility, kept the people in the crowd from speculating where they might be. Renzo Marolo, who had lived next door for more than thirty years, found the courage to do what no one else was willing to do and took the spare key from where everyone in the village knew it to be, under the pot of pink geraniums on the windowsill to the right of the front door. Calling ahead of him, he opened the door and stepped into the familiar house. He switched on the lights in the small living room and, seeing no one there, went and looked in the kitchen, though he couldn't have explained why he did so, as the room was dark, and he didn't bother to turn the light on. Then, still calling out the names of the two men in a kind of unmusical voluntary, he went up the single flight of steps to the upper floor and down the hall to the larger of the two bedrooms.

'Giulio, it's me, Renzo,' he called, paused a moment, then stepped into the bedroom and switched on the light. The bed was empty and unslept in. Unsettled by this, he went across the hall and turned on the light in Marco's room. Here, too, though a pair of jeans and a light sweater lay folded on a chair, both bed and room were empty.

Marolo went back downstairs and outside, closing the door quietly behind him and replacing the key. To the waiting people, he said, 'They aren't here.'

As a group, somehow comforted by the fact that there were a number of them, they moved back towards the water, where most of the inhabitants of Pellestrina were gathered on the edge of the pier. Some of the boats that had found safety in the deeper water pulled slowly back, taking their accustomed places. When all of them were again moored to the *riva*, the single empty space left by the sunken *Squallus* seemed larger than it had when there had been only the two damaged boats on either side. From the middle of the empty slot, the masts of the *Squallus* poked through the water at a crazy angle.

Marolo's son, sixteen-year-old Luciano, came and stood beside his father. Off in the distance, a waterfowl cried out. 'Well, *Papà*?' the boy asked.

Renzo had watched his son grow up in the shadow or, to use a more nautical metaphor, in the wake of Marco Bottin, who had always been two years ahead of him at school and was thus to be admired and emulated.

Luciano had thrown on a pair of cut-off jeans when his father's shouts woke him but had had no time to put on a shirt. He stepped closer to the water, turned and signalled to his cousin Franco, who stood at the front of the crowd, an enormous flashlight in his left hand. Franco stepped forward reluctantly, shy about putting himself so conspicuously under the scrutiny of the assembled Pellestrinotti.

Luciano kicked off his sandals and knifed into the water just to the left of the sunken prow of the *Squallus*. Franco stepped forward and played the light into the water below, where his cousin's body moved with fishlike ease. A woman stepped forward, then another, and then the entire first rank of people moved to the edge of the pier and stared down. Two men holding flashlights pushed their way through and added their beams to Franco's.

After what was little more than a minute but seemed an eternity, Luciano's head broke the surface of the water. Shaking his hair back out of his eyes, he shouted up to his cousin, 'Shine it back towards the cabin,' and was gone, ducking under the water as quickly as a seal.

All three lights moved along the hulk of the *Squallus*. Occasionally they caught a flash of white from one of the soles of Luciano's feet, the only part of his body that was not tanned to near-blackness. They lost him for an instant, then his head and shoulders burst from the water, and he was gone again. Twice more he shot up and filled his lungs, diving back towards the wreck. At last he surfaced and lay on his back for a moment, pulling in great, rasping lungfuls of air. When they saw this, the people holding the flashlights moved the beams away from him, letting him float there illuminated only by the curiosity of the onlookers and the faint paling of the sky.

Luciano suddenly slipped over on to his stomach and paddled like a dog, a motion strangely awkward in such a powerful swimmer, to the edge of the embankment. He reached the ladder nailed to the wooden embankment wall, and started to pull himself up the rungs.

The crowd parted in front of the ladder and at just that instant the sun emerged from the waters of the Adriatic. Its first rays, rising above the sea wall and cutting across the narrow peninsula, caught Luciano as he paused at the top of the ladder, transforming this fisherman's son into a godlike presence that had arisen gleaming from the waters. There was a collective intake of breath, as in the presence of the numinous.

Luciano shook his head, and water spattered to both sides. Then, looking at his father, he said, 'They're both in the cabin.'

3

The boy's announcement caused little surprise among the people standing at the side of the pier. Someone not of that place might have responded differently to the revelation that two people were lying dead in the waters below them, but the people of Pellestrina had known Giulio Bottin for fifty-three years; many of them had known his father; still others had known his grandfather. The men of the Bottin family had, and had always, been hard, merciless men, whose characters had perhaps been formed, surely influenced, by the brutality of the sea. If violence befell Giulio, there were few who would be surprised to learn of it.

Some had noticed a difference in Marco, perhaps caused by the fact that he was the only one of the Bottin who had ever remained in school more than a few years or who had ever learned from books more than to read a few words or set down a crabbed signature. There had also been the influence of his mother, dead now for five years. Originally from Murano, she had been a soft, loving woman who had married Giulio twenty years ago, some said because she had been involved with her cousin Maurizio, who had left her to go to Argentina, others because her father, a gambler, had borrowed heavily from Giulio and had repaid the loan by giving away his daughter in marriage. The events leading to their marriage had never been made clear, or perhaps there simply was no story to tell. But what had always been evident to everyone in the village was the almost total lack of love or sympathy between husband and wife, so perhaps the stories were merely a way of making sense of that absence of feeling.

Regardless of how she may have felt about her husband, Bianca had adored her son, and people, always quick to gossip, had said that this was the reason for Giulio's behaviour towards him: cold, hard, unforgiving, but completely in the tradition of the Bottin men towards their sons. At this point in the story, most people threw up their hands and said those two should never have married, but then someone else was sure to say that then there would have been no Marco and remember how happy he had made Bianca, and just one look at him and you'd know what a good boy he is.

No one would say that in the present tense again, not now, not with Marco lying dead at the bottom of the harbour in the burnt-out wreckage of his father's boat.

Gradually, as there came to be more light, there came to be fewer people, as they slipped back to their homes. Soon most of them had disappeared, but then the men returned and were seen briefly crossing the square towards their boats. Bottin and his son were dead, but that was no reason to miss a day's clam harvest. The season was already short enough, what with the laws controlling what they could do, and where, and when.

Within half an hour, the only boat remaining at the pier was the one to the left of the sunken *Squallus*: the gas tank had exploded with such force that a metal stanchion had been blown through the side of the *Anna Maria*, about a metre above the waterline. The captain, Ottavio Rusponi, had at first thought he would risk it and follow the other boats to the clam beds, but when he studied the clouds and held his left hand up to sense the wind, he decided not to, not with the rising wind from the east.

It wasn't until eight that morning, when Captain Rusponi called his insurance agent to report the damage to his boat, that anyone thought of calling the police, and it was the agent, not the captain, who did so. Later, those questioned about their failure to notify the authorities would claim that they thought someone else had done it. The failure to report the deaths of the two Bottin men would be taken by many as a suggestion of the esteem in which the family was held by the rest of the citizens of Pellestrina.

The Carabinieri were slow in getting there, coming down in a launch from their station on the Lido. There obviously had been some confusion when the deaths were reported, for the Carabinieri who came were in uniform, and no provision had been made to bring along anyone who could dive down to the wreckage, for no one had explained to them where the bodies were. The subsequent discussion was juridical as well as jurisdictional, no one being quite sure which arm of the law was meant to deal with a suspicious death in water. At last it was decided that the city police should be summoned to investigate, along with divers from the Vigili del Fuoco. Not the least of the reasons for this decision was the fact that the two Carabinieri who worked as divers were that day engaged in the illegal underwater collection of pottery shards from a newly discovered dumping ground behind Murano, a place where unsuccessful or badly fired pottery had been dumped during the sixteenth century. The passage of centuries had transformed junk into potsherds; by the same alchemy, the worthless had been rendered valuable. The site had been discovered two months before and reported to the Sopraitendenza ai I Beni Culturali, which had added it to the list of sites of archaeological value where diving was prohibited. By night, watch was meant to be kept on it, as well as on the other places in the *laguna* where the waters covered relics of the past. By day, however, it was not unknown for a boat bearing the markings of some agency of the law to anchor in the area. And who would question the presence of the industrious divers who gave every appearance of being there on official business?

The Carabinieri returned in their boat to the Lido, and after more than an hour, a police launch pulled into the waters behind the fleet of Pellestrina, now all safely berthed along the pier and all the captains home.

The pilot of the launch slowed as he approached a boat with the markings of the Fire Department that was already anchored and bobbing in the water just behind the only empty space in the long line of docked boats. He slipped his engine into reverse for an instant, to bring the boat to a stop. Sergeant Lorenzo Vianello walked to the side of the boat and looked down into the waters that filled the empty space, but the sun glistened brightly and all he could see were the tilted masts sticking out of the surface. 'Is that it?' he called to the two black-suited divers who stood on the deck of the Fire Department launch.

One of the divers called across something Vianello couldn't make out and then went back to the business of pulling on his left flipper.

Paolo Montisi, the police pilot, came out of the small cabin at the front of the police launch and glanced down at the sunken boat. He raised a protective hand to cut the sun's glare and looked down to where Vianello was pointing. 'That's got to be it,' he said. 'The man who called said it caught fire and sank.' He looked at the boats on either side of the empty space, and saw that their sides and decks were scarred and blackened by flames.

Beside them, the two divers fiddled with their masks, pulling tight the straps that held their oxygen canisters to their backs. They slipped the mouthpieces in, took a few exploratory breaths, and walked to the side of their boat. Vianello, tall and broad shouldered, stood beside his shorter colleague, still looking down into the water.

Indicating the two divers, he asked Montisi, 'Would you go into that water?'

The pilot shrugged. 'It's not too bad out here. Besides, they're covered,' he said, nodding with his chin towards the black-suited divers.

The first diver stepped over the side of the boat and, facing outward, the back of his rubber fins placed carefully on the rungs of the exterior ladder, walked down into the water, followed immediately by the other.

'Aren't they supposed to jump in backwards?' Vianello asked.

'That's only on Jacques Cousteau,' Montisi said and went back into the cabin. He came out a moment later, a cigarette cupped in one hand. 'What else did they tell you?' he asked the sergeant.

'A call came in from the Carabinieri on the

Lido,' Vianello began. Montisi interrupted him with an antiphonal, 'sons of bitches', but the sergeant pretended not to hear and continued, 'They said there were two bodies in a sunken boat and we should get some divers out here to have a look.'

'Nothing else?' Montisi asked.

Vianello shrugged, as if to ask whether much more could be expected from Carabinieri.

Silently, they watched the bubbles burst on the surface in front of their boat. Gradually, the tide pulled the boat backwards; Montisi let it drift for a few minutes but then went back into the cabin, fired the engine to life, and pulled the boat back into place directly behind the gap in the line of boats. He cut the engine and came back out on deck. He reached down and picked up a rope. Effortlessly, he tossed it towards the Fire Department boat, looping it around a stanchion the first time, and tied their own boat to the other. Below them, they could see motion, but it was no more than gleams and flashes, and they could make no sense of it. Montisi finished his cigarette and tossed the butt overboard, like most Venetians utterly careless about what he threw into the water. The two men watched the filter float, then dance, in the fizzing bubbles before freeing itself and drifting away.

After about five minutes, the divers surfaced and pulled back their masks. Graziano, the more senior, called up to the men on the police boat, 'There's two of them down there.'

'What happened?' Vianello asked.

Graziano shook his head. 'No idea. It looks like they drowned when the boat went down.'

'They're fishermen,' Montisi said in disbelief. 'They wouldn't get trapped in a sinking boat.'

Graziano's business was to dive into the water, not to speculate on what he found there, so he said nothing. When Montisi remained silent, the man bobbing on the surface beside Graziano asked, 'Do you want us to bring them up?'

Vianello and Montisi exchanged a glance. Neither of them had any idea of what had happened to take the two men down with their boat, but neither of them wanted to make a decision of this sort and thus run the risk of destroying whatever evidence might be down there with them.

Finally Graziano said, 'The crabs are there already.'

'OK, get them out,' Vianello said.

Graziano and his partner pulled on their masks, slipped the mouthpieces into place, and, like a pair of eider ducks, upended themselves and disappeared. The pilot went down the cabin steps, pulled open one of the seats along the side, and took out some complicated rigging from the end of which hung a double canvas sling. He came up the steps and back to Vianello's side. He raised the rope, slung it over the side of the boat, and lowered it into the water.

A minute later Graziano and his partner

bobbed to the surface, the body of a third man dangling limp between them. With motions so practised it made Vianello uneasy to watch them, they eased the arms of the dead man into the sling Montisi tossed down; one of them dived under the water to run a rope between the man's legs, then attached it to a hook on the front of the sling.

He waved to Montisi and the pilot and Vianello hauled the dead man up, amazed at how heavy he was. Vianello caught himself thinking that this was why it was called dead weight, but he forced himself, embarrassed, away from that thought. Slowly the body lifted out of the water, and the two men had to lean out from the deck to prevent it from banging against the side. They were not entirely successful, but finally they dragged him over the railing and laid him on the deck, his sightless eyes staring up at the sky.

Before they could take a closer look, they heard splashing below them. Quickly, they loosened the sling and threw it over the side again. Even more careful this time to keep the second body from the side of the boat, they hauled it up on to the deck and stretched it out beside the other.

Two crabs still clung to the hair of the first corpse, but Vianello was too horrified by the sight to do anything except stare. Montisi reached down and pulled them off, casually tossing them over the side of the boat into the water.

The divers climbed up the ladder on the side of the police boat and stepped over the gunwale and on to the deck. They unhooked their oxygen tanks and set them carefully down, pulled off their masks, then the black rubber hoods that covered their heads.

On the deck of the police launch, the four men looked at the bodies that lay at their feet. Vianello went into the cabin, and when he emerged he had two woollen blankets in his hands. He stuffed one under his elbow, signalled to Montisi, and shook out the first one. The pilot caught the other end, and together they lowered it over the body of the older man. Vianello took the second blanket, and together they repeated the process with the son.

It was only then, when they were fully covered and hidden from sight, that Graziano's partner, the youngest living person on the boat, said, 'No crab did that to his face.'

4

Vianello had seen the crushed fragments of bone showing through the bloodless wound on the older man's head, though his quick glance had discerned no sign of violence on the son's body. Nodding in acknowledgement of the diver's remark, he took out his *telefonino*, called the Questura, and asked to speak to his immediate superior, Commissario Guido Brunetti. While he waited, he watched the two divers climb on to their own boat. Brunetti finally answered, and the sergeant said, 'I'm out here on Pellestrina, sir. It looks like one of them was killed.' Then, to avoid any ambiguity, given the fact that the men had died in what appeared to be an accident, he continued, 'That is, murdered.'

'How?' Brunetti asked.

'The older one was hit on the head, hard enough to do a lot of damage. I don't know about the other one, the son.'

'Are you sure who they are?' his superior asked.

Vianello had been expecting the question. 'No, sir. That is, no one's given us a positive identification, but the man who called the Carabinieri said they were the owners of the boat, Giulio Bottin and his son, so we just assumed that's who they were.'

'See if you can get someone to confirm that.'

'Yes, sir. Anything else?'

'Just the usual. Ask around, see what people say and what they volunteer about them.' Before Vianello could ask, Brunetti added, 'Don't act as though it's anything more than an accident. And talk to the divers, tell them they aren't to say anything.'

'How long do you think that will last?' Vianello asked, looking across to the deck of the other boat, where the two divers, now stripped of their diving gear, were putting on their normal uniforms.

'Ten minutes, I'd guess,' Brunetti said, with a soft explosion of breath that, in other circumstances, might have been a laugh.

'I'll send them back to the Lido, then,' Vianello said. 'That will at least slow things down.' Before Brunetti could comment, the sergeant asked, 'What do you want to do, sir?'

'I want to keep this quiet as long as we can, that they were killed. Start asking around, but gently, and I'll come out. If there's a boat free, I should be there in an hour, maybe less.'

Vianello was relieved. 'Good, sir. Do you want Montisi to take the bodies to the hospital?'

'Yes, as soon as you get an identification. I'll call and tell them he's coming in.' Suddenly there was nothing more to be said or ordered. Repeating that he'd be there as soon as he could, Brunetti hung up.

He looked at his watch again, and saw that it was past eleven: surely his superior, Vice-Questore Giuseppe Patta, should be in his office by now. He walked downstairs without bothering to call ahead and went into the small anteroom that led to the Vice-Questore's much larger office.

Patta's secretary, Signorina Elettra Zorzi, sat at her desk, a book open in front of her. He was surprised to see her reading a book in the office, accustomed as he was to seeing her with magazines and newspapers. Because she had her chin propped on her cupped palms and her fingers pressed over her ears, it was not until she sensed his presence and sat up that he noticed she had cut her hair. It was shorter than usual, and if the roundness of her face and the vermilion of her lips had not declared her femininity, he would have judged the cut severe, almost masculine.

He didn't know how to acknowledge her new hairstyle and, like everyone else in a city where it had not rained for three months, he was tired of asking when it would rain, so he asked, nodding towards the book, 'Something more serious than usual?'

'Veblen,' she answered, *The Theory of the Leisure Class.*' He was flattered that she didn't bother to ask if he was familiar with the book.

'Isn't that a bit heavy?'

She agreed, then said, 'I used not to be able to get any serious reading done here, what with the constant interruptions.' She pursed her lips as her eyes travelled round her office in an arc that encompassed phone, computer, and the door to Patta's office. 'But things have improved, so I can start to make better use of my time.'

'That's good to know,' Brunetti said. Looking at the book, he added, 'I was fascinated by his view of lawns.'

She smiled up at him. 'Yes, and sports.'

He couldn't resist, 'And next, when you finish that?'

'I haven't decided.' A smile blossomed. 'Perhaps I could ask the Vice-Questore's advice.'

'Indeed,' Brunetti replied. 'I came to ask about him. Is he in?'

'No, not yet. He called about an hour ago and said he was at a meeting and would probably not be in until after lunch.'

'Ah,' Brunetti said, surprised not at the message but at the fact that Patta had bothered to call to leave it. 'When he comes in, please tell him I've gone to Pellestrina.'

'To meet Vianello?' she asked with her usual effortless omniscience.

He nodded. 'It looks like one of the men in the

boat was murdered.' He stopped there, wondering if she already knew all of this.

'Pellestrina, eh?' she asked, with an intonation that turned the question into a statement.

'Yes. Nothing but trouble, aren't they?'

'Not as bad as the Chioggotti,' she said with a shudder that was neither delicate nor artificial.

Chioggia, a mainland city the guidebooks never tired of calling 'the faithful daughter of Venice', had indeed remained loyal to her throughout the reign of La Serenissima. It was only now that animosity existed, violent and constant, as the fishermen of the two cities fought over ever-diminishing catches in waters which increasingly suffered the impositions of the Magistrato alle Acque, as larger and larger portions of the *laguna* were closed to fishing.

The idea had occurred to Brunetti, as it would to any Venetian, that these deaths had something to do with this competition. In the past there had been fights, and shots had been fired in anger, but nothing like this had happened. Boats had been stolen and burned, men had been killed in collisions on the water, but no one had yet been murdered in cold blood.

'*Una brutta razza*,' Signorina Elettra said, with the scorn that people whose families had been Venetian since the Crusades reserve for non-Venetians, regardless of their origin.

Brunetti exercised discretion and correctness in not giving voice to his agreement and left her to Veblen's analysis of the problems and inescapable corruptions of wealth. In the officers' room he found only one pilot, Rocca, and told him he needed to be taken out to Pellestrina. The pilot's face brightened at the news: it was a long run, and the day was glorious, a brisk wind coming from the west.

Brunetti stood on deck all the way out, gazing at the islands they passed: Santa Maria della Grazia, San Clemente, Santo Spirito, even tiny Poveglia, until he saw to their left the buildings of Malamocco. Though Brunetti had spent a great deal of his youth on boats and in the *laguna*, he had never fully mastered the art of piloting and so had never burned into his memory a map of the most direct routes between various points in the *laguna*. He knew that Pellestrina lay ahead of them, in the middle of this narrow spit of land, and he knew that the boat had to stay within the rows of slanting wooden pilings, but had they strayed into the expanse of water on their right, he would have found it embarrassingly difficult to get them safely back to Venice.

Rocca, his young face radiating simple pleasure at being outside and in motion on this beautiful day, called back to his superior, 'Where are we going, sir?'

'To the port. Vianello and Montisi are there. We should see them.'

On their left were trees; and the occasional car swept by. Ahead he began to make out the forms of boats, what seemed to be a long row of them, facing towards a cement-walled pier. He cast his eye along their blunt sterns, but he saw no sign of the police launch. They reached an opening in the line of boats, and beyond it, on the shore a few metres away, he saw Vianello, standing in the sun, one hand raised to shade his eyes.

Brunetti waved and Vianello started to walk to the right, towards the end of the line of moored boats, signalling for them to follow him. When they finally reached the open space at the end of the line of boats, Rocca pulled the launch up and Brunetti jumped on to the *riva*, momentarily surprised to feel its solidity under his feet.

'Has Montisi gone back?' he asked.

'One of their neighbours came on board the boat and identified them. It's who we thought: Giulio Bottin and his son, Marco. I sent him back to the hospital with them.' Vianello nodded toward Rocca, who was busy with a rope, mooring the boat to a metal stanchion. 'I can go back with you, sir.'

'What else?' asked Brunetti.

'I spoke to two or three people, and all of them pretty much told me the same story. They woke up with the noise of the explosion of the gas tank at about three. By the time they got out to the pier, the boat was in flames, and before they could do anything, it had sunk.'

Vianello started walking back towards the line of low houses that was the village of Pellestrina, and Brunetti fell into step with him. 'Then there was the usual nonsense,' Vianello began. 'No one bothered to call the Carabinieri, everybody thinking someone else had. So they weren't called until this morning.' Vianello stopped dead, looking at the houses, as if he couldn't believe that humans inhabited them. 'Incredible: two men get killed in an explosion, and no one calls us, no one calls anyone.'

He resumed walking. 'Anyway, the Carabinieri came out, then they called us and handed it over, said something about it being in our jurisdiction.' He waved ahead at the space between the boats. 'The divers brought them up.'

'You said the father had a wound on his head?'

'Yes. Terrible, the skull was crushed in.'

'What about the son?'

'Knife,' Vianello said. 'In the stomach. I'd say he bled to death.' Then, before Brunetti could ask, he added, 'It was like he was gutted. The knife went in low and was pulled up. His shirt was covering it when the body was brought up, but when we moved him, we saw it.' Vianello stopped walking again and looked over at the still waters of the *laguna*. 'He would have bled to death in minutes.' Remembering his place, he added, 'But the autopsy will decide that, I suppose.'

'Who have you spoken to?'

Vianello patted the pocket of his jacket where he kept his notebook. 'I've got their names in here: neighbours, mostly. A couple of men who have boats and who fished with them, well, who went out with them, because I don't get the impression that these men think of fishing as anything they're meant to share.'

'Did anyone tell you that?'

Vianello shook the idea away. 'No, no one said anything, at least not directly. But it was always there, this sense that they were forcing themselves to talk as though they felt some sense of loyalty or common bond because they were all fishermen, while at the same time I got the feeling they'd push anyone out of the way who tried to fish a spot where they wanted to or that they thought they had a right to.'

'Push out of the way?' Brunetti asked.

'Well, in a manner of speaking,' Vianello answered. 'I don't know enough about the way things work out here, but that's the feeling I get: there's too many of them and too few fish left. And it's too late for most of them to learn to do anything else.'

Brunetti waited to see if Vianello had anything else to say, but when it seemed that he had finished, Brunetti said, 'There used to be a restaurant off to the right here somewhere.'

Vianello nodded. 'I had a coffee there earlier while I was talking to one of them.'

'There's no sense in my pretending I'm just a passing tourist, is there?' Brunetti asked.

Vianello smiled at the absurdity of it. 'Everyone in the village saw you get off that launch, sir. And walk back here with me. Damned by the company, if I might dare to say it.'

'So we might as well go and have lunch together,' suggested Brunetti.

Vianello led the way back to the village. At the first row of houses he stopped in front of the large windows and wooden door of a restaurant. He pushed open the door and held it for Brunetti, then pulled it closed behind them.

A man in a long apron stood behind the zinc-covered bar, wiping at a squat glass with a cloth large enough to cover a small table. He nodded to Vianello then, an instant later, to Brunetti.

'Could we have lunch here?' the sergeant asked.

The man tilted his head towards a hallway that led away from the bar. He looked down at the glass again and returned to his careful work.

To the side of the bar was a doorway of a sort Brunetti had not seen in decades. Narrow, it was hung with a row of long strips of green and white plastic, each little more than a centimetre wide, ribbed on both sides. As he inserted his right hand to slip half of them aside, he heard the gentle clicking sound he recalled from his youth. Once these dividers had hung in the doorway of every bar and every trattoria, but during the last couple of decades, they'd all disappeared; he couldn't remember the last time he'd seen one. He held aside the still clattering strips until Vianello was through, then listened to them fall back into place.

The room they entered surprised him by its size, for it must have held thirty tables. The windows were set high in the walls, and plenty of light streamed in. Below them, fishermen's nets covered the walls, each embedded with shells, pieces of dried seaweed, and what looked like the petrified corpses of fish, crabs and lobsters. A low serving counter ran along one side of the room. In the back, a glass door, closed now, led to a pebble-covered parking lot.

Seeing that only one other table was occupied, Brunetti looked at his watch, surprised to find that it was only one thirty. There was some truth in the belief that exposure to sea air increases the appetite.

They walked across the room, pulled out chairs at a table halfway along the first row, and sat facing one another. A small vase of fresh wildflowers stood to the left of the bottles of olive oil and vinegar, and beside that was a wicker holder containing half a dozen paper-wrapped packs of grissini. Brunetti took one, ripped it open, and began to nibble at a breadstick.

The plastic strips parted and a young man in black jacket and trousers backed into the room. When he turned around, Brunetti saw that he had a plate of what appeared to be *antipasto di pesce* in each hand. The waiter nodded to the two newcomers and went to the table in the far corner, where he set the two plates down in front of a man and woman in their sixties.

The waiter came back towards their table. Brunetti and Vianello had realized that this was not the sort of place to bother with a menu, at least not this early in the season, so Brunetti smiled and said, as one always does in a new restaurant, 'Everyone says you can eat very well here.' He was careful to speak in Veneziano.

'I hope so,' the waiter said, smiling as he spoke and making no sign that he found the presence of a uniformed policeman in any way surprising.

'What can you recommend today?' Brunetti asked.

'The *antipasto di mare* is good. We've got cuttlefish milk or sardines if you'd like them, instead.'

'What else?' Vianello asked.

'There was still some asparagus in the market this morning, so there's a salad of asparagus and shrimp.'

Brunetti nodded at this; Vianello said he wouldn't have antipasto, so the waiter passed on to the *primi piatti*.

'*Spaghetti alle vongole, spaghetti alle cozze*, and *penne all' Amatriciana*,' he recited and then stopped.

'That's all?' Vianello couldn't help asking.

The waiter waved one hand in the air. 'We've got fifty people coming for a wedding anniversary tonight, so we've only got a few things on the menu today.'

Brunetti ordered the *vongole* and Vianello the *all' Amatriciana*.

The choice of main courses was limited to roast turkey or mixed fried fish. Vianello chose the first, Brunetti the second. They ordered a half-litre of white wine and a litre of mineral water. The waiter brought them a basket of *bussolai*, the thick oval breadsticks that Brunetti especially liked.

When he was gone, Brunetti picked one up, broke it in half, and took a bite. It always surprised him how they remained so crisp in this seaside climate. The waiter brought the wine and water, set them on the table, and hurried over to remove the plates from in front of the elderly couple.

'We come out to Pellestrina and you don't eat fish,' Brunetti said, making it a statement rather than a question, though it was.

Vianello poured them each a glass of wine, picked up his, and sipped at it. 'Very good,' he said. 'It's like what my uncle used to bring back from Istria on his boat.'

'And the fish?' Brunetti asked, not letting it go.

'I don't eat it any more,' Vianello said. 'Not unless I know it comes from the Atlantic.'

Lunacy had many forms, Brunetti knew, and most of them had to be detected in the early stages. 'Why?' he asked.

'I joined Greenpeace, you know, sir,' Vianello said by way of answer.

'And Greenpeace doesn't let you eat fish?' he asked, trying to make a joke of it.

Vianello started to say something, stopped, took another sip of wine, and said, 'That's not true, sir.'

Neither of them spoke for a long time, and then the waiter was back, bringing Brunetti his antipasto, a small mound of tiny pink shrimp on a bed of slivered raw asparagus. Brunetti took a forkful: they'd been sprinkled with balsamic vinegar. The combination of sweet, sour, sweet, salty was wonderful. Ignoring Vianello for a moment, he ate the salad slowly, relishing it, perpetually delighted by the contrast of flavours and textures.

He set his fork on the plate and took a sip of wine. 'Are you afraid to ruin my meal by telling me what polluting horrors lie in wait for me inside the shrimp?' he asked, smiling.

'Clams are worse,' said Vianello, smiling back but with no further attempt at clarification.

Before Brunetti could ask for a list of the deadly poisons that lurked in his shrimp and clams, the waiter took his plate away, then was quickly back with the two dishes of pasta.

The rest of the meal passed amiably as they talked idly of people they'd known who had fished in the waters around Pellestrina and of a famous footballer from Chioggia whom neither of them had ever seen play. When their main courses came, Vianello could not help giving Brunetti's a suspicious glance, though he had forgone the opportunity to comment further upon the clams. Brunetti, for his part, gave silent proof of the high regard in which he held his sergeant by not repeating to him the contents of an article he had read the previous month about the methods used in commercial turkey farming, nor did he list the transmissible diseases to which those birds are prone.

5

After they'd drunk their coffee, Brunetti asked for the bill. The waiter paused, as if from a habit too strong for him to control, and Brunetti added, 'I don't need a receipt.' The waiter's eyes grew wide as he registered this new reality: a man who must be a policeman, willing to aid the owner of the restaurant in avoiding the tax that was imposed whenever a receipt was issued. Brunetti could see this created a dilemma, which the waiter solved by saying, 'I'll ask the boss.'

He came back a few minutes later, carrying a small glass of grappa in each hand. Placing them on the table he said, 'Fifty-two thousand.' Brunetti reached for his wallet. It was a third of what it would have cost in Venice, and the fish had been fresh, the shrimp perfect.

He took sixty thousand lire from his wallet and when the waiter reached into his pocket for change, Brunetti waved his gesture aside with a muttered, '*Grazie.*' He raised his grappa and took a sip. 'Very good,' he said. 'Please thank the owner for us.'

The waiter nodded, took the money, and turned to go.

'Are you from here?' Brunetti asked, with no attempt to make it seem an idle question.

'Yes.'

'We're out here because of the accident,' Brunetti said, indicating the general direction of the water. Then, with a smile he added, 'Though I don't imagine that's much of a surprise.'

'Not to anyone here, it's not,' the waiter said.

'Did you know them?' Brunetti asked. He pulled out another chair, motioning to the waiter to sit. The couple at the other table were long gone, the tables all set for the anniversary party, so there was little for him to do. He sat, then turned his chair slightly to face Brunetti.

'I knew Marco,' he said. 'We went to the same school. He was a couple of years behind me, but we knew one another because we used to come back on the same bus from the Lido.'

'What was he like?' Brunetti asked.

'Bright,' the waiter said seriously. 'Very bright and very nice. Nothing like his father, nothing at all. Giulio never talked to anyone if he could help it, but Marco was friendly with everyone. He used to help me with my maths homework, even though he was younger.' The waiter placed the notes that were still in his hand on the table, lining the fifty up beside the ten. 'About the only thing I could ever do was add these up.' Then, with a sudden smile that revealed chalky, gray teeth, he said, 'And most of the time, if I added them, I'd get fifty. Or seventy.' He slipped the bills into his pocket and glanced back at the kitchen, from which came the sudden hiss of frying food and the clang of a pot on the stove. 'But I don't need to know maths here, beyond addition, and the boss does that.'

'Was he still in school, Marco?'

'No, he finished last year.'

'And then what?'

'Went to work with his father,' the waiter said, as though that were the only choice open to Marco or the only choice a Pellestrinotto could ever conceive of. 'They've always been fishermen, the Bottins.'

'Did Marco want to fish?'

The waiter looked at Brunetti, his surprise evident. 'What else could he do? His father had the boat, and Marco knew all about fishing.'

'Of course,' Brunetti agreed. 'You said Bottin never talked to anyone. Was there more to it than that?' Brunetti refused to allow the waiter to play dumb: he clarified his question: 'Did he have many enemies here?'

The waiter shrugged, his reluctance visible in his gesture, but before he could say anything, Vianello broke in, speaking to Brunetti with practised audacity: 'Sir, he can't answer a question like that.' The sergeant glanced protectively at the waiter. 'This is a small place; everyone's going to know he talked to us.'

Picking up the cue, Brunetti answered, 'But you said you've already got the names of a couple of people.' He sensed the waiter's interest increase, saw it in the way he pulled his feet under the chair and fought to keep himself from leaning forward. 'All he'd be doing is confirming what you've already been told.'

Vianello ignored the waiter, keeping his eyes on Brunetti. 'If he doesn't want to talk, he doesn't want to talk, sir. We've already got names.'

'Which ones?' the waiter broke in.

Vianello slid his eyes across to the waiter and gave him a minimal shake of the head, a gesture he tried to hide from Brunetti.

'What names?' the waiter asked in a stronger voice. When neither of the policemen answered him, he demanded, 'Mine?'

'You've never told us your name,' Brunetti said.

'Lorenzo Scarpa,' he said. Vianello's eyes opened and he turned to look at the waiter in badly disguised shock.

When he saw Vianello's reaction, the waiter said in a tight voice, 'It was nothing. Giulio was in here one night, at the bar, and he'd been drinking. My brother never said anything to him. Bottin just wanted to get into a fight, so he invented it, said that Sandro made him spill his wine.' He looked back and forth between the knowing faces of the two policemen. 'I tell you, nothing happened, and nothing ever got reported. People stopped them before anything happened. I was in the back, working. I didn't get out here until it was all over, but no one was hurt.'

'I'm sure that's true,' Vianello said with a smile he did his best to make appear amiable. 'But that's not what's been suggested might have happened.'

'What was that? Who told you?'

Vianello shook his head with apparent reluctance, as if to suggest to the waiter that he would gladly have named his informant, but with his superior sitting right there at the table across from him, there was no way he could help his friend the waiter, no matter how much he might want to.

'Was it that bastard, Giacomini? Just tell me that? Was it him?'

Again apparently unable to disguise his surprise at the name, Vianello shot the waiter a quick glance, almost as if to warn him to stop. But beyond caring about caution, the waiter went on, 'He wasn't even here, Giacomini. He just wanted to cause Sandro trouble, the bastard. And he knew there was bad blood between them because of that time off Chioggia. But he's lying; he's always been a liar.' The waiter pushed himself back from the table and got to his feet, as if to stop himself from saying anything more. Suddenly formal, all thought of his brother abandoned, he asked, 'Would you like another grappa?'

Brunetti shook his head, then got to his feet, the sergeant quickly following him. 'Thank you,' Brunetti said, leaving it unclear if he meant for the service or for the information. He paused a moment, making it obvious that Vianello had no choice but to precede his superior from the room.

Outside, Brunetti walked for a few minutes until they stood at the edge of the water, where they were safely away from the restaurant and all of the houses. Looking in the general direction of Venice, he put one foot up on the sea wall and reached down to flick a pebble from inside the sole of his shoe.

'Well?' he asked.

'All news to me,' Vianello said with a small smile. 'No one was willing to tell me a thing.'

'That's what I assumed,' Brunetti said then added, knowing that Vianello would be pleased to hear it, 'You played that very well.'

'It wasn't very hard, was it?' the sergeant asked by way of answer.

'I'd like to know how bad their fight was, especially as he was so eager to convince us it was nothing.' Brunetti continued to gaze off towards the invisible city, but it was clear his remarks were meant for Vianello.

'He was pretty insistent, wasn't he, sir?'

Brunetti had thought so at the time, but now he began to wonder if perhaps the waiter had been smarter than he'd thought and had dropped Giacomini's name and the story of the fight with Bottin in order to deflect them from something else. 'You think he was trying to lead us away from something, Sergeant?'

'No, I think he was genuinely worried,' Vianello answered, as if he'd already considered and dismissed the same possibility. Then, with a scorn typical of those born on the major Venetian islands, he added, 'Pellestrinotti aren't bright enough for something like that, anyway.'

'We're not allowed to say things like that any more, Sergeant,' Brunetti said mildly.

'Regardless of whether they're true?' the sergeant asked.

'Because they're true,' Brunetti answered.

Vianello reflected for a moment upon this and then asked, 'What now, sir?'

'I think we go and see what else we can learn about the fight between Sandro Scarpa and Giulio Bottin.' Brunetti turned away from the *laguna* and back towards the rows of low houses.

Vianello fell into step beside him, saying, 'There's a kind of general store behind the restaurant. The sign said it opened at three, and someone told me that Signora Follini always opens on time.' He led the way to the left of the restaurant and into a sandy courtyard lined on two sides by doors and on the other left open to provide a long view towards the sea wall and, beyond it, the Adriatic. Because of the height of the distant sea wall, they could not see the water on that side of the island, but there was a sharp scent of iodine in the air and a general moistness that spoke of the presence of the sea.

Brunetti had not been out here for years,

perhaps for more than a decade, not since the kids were smaller and he and Paola and his brother Sergio and his family used to crowd together into Sergio's boat on Sunday afternoons, saying they wanted to explore the islands but knowing themselves to be, all the while, in search of good restaurants and fresh fish. He remembered sunburnt, cranky children, asleep in the bottom of the boat like puppies, drugged by too much sun and the endless tedium of adult conversation. He remembered Sergio erupting from the water and hurling himself over the side of the boat, both legs lashed red by an enormous jellyfish that had trailed up against him in the clear waters. And he remembered, with a surge of recalled joy, making love with Paola in the bottom of the boat one August afternoon when Sergio had taken all the children to pick blackberries on one of the smaller islands.

A bell pealed out as Vianello opened the door to the small shop. They went in, uniformed officer first to announce the reason for their visit.

From another room a woman's voice called out, '*Un momento,*' followed by the sound of a closing door and then a sharper, smaller sound, something being set down on a hard surface. After that, silence. Brunetti took a look around the shop and saw dusty rows of boxes of rice, double packs of flypaper, an object that looked like an umbrella stand filled with brooms and mops, and a low shelf upon which lay four copies of yesterday's *Gazzettino*. Everything smelled faintly of old paper and dried legumes.

After the promised moment, a woman emerged, pushing aside the white cotton curtain that separated the shop from the rooms behind it. She wore a short green dress with a scooped neck, and shoes with heels uncomfortably high for a woman who stood behind a counter all day. 'Buon giorno,' she said in their direction, stopping just in front of the curtain. She stood silently for a moment, and Brunetti saw that she was a woman in the most recent flower of her youth, though its apparent blossoming had been much repeated, no doubt at ever shorter intervals.

Her hair was dandelion blonde, though it seemed brighter still because of the deep tan of her skin. Brunetti had once taken a three-day seminar in advanced methods of suspect identification, two hours of which had concerned the means criminals use to disguise their appearance. He had been, quite frankly and perhaps because he spent so much of his life observing women, fascinated by the varieties of plastic surgery by which a face could be transformed and identity disguised. He noted some of those techniques on display here, and it occurred to him that the police could have used this woman's face as an exhibit, for the signs of the work done were so easily detectable.

Her eyes had a faint Oriental cast to them, and she was doomed forever to respond to life with a small smile that parted her lips in perpetual happy anticipation. A butcher could have sharpened his knives on the long line of her jaw. Her nose, pert and upturned, would have done wonders for the face of a woman thirty years her junior. On hers, it struck a note of visual dissonance, placed as it was over a broad, thick-lipped mouth. Brunetti judged her to be a few years older than himself.

'May I help you?' she asked, moving behind the low counter.

'Yes, Signora Follini,' Brunetti answered, stepping forward. 'I'm Commissario Guido Brunetti. I'm here to investigate the accident that took place this morning.' He started to reach for his wallet to show her his warrant card, but she waved him away impatiently.

She glanced at Vianello then returned her attention to Brunetti.

'Accident?' she asked neutrally.

Brunetti shrugged. 'Until we have reason to believe it was something else, that's how it's being treated,' he answered.

She nodded but offered nothing further.

'Did you know them, Signora?'

'Bottin and Marco?' she asked unnecessarily. 'Yes.'

'They came in here,' she said, as if that were enough.

'As customers, you mean?' he asked, though in a place as small as Pellestrina, eventually everyone would be her customer.

'Yes.'

'And beyond that? Were they friends of yours?'

She paused and thought for a moment. 'Perhaps you could say Marco was a friend.' She put special emphasis on the word 'friend', as if to suggest the interesting possibility that they had been more than that, then added, 'But definitely not his father.'

'And why was that?' Brunetti asked.

This time it was her turn to shrug. 'We didn't get along.'

'About anything in particular?'

'About everything in particular,' she said, smiling at the speed of her own response. Her smile, which exposed perfect teeth and permitted the appearance of only two small wrinkles at the corners of her mouth, gave Brunetti a suggestion of what she might have been had she not decided to devote her middle years to the reacquisition of her earlier ones.

'And why was that?' he asked.

'Our fathers had a fight when they were young men, about fifty years ago,' she said, her delivery this time so deadpan that Brunetti had no idea if she was being serious or making fun of the way things were supposed to be in small villages.

'I doubt that either you or Giulio could have been much affected,' Brunetti said, then added, 'You couldn't even have been born at the time.'

He had spoken with the excessive sincerity of flattery. Her smile this time created pairs of wrinkles, though very small ones. Paola had taught a class in the sonnet last year, and Brunetti remembered one – he thought it was

49

English – that said something about the denial of age, a form of deceit that had always seemed particularly pathetic to Brunetti.

'But didn't you have to deal with him, the older Bottin?' Brunetti asked. 'After all, this is a small village: people here must see one another every day.'

She actually put the back of her hand to her forehead when she answered, 'Don't tell me about that. I know, I know. From long experience, I know what people in small villages are like. All they need is the tiniest thing, and they invent lies about everyone.' Her studied performance of this lament raised in Brunetti's mind a certain curiosity as to the whereabouts, or the actual existence, of Signor Follini. She glanced at Vianello and opened her mouth to continue.

'And Signor Bottin?' Brunetti cut her off by asking. 'Did they invent lies about him, as well?'

Seemingly unoffended by Brunetti's interruption, she said with some asperity, 'The truth would have sufficed.'

'The truth about what?'

Her expression showed him just how eager she was to tell him, but then he saw the precise moment when the discretion that is learned from life in small villages returned to her.

'Oh, the usual things,' she said with an airy wave of the hand, and Brunetti knew it was useless to try to get anything more from her.

Nevertheless, he asked, 'What things?'

After a long pause which she clearly was

using to choose examples as meaningless as she could make them, she said, 'That he was unkind to his wife and harsh with his son.'

'I would guess those things could be said about most men.'

'I doubt they're said about you, officer,' she said, leaning forward over the counter suggestively.

Vianello chose this moment to interrupt. 'The pilot said we had to get back, sir,' he said in a quiet voice, though loud enough for her to hear.

'Yes, of course, Sergeant,' Brunetti answered in his most official tone. Turning back to Signora Follini and giving her a brief smile, he said, 'I'm afraid that's all for now, Signora. If we have any further questions, someone will come out again.'

'Not you?' she asked, attempting to sound disappointed.

'Perhaps,' Brunetti answered, 'if it's necessary.'

He thanked her for her time and, Vianello preceding, they left the store. Vianello turned left and then right, already familiar with the few streets that made up the centre of Pellestrina.

'And not a moment too soon, Sergeant,' Brunetti said with a laugh.

'I thought it best to try to get us out by means of cunning, sir.'

'And if that hadn't worked?'

'I had my gun,' Vianello answered, patting his holster.

Ahead of them loomed the sea wall, and on

impulse Brunetti crossed the narrow road that led down to the end of the peninsula and started up the steps cut into the side of the wall. At the top, he moved aside to make room for Vianello on the narrow cement walkway that ran off in both directions.

Beyond them stretched the quietly moving waters of the Adriatic; dotted in the middle distance were tankers and cargo ships. And beyond those lay the open wound of the former Yugoslavia.

'It's strange, isn't it, sir, the way women like that seem absurd if they have "*un lifting*" but when they're richer or more famous, they don't?'

Brunetti considered two friends of his wife's known for their frequent disappearances to Rome and for their subsequent transformations. Because they were wealthy, the work was better done than it had been on the face of Signora Follini, so the results were less obvious and thus more successful. To him, however, the desire that prompted them was the same and no less pathetic.

He made a noncommittal noise and asked, 'What did the people you spoke to tell you? Anything about her?'

'No, sir. You know how it is in places like this: no one is willing to say anything that might be repeated to the person they said it about.'

'So much for police secrecy,' Brunetti said with a wry shake of his head.

'But you can understand it, can't you, sir? If it

ever gets to trial, we have to say how we got a name in the first place or why we began to investigate a particular person. The trial goes on and what happens, happens. But they still have to live here, among people who see them as informers.'

Brunetti knew better than to give Vianello his standard lecture about civic duty and the responsibility of the citizen to help the authorities in their investigation of crime. The fact that this was a murder, a double murder, would make not the least bit of difference to anyone who lived here: the highest civic duty was to live in peace and not be harassed by the state. A person was much safer trusting family and neighbours. Beyond that ring of safety lay the dangers of bureaucracy and officialdom and the inevitable consequences of being embroiled with either.

Leaving Vianello to his own reflections, Brunetti stood a while longer, looking out at the sea. The ships were a bit further along in their journeys towards their destinations. They were alone in that, it seemed to him.

6

Reflecting that his distaste for what Vianello had just told him in no way altered its truth, Brunetti decided there was little purpose in their remaining in Pellestrina any longer, so he suggested they start back to Venice. Vianello displayed no surprise at this and they turned back down the steps, across the road, and through the narrow village until they were once again on the side facing Venice, where the police boat awaited them. On the trip across the *laguna*, Vianello gave him the names of the people he had questioned and a quick summary of the banalities they had given him. Bottin's brother, he had learned, lived in Murano, where he worked in a glass factory; the only other people related to him, the family of his late wife, lived on that island as well, though no one had seemed able to tell him what they did there.

The people to whom Vianello had spoken had not been uncooperative in any way: they had all answered whatever questions he put to them. But no one had volunteered any information beyond that contained in the simplest, most direct response. There had been no extraneous detail, no release of the tide of gossip in which all social life swims. They had been clever enough not to answer in bare monosyllables and managed to suggest that they were doing everything they could to recall whatever might be of use to the police. And all the while, Vianello had known what they were doing, and it was likely that they knew he knew.

The launch turned left into the main canal leading back towards San Marco just as Vianello finished giving his account, and spread before them was the sight that had welcomed most arriving eyes ever since the great centuries of the Serenissima. Bell towers, domes, cupolas – all disported themselves for the eyes of the passengers and crew of the arriving boat, each one seeming to jostle the others aside, in the manner of small children, the better to catch the attention of the approaching visitors. The only difference between what the two policemen saw and what would have been visible to those who followed the same channel five hundred years ago was the flock of construction cranes which loomed above the city and, on top of every building, television antennae of every height and configuration.

Seeing the cranes, stark and angular, Brunetti was struck by how seldom he ever saw them in motion. Two of them still towered above the hollow shell of the opera theatre, as motionless as all attempts to rebuild it. Thinking of the proud boast blazoned across the front page of *Il Gazzettino* the day after the fire, that the theatre would be rebuilt where it was and as it was, within two years, Brunetti didn't know whether to laugh or weep, a decision he had had far more than two years to consider. Popular belief, itself interchangeable with truth, had it that the motionless cranes cost the city ten million lire a day, and popular imagination had long since abandoned any attempt to calculate the final cost of restoration. Years passed, the money seeped away, and yet the cranes stood motionless, rising silently above the endless yammering and legal squabbling about who would get to perform the reconstruction.

Both of them stopped talking and watched the city draw near. No city is more self-regarding than Venice: cheap and vulgar self-portraits lined the sides of many streets; almost every kiosk peddled garish plastic gondolas; hacks whose berets falsely proclaimed them to be artists sold horrible pastels at every turn. At every step she pandered to the worst and flashed out the meretricious. Added to this was the terrible aftermath of all of these dry weeks: narrow *calli* that stank of urine, both dog and human; a thin layer of dust that was forever underfoot, no matter how many times the streets were swept. And yet her beauty remained unblemished, just as it remained supreme.

The pilot cut to the right and drew up in front of the Questura. Brunetti waved his thanks and jumped on to the embankment, quickly followed by Vianello.

'And now, sir?' the sergeant asked as they passed through the tall glass doors.

'Call the hospital and check when they're going to do the autopsies. I'll set Signorina Elettra to work on the Bottins.' Before Vianello could ask, he added, 'And on Sandro Scarpa, and while she's at it, Signora Follini.'

At the top of the first flight of steps, Brunetti turned off towards Patta's office, and Vianello went down to the uniformed men's office.

'Still thrashing it out with Veblen?' Brunetti asked as he came into Signorina Elettra's small office.

She picked up an envelope and used it to mark her place, then set the book aside. 'It's not easy reading. But I couldn't find it in translation.'

'I could have lent you mine,' Brunetti offered.

'Thank you, sir. If I had known you had it . . .' she began, then let the sentence drop. She wouldn't have asked her superior to bring her a book to read at work.

'Has the Vice-Questore come in yet?'

'He was here for a half-hour after lunch, but then he said he had to go to a meeting.'

One of the things Brunetti liked about Signorina Elettra was the merciless accuracy of her speech. Not, 'had to go to a meeting', but the more precise, 'said he had to go to a meeting'.

'Are you free, then?'

'As the air itself, sir,' she said, folding her hands in front of her like a diligent pupil and sitting up very straight in her chair.

'The murdered men were Giulio Bottin and his son, Marco. Both are from Pellestrina and both are fishermen. I'd like you to find whatever you can about them.'

'Everywhere, sir?'

Assuming this to mean everywhere she had access to with her computer or through her network of friends and connections, he nodded. 'And Sandro Scarpa, also of Pellestrina and probably a fisherman. See if the name Giacomini comes up in anything about them; I don't have a first name. And a Signora Follini, who runs the store there.'

At the name, Signorina Elettra raised her eyebrows in an open avowal of interest.

'You know her?' Brunetti asked.

'No, not really, no more than to say hello to.'

Brunetti waited for her to add something to this but when she did not, he went on, 'I don't know if it's a married name or not.' Signorina Elettra shook her head to indicate she had no clearer idea. 'I guess she's about fifty,' Brunetti offered, then couldn't resist adding, 'Though you'd probably have to drive bamboo shoots under her fingernails to get her to admit it.'

She looked up, startled, and said, 'That's a very unkind thing to say.'

'Is it any less unkind if it's true?' he asked.

She considered for a moment and then answered, 'No, probably more so.'

In defence of his remark, he said, 'She flirted with me,' putting ironic emphasis on 'me' to suggest the absurdity of the woman's behaviour.

Signorina Elettra glanced at him quickly. 'Ah,' was the only thing she allowed herself to say and then just as quickly asked, 'Any other names, sir?'

'No, but see if you can find if they owned the boat free and clear.' He thought for a moment, exploring possibilities. 'And see if any sort of insurance claim was ever made on it.'

She nodded each time he spoke but didn't bother to write any of this down.

'Do you know anyone out there?' he asked suddenly.

'I have a cousin who has a house in the village,' she answered modestly, disguising any pleasure she might have felt in finally being asked this question.

'In Pellestrina?' he asked, with interest.

'Actually, she's my father's cousin. She shocked the family, ages ago, by marrying a fisherman and moving out there. Her eldest daughter married a fisherman, too.'

'And do you visit them?'

'Every summer,' she said. 'I usually spend a week there, sometimes two.'

'How long have you been doing this?' he asked, his mind running well ahead of his question.

She permitted herself to smile. 'Ever since we were kids. And I have even gone fishing on her son-in-law's boat.'

'You? Fishing?' Brunetti asked, as astonished as if she'd said she had taken up Sumo wrestling.

'I was younger then, sir,' she said, then, casting into the deep waters of memory, she added, 'I think it might have been the season Armani tried navy blue.'

He conjured her up then, wide-cut slacks, no doubt a mixture of silk and cashmere, cut low on the hip like the ones sailors wore. Not a white cap, certainly not that, but a captain's hat, brim covered in gold braid. He abandoned this vision, returned to her office, and asked, 'You still go out there?'

'I hadn't made plans yet to go out this summer, sir, but if you ask it like that, I suppose I can.'

Brunetti had had no idea at all of asking her to go and had inquired out of simple curiosity, wondering if she knew someone who would be willing to talk to them openly. 'No, nothing like that, Signorina,' he said. 'I was just surprised at the coincidence.' Even as he spoke, however, he was considering what she had just told him: a cousin in Pellestrina, a cousin married to a fisherman.

She interrupted his thoughts by saying, 'I

hadn't made any other plans for vacation, you know, sir, and I really do love it there.'

'Please, Signorina,' he said, forcing himself to sound convinced and, he hoped, convincing, 'it's hardly anything we could ask of you.'

'No one's asking, sir. I'm merely trying to decide where to go for the first part of my vacation.'

'But I thought you just came back from . . .' he began, but she stopped him with a glance.

'There are so few days I manage to take,' she said modestly, and at the words, he blotted from his memory the postcards that had arrived at the Questura from Egypt, Crete, Peru and New Zealand.

Before she could suggest anything, he said, 'I hardly think any of this is proper, Signorina.'

She gave him a look that combined shock and injury. 'I'm not sure it's anyone's business where I choose to spend my vacation, sir.'

'Signorina,' he began by way of protest, but she cut him short with her most efficient voice.

'We can discuss this again at some other time, sir, but first let me see what I can find out about those people.' She turned her head to one side, as if hearing a sound Brunetti could not. 'I think I remember something about the Bottins, a few years ago. But I'll have to think about it.' She gave him a broad smile. 'Or I can ask my cousin.'

'Of course,' Brunetti agreed, not at all pleased at the way she had outmanoeuvred him. Habitual caution made him ask, 'Do they know you work here?'

'I doubt it,' she answered. 'Most people really aren't interested in other people or what they do, not unless it bothers or affects them in some way.' Brunetti had concluded much the same thing, through years of experience. He wondered if her belief was theoretical or practical; she seemed so young and so untender.

She looked up at him and said, 'My father never approved of the fact that I left the bank, so I doubt he's told anyone where I'm working. I imagine most of my family still think I work there. If they bother to think about it at all, that is.'

Brunetti had become aware of what his enthusiasm had led her to contemplate, and again he protested. 'Signorina, this is not a good idea. These two men were murdered.' Her glance was cool, uninterested. 'And you're really not a member of the police, not officially, that is.' As he had seen done in countless films, she turned up her palm, bent her fingers, and examined her nails, as though they were the most interesting thing in the room. With her thumbnail, she flicked an invisible speck from another nail, then glanced in his direction to see if he was finished.

'As I was saying, sir, I think I'll be on vacation next week. The Vice-Questore will be gone, so I don't think he'll be much inconvenienced by my absence.'

'Signorina,' Brunetti said, his voice calm and official, 'there could be a certain measure of danger involved here.' She didn't answer. 'You don't have the skills,' he said.

'Would you rather send Alvise and Riverre?' she asked drily, naming the two worst officers on the force. Then she repeated, 'Skills?'

He began to speak, but she cut him off again. 'What skills do you think I'm going to need, Commissario: to fire a gun or restrain a suspect or jump from a third-floor window?'

He refused to answer, not wanting to provoke her further and reluctant to admit he was responsible in any way for her hare-brained idea.

'What sort of skills do you think I've been using here since I was hired? I don't go out and arrest people, but I send you to the people you should arrest, and I give you the evidence that will help convict them. And I do it, sir, by asking people questions and then thinking about what they tell me and using that to go and ask other questions of other people.' She paused but he said nothing, merely nodded to show that he was listening to what she said.

'If I do it with this,' she said, waving a red-nailed hand above her computer keyboard, 'or I go out to Pellestrina to spend time with people I've known for years, there's really little difference.'

When he saw that she had stopped, he said, 'I'm concerned about your safety, Signorina.'

'How gallant,' she said, stunning him with her tone.

'And I don't have the authority to send you

out there. It would be completely irregular.' He marvelled at the realization that he didn't have the authority to stop her.

'But I have the authority to grant myself a week's vacation, sir. There's nothing irregular about that.'

'You can't do that,' he insisted.

'Our first fight,' she said with a falsely tragic face, and he was forced to smile.

'I really don't want you to do this, Elettra,' he said.

'And the first time you've used my name.'

'I don't want it to be the last,' he shot back.

'Is that a threat to fire me or a warning that someone out there might kill me?'

He thought about his answer for a long time before he gave it. 'If you'll promise not to go out there, I'll promise never to fire you.'

'Commissario,' she said, returning to her usual formality, 'tempting as that offer is, you must understand that Vice-Questore Patta would never let you fire me, not even if I were discovered to be the person who killed those two men. I make his life too comfortable.' Brunetti was forced to admit, at least to himself, the truth of this.

'If I charge you officially with insubordination?' he asked, though both of them knew his heart wasn't in it.

As if he had not spoken, she continued, 'I'll need some way to keep in touch with you.'

'We can give you a *telefonino*,' he said, caving in.

'It'll be easier for me to use my own,' she said. 'But I'd like to have someone there, just in case what you say is true and there is some danger.'

'Some of our men will be sent out to investigate. We can tell them you're there.'

Her answer was instant. 'No. I don't trust them not to talk to me if they see me or, if you tell them to ignore me, make such a production of it that they'll call attention to me in any case. I don't want anyone here to know what I'm doing. If possible, I don't want them even to know I'm there. Except you and Sergeant Vianello.'

Did her reluctance, he wondered, result from information he didn't have about the people who worked in the Questura or from a scepticism about human nature even more profound than his own? 'If I assign myself the investigation, then I'll be the one to go out to talk to people, just Vianello and I.'

'That would be best.'

'How long are you planning on staying out there?'

'I can stay as long as I usually do, I suppose: a week, perhaps a bit more. It's not as if the people in the village are going to see me get down from the orange bus and come up to tell me the name of the person who did it, is it, sir? I'll just go out and stay with my cousin and see what's new and what people are talking about. Nothing at all unusual about that.'

There was little left to settle. 'Would it be too

melodramatic if I asked if you'd like to take a gun with you?' he asked.

'I think it would be far more melodramatic if I accepted, sir,' she said, and turned away, as glad as he to be finished with all of this. 'I'll start seeing what I can find about the Bottins, shall I?' she asked, reaching out to swing the screen of her computer towards her.

7

'You're going to let her do *what*?' Paola protested that night after dinner, when he had finished telling her about his trip to Pellestrina and his subsequent conversation – he wanted to call it a confrontation but thought that was an exaggeration – with Signorina Elettra in the office. 'You're going to let her go out to Pellestrina and play detective? Alone? Unarmed? With a killer running around? Are you out of your mind, Guido?'

They were still sitting at the table, the children gone off to do whatever it is dutiful and obedient children do after dinner in order to avoid their share of the housework. She set her glass, still half full of Calvados, back on the table and stared across at him. 'I repeat: are you out of your mind?'

'There was no way I could stop her,' Brunetti insisted, conscious of how weak the admission made him sound. In his recounting of the incident, he had omitted to mention that the original idea had come from him and had given Paola a modified version in which Signorina Elettra insisted on her own initiative that she take a more active part in the investigation. Brunetti heard himself emerging from his telling of the tale as the hapless boss, outwitted by his secretary and too indulgent to endanger her career by imposing upon her the necessary discipline.

Long experience with the prevarications of men in positions of power led Paola to suspect that what she heard was at some variance with the truth. She saw no profit, however, in questioning his account of the incident when it was only the results that interested her.

'So you're going to let her go?' she repeated.

'I told you, Paola,' he said, thinking it would be better to wait until this was over before he poured himself another Calvados, 'it's not at all a case of letting her; it's a case of not being able to stop her. If I hadn't given in, she would have taken a week of vacation and gone out there on her own anyway to start asking questions.'

'Then is she the one who's out of her mind?' Paola demanded.

Though there were many questions Brunetti would have liked answered about Signorina Elettra, this was not among them. Rather than say that, he gave in to his baser nature and poured himself another drop of Calvados.

'What does she think she's going to be able to do?' Paola asked.

He set his glass down untouched. 'The way she explained it to me, she hopes to employ the same tactics and techniques she does with her computer: ask questions, listen to the answers, then ask more questions.'

'And what if, while she's asking one of these questions, someone decides to stick a knife into her stomach the way they did with that fisherman's son?' Paola demanded.

'That's exactly what I asked her,' Brunetti said, which was certainly true in intention if not in fact.

'And?'

'She's convinced that the fact that she's been going out there every summer for years is enough.'

'To what – shroud her in a cloak of invisibility?' Paola rolled her eyes and shook her head in astonishment.

'She's not a fool, Paola,' Brunetti said in Signorina Elettra's defence.

'I know that, but she's only a woman.'

He had been leaning forward to pick up his glass when she spoke, but her remark stopped him cold. 'This from the Rosa Luxemburg of feminism?' he asked. 'She's *only* a woman?'

'Oh, fight fair, Guido,' Paola said with real anger. 'You know what I mean. She'll be out there with a *telefonino* and her wits, but someone else is out there with a knife, and this someone has already murdered two people. Those aren't odds I'd want to give to anyone I cared about.'

He registered her last remark and let it pass for the moment. 'Perhaps you should have talked to her, instead of me.'

'No,' Paola said, ignoring his sarcasm. 'I doubt that would have done any good.' Paola had met Signorina Elettra only twice, both times at official dinners given by Patta for members of the Questura staff. Each time, though they had been introduced to one another and had managed to speak for a few moments, they had been seated at different tables, something Brunetti had always viewed as a conscious decision on Patta's part to keep the two women from talking about him.

Ever practical, Paola leaped over theory and recrimination and set herself to deal with reality. 'Is there any way you can see that someone could be put there to keep an eye on her?'

'I'm not sure at this point that that will be necessary.'

'When and if it does become necessary, it will be too late to do anything about it,' Paola said, and he was forced to agree, though he didn't tell her this.

'Well?' she insisted.

'I spoke to Vianello to see if there's anyone on the force who lives out there.' He shook his head to indicate the answer. 'Besides, she was very insistent that she doesn't want anyone except me and Vianello to know where she is and what she's doing.' Before Paola could ask, he explained. 'She said no one in her family knows what she does, though I find that hard to believe. I'd agree it's unlikely that her relatives on Pellestrina know, especially if she sees them only once a year, but I'm sure that some members of her family must pay attention to what she does.'

'And if they do know or someone asks her about it, or someone finds out she works at the Questura?' Paola asked.

'Oh,' he said instantly, 'I'm sure she'd be able to invent something to explain it. She's an excellent liar; I've listened to her do it for years.'

'But what if she's in danger?' Paola asked, bringing him back to earth.

'I certainly hope she isn't.'

'That's not an answer, Guido, and it's not enough.'

'There's nothing we can do. She's decided this and I don't think she can be stopped.'

'You sound very cavalier about it, I must say.'

Brunetti was uncertain of how his wife would respond to any revelation of his feelings for another woman, so he made no attempt to defend himself.

'It would be terrible if anything happened to her,' Paola said.

Biting back the confession that it would break his heart, Brunetti reached forward and picked up his Calvados.

The next morning, Brunetti got to the Questura after nine, delayed by phone calls to three different informers, calls he was always careful to make from public phones and only to their *telefonini*. Though all had read about the crime, none of them could give him any information about the Bottins or their murder. All promised to call him if they heard anything, but none was optimistic because the crime had taken place so far away. As far as his Venetian contacts were concerned, it might as well have taken place in Milan.

The subject of his discussion with Paola was not in her office when he got there, so he went up to his own and read quickly through the newspapers. The national papers had under-standably not bothered with the Bottins, but *Il Gazzettino* had given them half of the first page of the second section. In the hyperventilated style the local paper reserved for crimes of violence, the article began by asking if the Bottin men had felt some sort of strange premonition or if they had known, when they woke up the previous morning, that it would turn out to be the last day of their lives. Since these questions had become, by now, the paper's opening trope in any account of any violent death, Brunetti muttered, 'Probably not.'

The story repeated the facts Brunetti had already learned: the father had died from a blow to the head, the son from a knife wound. Both had been dead when the boat was set on fire and sunk. The newspaper account told him nothing new, though it did contain small photos of the two dead men. Bottin had the rough-featured look of a man who had spent too much time in the open. His expression showed the usual sullen hostility to be seen in photos on official documents. Marco, on the other hand, was smiling, two deep dimples visible just at the corners of his mouth. While the father was dark, his neck short and thick, Marco seemed made of finer, lighter materials. His fineness of feature would probably have disappeared, Brunetti realized, after two decades on the sea, but there was an easy grace about the tilt of Marco's head that made Brunetti curious about his mother and about the forces that had led him to share in the brutality of his father's fate.

8

Signorina Elettra didn't come into his office until more than two hours after he arrived. When he saw her, Brunetti found it impossible to resist the impulse to approach her, and he raised himself from his chair. Propriety, however, restrained him. 'Good morning,' he said casually, hoping, by the ordinariness of his greeting, to carry them back to simpler times, before she'd got the idea – no, he'd be honest here – before he'd given her the idea of going out to Pellestrina.

'Good morning, sir,' she said in an entirely normal way. He saw in her hand a few sheets of paper.

'The Bottins?' he asked.

She held them up. 'Yes. But very little, really,'

she said apologetically. 'I'm still working on the others.'

'Let me see,' he said, as he sat down, very carefully keeping his tone level.

She placed the papers in front of him, then turned and made towards the door. Brunetti watched her leave, the narrowness of her back exaggerated by a light blue sweater with thin white vertical stripes. He remembered, then, asking her, some years ago, about the new millennium and what her plans and hopes for it were. Her plans, she'd answered, were to see how well baby blue, the announced colour of the new decade, suited her, and her only hope was that it would. When pressed, she'd admitted that she did have one or two other little things to hope for, but she hardly thought they were worth talking about, and that had been the end of that. Well, it suited her, baby blue, and Brunetti found himself wishing that, whatever other hopes she might have had, they'd all been granted her.

The Bottins, when he looked through the papers, were revealed as rather unexceptional men: they owned both the house on Pellestrina and the *Squallus* jointly, though they had separate bank accounts. Both owned cars, though Marco was also sole owner of a house on Murano, left to him by his mother.

Beyond the realm of the financial, Giulio began to stand out: he was known to the Carabinieri on the Lido and was the subject of a number of *denuncie*, three of them resulting from fights in bars and one from an incident that had taken place between two boats on the *laguna*, though the other boat had not been Scarpa's. Bottin seemed, however, to have lived a charmed life so far as the police were concerned, for, however well known he was to them, formal charges had never been made against him, which suggested a lack of evidence or reluctance on the part of witnesses to testify. Marco had never been reported to the police.

Brunetti searched for a report of whatever had happened between the boats on the *laguna*, but no details were provided. He stopped himself from calling Signorina Elettra to ask her who might be able to provide this information, hoping she'd somehow forget about going.

Instead, he called down to the squad room and asked for Montisi to be sent up to his office.

The pilot knocked on the door a few minutes later, came in without bothering to salute or acknowledge Brunetti's rank, and took the seat Brunetti pointed out to him. He sat with his feet flat on the floor in front of him, his hands grasped around the arms of his chair, almost as if long exposure to the sea had made him eternally expectant of some sudden shift of tide or current. Brunetti could see the short stump of Montisi's little finger, the last two joints lost in some long-forgotten boating accident.

'Montisi,' Brunetti began, 'do you have any friends who are fishermen?'

Montisi showed no curiosity. 'Fishermen, yes. *Vongolari*, no.' The heat with which he answered surprised Brunetti, as did the distinction he drew.

'What's wrong with the *vongolari*?' he asked.

'They're *figli di puttane*, every one of them.'

Brunetti had heard a similar opinion of the clam fishermen from Vianello, among others, but he'd never heard it expressed with such disgust.

'Why?'

'Because they're hyenas,' Montisi answered. 'Or vultures. They suck up everything with their damned vacuum cleaner scoops, rip up the breeding beds, destroy whole colonies.' Montisi paused, pulled himself forward in his chair, then went on. 'They don't think about the future. The clam beds have fed us for centuries and could feed us for ever. They just dig and dig like wild animals, destroying everything.'

Brunetti remembered his lunch on Pellestrina. 'Vianello won't eat them any more, clams.'

'Ah, Vianello,' Montisi said dismissively. 'He does it for health reasons.' On Montisi's lips, this sounded like an obscenity.

Not quite sure how he was meant to respond, Brunetti asked, 'Is it safe to eat them, then?'

Montisi shrugged. 'At my age, it's safe to eat anything.' He paused, then went on, 'No, I suppose it isn't safe to eat some of them. The bastards dig them up right in front of Porto Marghera, and God knows what's been pumped or dumped into the water there. I've seen the bastards, anchored there at night, with no lights, scooping them up, not fifty metres from the sign saying that the waters are contaminated and fishing's forbidden.'

'But who'd eat them?' Brunetti asked, thinking again of the clams he'd eaten on Pellestrina.

'No one who knew,' the pilot answered. 'But who does know? Who knows where anything in the market comes from any more? A pile of clams is a pile of clams.' Montisi looked up at him then, smiled, and added, 'No passports. No health cards.'

'But isn't there some control, doesn't someone check them?'

Montisi smiled at such innocence from one no longer young but did not deign to answer.

'No, tell me, Montisi,' Brunetti insisted. 'Aren't there health inspectors?' Even as he spoke, Brunetti realized how little he knew about this subject. He'd fished in the *laguna* since he was a boy, but he knew nothing at all about the business of fishing there.

'There are all sorts of inspectors, Dottore,' Montisi answered. Holding up his right hand, he counted them out on his fingers. 'There are inspectors who are supposed to make random checks of the fish that are already on sale in the market: are they really fresh when they're being sold as fresh? There are the inspectors who are supposed to check whether there are any dangerous substances in the fish: heavy metals or poisons or chemicals – all those things that flood into the *laguna* from the factories. Then there are the inspectors from the Magistrato alle

Acque, whose job it is to see that the fishermen fish only where they're supposed to.' He closed his hand into a fist and added, 'These are the ones I know about, but I'm sure, if you looked, you could find all sorts of other inspectors. But that doesn't mean anything gets inspected or, if it does, that whatever they find gets reported.'

'Why not?' Brunetti asked.

Montisi's smile was compassion itself. Instead of speaking, however, he contented himself with rubbing his thumb across the end joint of his first three fingers.

'But who pays?' Brunetti asked.

'Use your imagination, Dottore. Anyone who does something they don't want people to know about or something that would hurt their business if people found out about it: someone with a boat or a fish stall at Rialto, or a business that ships contaminated flounder to Japan or some other country hungry for fish.'

'Are you sure about this, Montisi?'

'Does that mean am I sure this happens or do I know the names of the people who do it?'

'Both.'

Montisi gave his superior a long, reflective look before he answered. 'I suppose, if I thought about it, I could come up with the names of people, friends of mine who work in the *laguna*, who I think might have given money to see that someone overlooked something. And I suppose, if I asked around a bit, I could come up with the names of the people they gave it to.' He stopped.

'But?'

'But two of my nephews are fishermen, have their own boats. And I retire in two years.'

When Brunetti realized that was all the answer Montisi was willing to volunteer, he asked, 'What does that mean?'

'It means my life is on the *laguna*, not here at the Questura; at least it won't be two years from now.'

Brunetti found it a reasonable enough stance. But he tried, nevertheless. 'But if these fish are contaminated in some way, then isn't it dangerous for people to eat them?'

'Does that mean what I think it does, sir?' Montisi asked quietly.

'What?'

'That you're appealing to my duty as a citizen to help get rid of a public danger? It sounds to me like you're asking me to act like I'm Greenpeace and tell you who these people are so that you can stop them from doing something that's dangerous to people and the environment.'

Though there was not a hint of sarcasm in the way he spoke, Brunetti could not help but feel that Montisi's remark made a fool of him. 'Yes, I suppose it's something like that,' he admitted unwillingly.

Montisi moved around in the chair, pulled himself upright, and placed his palms flat on his knees, though his feet were still firmly braced in anticipation of a sudden wave. 'I'm not an educated man, sir,' he began, 'so I'm sure my thinking on this isn't very clear, but I don't see what difference it makes.' Brunetti chose not to interrupt, so the pilot went on. 'Remember when there was talk of closing the chemical plants because of the pollution they caused?' He glanced across at Brunetti and waited for an answer.

'Yes.' Of course he remembered. Investigators had, a few years ago, found all manner of toxic material seeping, pouring, flooding into the *laguna* from the various chemical and petro-chemical plants on the mainland. There'd even been a list in the papers of the workers who had died from cancer during the last ten years, a number so high as to soar off the charts of all probability. A judge had ordered the plants closed, declaring them a danger to the health of the people who worked there, leaving moot the question of the damage they did to the people who lived around them. And within a day there had been a mass protest and the threat of violence from the workers themselves, the very men who handled, breathed in, got splashed by the toxins that were said to be killing them. They demanded that the factories be kept open, that they continue to be allowed to work, and insisted that the long-term possibility of disease was less dangerous than the immediate one of unemployment. And so the plants remained open, the men continued to work, and very little more was said or written about this other tide that flowed into the *laguna*.

Montisi had gone silent, and so Brunetti prompted him. 'What about it?'

'Luca has a patient,' Montisi began, naming

his son, a doctor with an office in Castello. 'He's got some rare form of lung cancer. Never smoked a cigarette in his life. His wife doesn't smoke, either.' He waved his right hand in the general direction of the mainland. 'But he's worked out there for twenty years.'

Montisi stopped; Brunetti asked, 'And?'

'And though Luca's got statistics that say this form of cancer is found only in people who have had long exposure to one of the chemicals they use out there, he still refuses to believe it could have been caused by the place where he works. His wife says it's God's will, and he says it's just bad luck. Luca gave up talking to him about it when he saw that it didn't make any difference to them what it was that was going to kill him. He says there's no way he could make him believe his work had anything to do with it.'

This time, Montisi didn't bother to wait for Brunetti to ask for clarification. 'So I don't think it makes any difference if someone warns people that the clams are dangerous, or the fish or the shrimp. They're going to say that their parents always ate them and they lived to be ninety or they're going to say that you can't worry about everything. Or they're going to get angry that you're trying to take people's jobs away from them. But the one thing you're not going to do is stop people from doing what they want to do, whether it's eat fish that glows in the dark or pay a bribe so they can go on catching and selling it.'

This, Brunetti realized, was the longest speech he'd heard Montisi give in all the years he'd known him. Because the pilot had begun it by mentioning his nephews and the fact of his imminent retirement, Brunetti refused to believe that his explanation was completely truthful.

'When you retire,' Brunetti began, 'are you going to work with your nephews?'

'I've got a pilot's licence,' Montisi answered. 'I can't afford to buy a taxi. I don't think I'd like the work, anyway. They're another bunch of greedy bastards.'

'And you know the *laguna*,' Brunetti suggested.

'And I know the *laguna*.'

Resigned, Brunetti asked, 'Is there anything you can tell me?'

Montisi, he knew, was not as tough as he appeared to be. Over the years, Brunetti had occasionally seen him discard the carapace he wore, abandon the disguise of dour old sea dog who was never surprised by the crimes of men. 'It might help, you know,' Brunetti added, doing his best to make it sound as if he was suggesting, rather than pleading.

Montisi pushed himself to his feet. Before he turned to the door, he said, 'It's not a question of which fishermen do this, sir; it's more a question of which ones don't.' He aimed his right hand in the general direction of his forehead in what Brunetti supposed was meant to be a salute, then added, 'It's too big for you, and it's too big for us.' He said good morning and left the office.

This left Brunetti little wiser than before he asked the pilot to come up. He realized now how foolish he had been to hope that appeals to loyalty to the police or the public good would have any effect when in competition with tribe or, worse, family. He supposed it was a step towards civilization, the ability to think of tribe or family rather than of the self, but it seemed such a tiny step. As always, when he caught himself making these sweeping generalizations about human behaviour, usually when he needed some justification for criticizing the behaviour of someone he knew, he ended up asking himself if, in the same circumstances, he'd behave any differently. The usual conclusion he came to, that he probably would not, put an end to his reflections and left him feeling slightly uncomfortable with an ever-judgmental self. After all, there was very little evidence that public institutions or government took even the least interest in the public good.

He reflected on his brief conversation with Montisi. Certainly, over the years, he'd read numerous accounts of the violence in those waters: boats running aground or into one another; men fallen or knocked overboard and then either saved or drowned; shots fired from boats that were not seen, coming from men whose identity was never discovered. For the most part, however, the *laguna* was generally perceived as a benign presence by the people who lived their lives surrounded by it, many of whom owed their lives and fortunes to it.

In the face of his growing curiosity, he abandoned the superstitious idea that he could somehow influence Signorina Elettra's decision and called down to her to ask if she would check the files of the *Gazzettino* for the last three years and see what she could find about the *laguna*, fishermen, and the *vongolari*, specifically anything that had to do with acts of violence among the fishermen themselves and between them and the police. He knew he'd read more than one article, but because reports of violence on the water often were made to the harbour police or the Carabinieri, he had paid little attention to them.

Child of its waters, Brunetti still idealized the *laguna* as a peaceful place. Did people in India, he wondered, think of Mother Ganges in this manner, as the liquid source of all life, the giver of food and bringer of peace? He'd recently read an article in one of Paola's English magazines on the pollution of the Ganges and the way it was now, in many places, irreversibly fouled, sure to carry disease, if not death, to the people who bathed in or drank its waters, while a lethargic government concerned itself with posturing and empty phrases. He contemplated this but before he could begin to bask in a sense of European superiority, he recalled Vianello's refusal to eat molluscs and Montisi's explanation of the forces that allowed them to be dredged from the bottom of the *laguna*.

From his lower drawer he took out the phone book. Feeling not a little foolish, he opened it at the Ps and, quickly turning the pages, found 'Police'. The sub-listings, for San Polo, Railway and Frontier, were not very promising. Nor did he think there would be much joy on offer from the Postal Police or the Highway Police. He shut the directory, dialled the switchboard downstairs, and asked the operator to whom calls about trouble in the *laguna* were directed. The man on duty explained that it depended what sort of problem got called in: accidents were reported to the Capitaneria di Porto; crimes were dealt with either by the Carabinieri or, and here the operator's voice grew a bit strained, by themselves.

'I understand,' Brunetti said. 'But who goes out to investigate?'

'It depends, sir,' the operator said, his voice a study in discretion. 'If we don't have a boat available, then we call the Carabinieri and they go.'

Brunetti knew too well why the Carabinieri divers had been unavailable to examine the wreck of the *Squallus*, so he merely made a note of this, believing it wiser not to comment.

'And in the last few years . . .' Brunetti began, then stopped himself and said, 'No, forget it. I'll wait for Signorina Elettra.'

Just as he hung up, he thought he heard the operator's voice, disembodied by distance, say, 'We're all waiting for her', but he couldn't be sure.

Like all Italians, Brunetti had grown up hearing Carabinieri jokes: Why are two *Carabinieri* always sent to investigate? One to write and one to read. He understood that the

Americans told the same jokes about Poles, and the English told them at the expense of the Irish. During his career, Brunetti had seen much to prove the truth of this piece of folk wisdom, but it was only in recent years that anything had weakened his faith in a second belief: that, however stupid, however dim they might be, the Carabinieri were rocklike in their honesty.

Becalmed, he could invent nothing with which to busy himself, and so he pulled towards him a sheaf of unread papers and reports and began to glance through them, skimming the texts, paying little attention save to find the place at the end where he was meant to initialize them before passing them on to the next reader. When the kids were younger, he'd been told that the homework they did had all to be collected by their school, put into an archive and kept for ten years. He couldn't remember now who'd told him, though he did remember having visualized, at the time, an enormous archive, as large as the city itself, where all official papers were stored. The Roman historians he so loved had often described an Italian peninsula densely, in parts impenetrably, covered in trees: oak, beech, chestnut; all gone now, of course, cut down to clear land for farming or to build boats. Or, he thought sadly, to be turned into paper to add to the already stored documents that, if unchecked, might some day cover the entire peninsula once again. He'd consigned his fair share of papers to that archive in his time, he thought, as he put his initials on another sheet and set it aside. He glanced at his watch and, reluctant to be perceived as nagging at Signorina Elettra for the information he'd requested, decided to go home for lunch.

9

He found Paola at the kitchen table, head bent over a copy of either *Panorama* or *Espresso*, the two weekly magazines to which she subscribed. Her custom was to let back issues pile up for at least six months before reading them, for she insisted that this was sufficient time to put things into proper perspective and thus allow the current pop star to die of an overdose and lapse into well-merited obscurity; to permit Gina Lollobrigida to launch and abandon yet another career, to wipe the slate clean of all talk of plans for the current political *riforma* and replace it with an entirely new one.

Glancing down, he saw a photo of two men wearing the distinctive white coats of chefs and the red and white banded hoods of Father

Christmas. On the page to their left was a heavily laden table: the evergreens and red candles told him that Paola's reading had finally taken her as far as the end of last year.

'Oh, good,' he said as he bent to kiss the top of her head. 'Does this mean we're having goose for lunch?' When she ignored him, he added, 'Bit hot for that, isn't it? Though whatever it is, it smells wonderful.'

She looked up and smiled. 'Would that goose were what they suggested for Christmas dinner,' she added, tapping at one of the pages with a disapproving forefinger. 'I can't believe these people.'

As this was a frequent response to her reading of these magazines, Brunetti turned his attention to a bottle of Pinot Grigio which he took out of the refrigerator. Pulling two glasses from the cabinet behind, he filled them halfway. As he set Paola's beside her, he made an inquisitive noise.

She chose to construe this as a sign of interest and replied, 'They're telling us that we should abandon all new ideas about eating and return to the way our parents and grandparents ate.' Brunetti, who had had enough of nouvelle cuisine to last a lifetime, could not have agreed more strongly. Knowing that Paola, a more adventurous eater, differed from him in this, he kept his opinion to himself.

'Listen to what they suggest as a way to begin a Christmas dinner in the style of our grandparents.' She picked up the magazine and shook it angrily, as if the attempt would shake some sense into it. '"Goose liver with small pear tarts *al Taurasi* – whatever or whoever that is – with pineapple flavoured with limoncello."' She looked up at Brunetti, who had the presence of mind to shake his head in what he thought was a damning fashion.

Encouraged, she went on, 'Then listen to this. "Sartù – whatever that is – of rice with slices of eggplant with eggs and tiny meatballs *di annecchia* with a sauce of San Marsano tomatoes."' Overcome with disgust at this final excess, she tossed the magazine on to the table, where it closed, thus providing Brunetti with a sight of the prosperous female breasts which served both magazines as a sort of obligatory cover logo. 'Where do they think our grand-parents lived – at the court of Louis the Fourteenth?' she demanded.

Brunetti, who knew that at least one of Paola's great-grandparents had served at the court of the first king of Italy, again chose silence as a response.

Pushing the magazine farther away, she asked, 'Why is it so difficult for them to remember what a poor country Italy was, and not so long ago?'

This seemed something more than a rhetori-cal question, and so Brunetti answered, 'I think people prefer to remember happy times, well, happier times, and if they can't remember them, then to change the memories and make them happier.'

'Old people seem to,' Paola agreed. 'If you

listen to the old women at Rialto, all you hear is how much better things were in the past, how much better they lived, even with less.'

'Or maybe it's because most of the journalists are young, so they really don't remember how things were.'

She nodded. 'And we certainly have no sense of historical memory, not as a society, that is. I had a look at Chiara's history book last week, and it frightened me. In the chapters on this century, it just glides right past the Second World War. Mussolini makes a walk-on appearance in the Twenties, then he's led astray by the wicked Germans, and then it's all over and Rome is free again. Though not before our valiant troops fought like lions and died like heroes.'

'We were never taught anything at all about it in school, not that I can remember,' Brunetti said, pouring himself another half-glass of wine.

'Well,' Paola said after taking a sip of her own, 'when we were in school, the Right was in power, so they'd hardly want an honest discussion of Fascism. And once they formed their alliance with the Left, it would be inconvenient to talk about Communism.' Another sip. 'And since we changed sides during the war, I suppose they have to be careful who they present as the bad guys or the good guys.'

'Who's "they"?' Brunetti asked.

'The people who write the history books. Or, rather, the politicians who decide who will write the history books, at least the ones that get used in the schools.'

'And the idea of simple historical truth?' Brunetti asked.

'You spend most of your time reading history, Guido: that should be enough to show you there is no such thing.'

He had only to call to mind the difference between the Protestant and Catholic histories of the Papacy to see how right she was. But that was religion, where everyone is expected to lie; here, they were talking about living memory: people were still alive who had taken part in the events they were talking about; the fathers of most of his friends had fought in the war.

'Maybe it's harder to distinguish the truth when you know it from your own experience,' he suggested, then, seeing her confusion, he added, 'If it's just records of people you never knew, from hundreds of years ago, then you can be honest, or at least you're more likely to be honest.'

'Like the Church's account of the Inquisition?' she inquired.

He grinned at his defeat and asked, 'If not goose, what are we having?'

Gracious in her victory, she said, 'I thought we'd eat the food of our forefathers.'

'Specifically?'

'Those *involtini* you like so much, with prosciutto and artichoke hearts in the centre.'

'I doubt that any ancestor of mine ever ate such a thing,' he confessed.

'There's polenta to go with them. To preserve historical truth.'

Both children were present at lunch, but they were curiously subdued, concerned with the last weeks of school and the final exams of the year. Raffi, who hoped to begin university in the autumn, had become something of a phantom during the last months, emerging from his room only for meals or to ask his mother's help with a difficult translation from the Greek. His romance with Sara Paganuzzi was kept alive, it seemed, only by means of late night phone calls and occasional before-dinner meetings in Campo San Bortolo. Chiara, who was coming into the full inheritance of her mother's beauty more with every passing month, was still so caught up in the mysteries of mathematics and celestial navigation that she remained ignorant of the power her beauty was likely to give her.

When lunch was finished, Paola moved out on to the terrace, taking their coffee and luring her husband along with her. The early afternoon sun was so hot that Brunetti removed his tie before he joined her, the first sure sign that summer was on the way.

They sat in easy silence. Voices drifted towards them from a terrace to their left; occasionally one of the sheets hung to dry from the window of the apartment beneath them snapped in the freshening breeze which, alas, held no promise of rain.

'I'm probably going to spend a fair amount of time out in Pellestrina,' Brunetti said.

'When?'

'Starting this week, even as early as tomorrow.'

'To keep an eye on her?' Paola asked, without renewing her objections to Signorina Elettra's decision to go out to Pellestrina.

'Partly, though I'm not sure when she plans to get there.'

'What else?'

'To talk to people and see what they say.'

'Will they talk to you if they know you're a policeman?'

'Well, they can't refuse to talk to me, not really, though they can refuse to tell me the truth, or say they can't remember anything about the Bottins. That's the usual technique.'

'Then why talk to them?' Paola asked.

'Because of what they don't tell me or what they lie to me about.' He closed his eyes and lay back in the sun, letting it beat down on his face for the first time that year. After a long time, he said, 'I guess it makes me like one of those historians or forces me to behave the way they do.' He waited for Paola to ask for clarification, and when she did not, he glanced at her to see if she'd fallen asleep. But she had not. She sat beside him, attentive, waiting for him to continue.

'I've got to listen to all of the variant accounts, weigh the evidence, adjusting my response according to who profits from the different versions.'

'And keeping in mind that everyone is lying to you?'

'Or is likely to be lying to me,' he agreed.

'And then?'

'And then I see what Signorina Elettra has been told.'

'And then?' she repeated.

'I've no idea.'

'And you'll be back at night?'

'I should be. Why?'

She gave him a long look then, surprised at his question. 'In case I finally decide to run off with the postman. I'd like to know you'll still be here to feed the kids.'

Late in the afternoon, Signorina Elettra called up to Brunetti and told him that Vice-Questore Patta wanted to see him in his office. Brunetti seldom greeted such a summons with pleasure, but he was so bored with the reading and initialling of reports that he welcomed even this opportunity to escape. Quickly he went downstairs and into Signorina Elettra's office.

She greeted him with a smile. 'He wants to tell you who will be in charge while he's away.'

'Not me, I hope,' Brunetti said; it would complicate his plans to spend time in Pellestrina.

'No, he's already spoken to Marotta,' she said, naming a commissario from Turin who had been assigned to the Venice Questura earlier in the year.

'Am I meant to be offended?' Brunetti asked. Marotta was by far his junior and a non-Venetian, so his appointment could be intended as nothing but a calculated insult.

'Probably. Or at least I think he'd like you to be.'

'Then I'll do my best to appear so,' Brunetti said. 'I'd hate to disappoint him just as he's going off on vacation.'

'It's not a vacation, sir,' she said in a voice laden with reprimand. 'It's a conference about new methods of crime prevention,' she insisted, making no mention of the details of the invitation.

'In London,' Brunetti added.

'In London,' she confirmed.

'In English,' Brunetti said.

'Yes,' she agreed in that language.

'Which the Vice-Questore speaks as well as he speaks Finnish.'

'Probably better than Finnish. He can say, "Bond Street", "Oxford Street", and "The Dorchester".'

'And "The Ritz",' Brunetti suggested. 'Don't forget that.'

'You've discussed this with him?' she asked.

'Which, the conference or his English?'

'The conference and who should go.'

'I didn't want to waste the time. He told me a few weeks ago that he was going, and before I could raise the question of the language, he told me that his wife had agreed to go along as interpreter.'

'He never told me that,' Signorina Elettra said, barely disguising her surprise and, he thought, irritation. 'Does she speak English?'

'As well as he,' Brunetti said and turned to knock at Patta's door.

The Vice-Questore, as always when in the act of mistreating Brunetti – to whom the invitation had been addressed – cast himself in the role of the injured party. To create the proper visual setting for this, he chose to remain seated at his desk, putting himself lower than Brunetti.

'Where have you been for the last few days?' he asked as soon as he saw Brunetti, who recognized the technique of the pre-emptive strike. Patta himself, wearing a grey suit Brunetti had never seen before, looked as though he'd been spending the last few days getting ready for his trip to London. His greying hair was freshly cut, and his face wore the early summer glow that comes from the careful attention of tanning lamps. As ever, Brunetti was struck by how absolutely right Patta looked for the job of senior police official; senior anything, for that matter.

'We had a call from Pellestrina, sir. Two men were murdered on their boat.' Brunetti tried his best to sound uninterested. 'The call came to us, so I had no choice but to go out and have a look.'

'That's out of our jurisdiction,' Patta said, though they both knew this was not true.

'The Carabinieri were also called,' Brunetti said with a small smile meant to display both relief and agreement with Patta's objection. 'So it's entirely likely that the case will be given to them.'

Something about the way Brunetti spoke made Patta suspicious, the way a dog is when he hears an unfamiliar tone in a familiar voice. 'Does it look like a simple case?'

'I've no idea, sir. Things like this usually turn out to be the result of either jealousy or greed.'

'If that's the case, then it might be a simple thing to solve. Perhaps we could keep it.'

'Oh, I've no doubt that it will be a simple case, sir. In fact, some of the people out there have already given us the name of a man who had trouble with one of the victims.'

'And?' Patta demanded, eager now that it sounded easy. The quick solution of a murder would be a coup for the Questura of Venice. Brunetti could almost see him writing the headline: 'QUICK ACTION BY VICE-QUESTORE SOLVES MURDER CASE.'

'Well, sir, with you away next week, I thought it might be better if the Carabinieri handled it.' Brunetti paused, waiting to see if Patta would pick up on his comment and discuss the hierarchy of command during his absence.

'And let them get the credit?' Patta demanded, making no attempt to hide his indignation and with no reference to the following week. 'If this is as simple as you say,' he began, raising a hand to stop Brunetti's protest, 'then it's definitely something we should investigate. The Carabinieri will make a complete hash of it.'

'But, sir,' Brunetti objected weakly, 'I'm not sure we can spare anyone to go out there.' One of Brunetti's favourite characters had always been Iago, whose skill he had long admired and often sought to emulate. Clasping Iago's image, as it were, to his bosom, Brunetti went on, 'Perhaps Marotta could take it. It would be good to send someone who couldn't possibly have any involvement with the people there. He's from Turin, isn't he, sir?' When Patta nodded, Brunetti went on, 'Good, then there's no chance that he'd know or be related to anyone in Pellestrina.'

Patta had had enough. 'Oh, for God's sake, use your head, Brunetti. If we send *un torinese* out there, no one will say a word to him. It's got to be someone local.' As if as an afterthought, Patta added, 'Besides, Marotta'll be taking my place during my absence, and he can't go running off to the ends of the *laguna* to interview people who don't know how to speak anything but dialect.' If these people also believed that the earth was flat as well as the centre of the universe, Patta's contempt for them could not have been more audible.

Ignoring Patta's remark and not at all certain that he should risk it, Brunetti nevertheless asked, 'But who, sir?'

'There are times when you're incredibly blind, Commissario.' Patta spoke so condescendingly that Brunetti could but admire his superior's self-restraint in not having said 'stupid'. 'You're Venetian. You've already been out there.'

With the exercise of equal self-restraint, Brunetti stopped himself from raising his hands to display shock and astonishment. It was a gesture he'd often seen in silent films from the Twenties and one he'd always wanted to use. Instead, voice deeply serious, he said, 'I'm not sure, sir.' A small goad, he had often noticed, worked on Patta far more effectively than a stronger impetus.

'Well, I am. It's a simple case, and we can use all the good publicity we can get, especially after those fools in the *magistratura* let all of the *mafiosi* out of prison.' The papers had been filled with little else for the last few days. Fifteen Mafia leaders, all condemned to life imprisonment, had been ordered to be released when a minor legal irregularity was discovered in the processing of their appeal. One of them, the papers never ceased to report, had confessed to the murders of fifty-nine people. And now all of them were free. Brunetti recalled Signorina Elettra's words, 'As free as air.'

'I'm not sure the two cases are related, sir,' Brunetti objected.

'Of course they're related,' Patta said, voice raised angrily. 'Any sort of bad publicity reflects on all of us.'

Was that all it was for Patta, Brunetti wondered, bad publicity? These laughing monsters are set free to return to feast on the bodies of their enemies, and all Patta can see is bad publicity?

Before principle could spur Brunetti to protest, Patta continued, 'I want you to go out there and settle this. If you've already got the name of someone, see what you can find out about him. Get this taken care of quickly.' Patta picked up a file from his desk, opened it, took his Mont Blanc from his breast pocket, and began to read. Good sense prevented Brunetti from raising an objection to Patta's peremptory commands or to the rudeness of his dismissal. He'd got what he had come for: the case was his. But not for the first time he left Patta's office feeling cheapened by having so easily manipulated the other man, by having again donned the cap and bells of the fool in order to achieve what he knew to be his by right. Marotta's temporary assignment had never been discussed, which meant Patta had been deprived of the opportunity to gloat over what he would perceive as a victory. But at least Brunetti had been spared the need to pretend to be offended by the decision. Command was the last thing he sought, but this was a piece of information he chose never to reveal, by word or deed, to his superior. Incapable by both nature and inclination of worshipping at the altar of the bitch goddess, Success, Brunetti had more modest desires. He was a man of short views, interested in the here, the now, the concrete. He left larger goals and desires to others, contenting himself with smaller ones: a happy family, a decent life, the attempt to do his job as well as he could. It seemed to him little enough to ask of life, and he settled for those hopes.

10

The next morning, Brunetti and Vianello left for Pellestrina a little after nine. Though both knew they were engaged in the investigation of two savage murders, the glory of the day once again conspired to lighten their hearts and fill them with a schoolboy sense of adventure and fun. No office to be stuck in, no Patta calling to demand instant progress, and no fixed times to be anywhere; even Montisi, grumbling at the helm that they'd be slowed down by cross-tides, couldn't dim their mood. The morning did not disappoint. The trees in the Giardini were covered with new leaves, and occasionally a sudden breeze set them shimmering, their undersides twinkling in the light reflected from the water.

As they approached the island of San Servolo, Montisi arched the boat in a wide curve to the right and took them past Santa Maria della Grazie and San Clemente. Even the thought that these islands had been used for centuries to isolate the sick in mind and body from the rest of the population of Venice did nothing to dampen Brunetti's spirits.

Vianello surprised him by saying, 'Soon there'll be no more chance to go blackberrying.'

Confused, thinking that the rush of the wind might have caused him to misunderstand, Brunetti leaned towards him and asked, 'What?'

'There,' Vianello said, pointing off to their right to the larger island that lay in the farther distance. 'Sacca Sèssola. We used to go out there when we were kids to pick blackberries. It was abandoned even then, so they grew like crazy. We'd pick kilos in a day, eat until we were sick with them.' Vianello raised his hand to shade his eyes from the sun. 'But someone told me it's been sold, auctioned off to a university or some company, and they're going to make it into a convention centre or something like that.' Brunetti could hear his sigh. 'No more blackberries.'

'But more tourists, I suppose,' Brunetti said, referring to the deity currently worshipped by those who ran the city.

'I'd rather have blackberries.'

Neither of them spoke until they saw the single campanile of Poveglia on their right, when Vianello asked, 'How are we going to do this, sir?'

'I think we should try to find out more about the waiter's story, about his brother and anything that might have come of that argument. See if you can find the brother and see what he says, and I'll go back and talk to Signora Follini.'

'You're a brave man, Commissario,' Vianello said, deadpan.

'My wife has promised to call the police if I'm not home by dinnertime.'

'I doubt that even we would be any good against Signora Follini.'

'I'm afraid you might be right, Sergeant, but still, a man must do his duty.'

'Like John Wayne.'

'Precisely. After I've spoken to her, I'll try the other bar: I think there was one up the street from the restaurant, on the other side.'

Vianello nodded. He'd seen it, but it had been closed the day they were there. 'Lunch?' he asked.

'Same place,' Brunetti answered. 'If you don't mind having to pass over the clams and fish.'

'Believe me, sir, I don't mind in the least.'

'But it's the food we grew up with,' Brunetti surprised himself by insisting. 'You must mind not eating it any more.'

'I told you, sir,' Vianello said, turning to look him in the face as he spoke, one hand holding his hat down against a sudden gust of wind, 'everything I've read tells me not to eat them.'

'But you've still got to miss them, want to eat them,' Brunetti insisted.

'Of course I miss them. I wouldn't be human

105

if I didn't. People who stop smoking always miss cigarettes. But I think they'll kill me, really I do.' Before Brunetti could question or ridicule, he continued, 'No, not one plate of them and not fifty plates of them. But they're loaded with chemicals and heavy metals. God knows how they live themselves. I just don't want to eat them; the idea makes me faintly sick.'

'Then how can you miss them?'

'Because I'm Venetian, and they're what I grew up eating, as you said. But they weren't poisoned then. I loved them, loved eating them, loved my mother's spaghetti with clam sauce, her fish soup. But now I know what's in them, and I just can't eat them.' Aware that he still hadn't satisfied Brunetti's curiosity, he said, 'Maybe it's what Indians feel about eating cows.' He thought about it for a while, then corrected himself. 'No, they never eat them to begin with, so they can't stop, can they?' He considered the question further, finally gave up. 'I can't explain what it's like, sir. I suppose I *could* eat them if I wanted to; it's just that I don't want to.'

Brunetti started to say something, but Vianello asked, 'Why does it confuse you so much? You wouldn't react like this if someone stopped smoking, would you?'

Brunetti considered this. 'I suppose not.' He laughed. 'It's probably because it's about food, and I find it hard to believe that anyone could stop eating something as good as clams, regardless of the consequences.'

That seemed to settle the issue, at least for the

moment. Montisi gave the engine full throttle, and its noise blocked out any further attempt to talk. Occasionally they passed boats on either side, anchored in the water, men sitting idly with fishing rods in their hands, engaged more in contemplation than in the attempt to catch fish. Hearing the speed of the approaching boat, most of the men looked up, but when they saw that it was a police boat they returned their attention to the water.

Too soon, as far as Brunetti was concerned, they saw the long dock of Pellestrina. A narrow gap showed the place where the *Squallus* still lay on the bottom, the masts emerging from the water at the same crazy angle. Montisi took them to the end of the pier, cut the motor, and glided silently until they were less than a metre from the *riva*, when he suddenly shot the motor into reverse for a few seconds, then as quickly shut it down. The boat drifted silently to the dock. Vianello tossed a mooring rope around the metal stanchion, easily pulling the boat into place. With quick precision, he knotted the rope and dropped it on deck.

Montisi leaned out of the cabin and said, 'I'll wait for you.'

'That's all right, Montisi,' Brunetti said. 'I've no idea when we'll finish; we can take the bus back to the Lido and the boat from there.'

'I'll wait for you,' Montisi repeated as if Brunetti had never spoken or he hadn't heard what his superior said.

Since Montisi's duties were those of a pilot

only, Brunetti could hardly ask him to move among the population of Pellestrina, asking for information about the murder of the Bottins. Nor did he want to order him to return to the Questura, even though the boat might be needed there. He compromised by asking, 'What'll you do all day?'

Montisi turned and pulled open the lid of the locker to his left. He bent down and pulled out three fishing rods and a small plastic-covered pail. 'I'll be out there,' he said, indicating the water to their right. He looked directly at Brunetti and said, 'If you like, I could go and have a coffee in the bar after I'm done fishing.'

'That might be a good idea,' Brunetti agreed and stepped up on to the pier.

He and Vianello walked towards the clustered houses of the small village. Brunetti looked down at his watch. 'It's after eleven now. I'll meet you at the restaurant.'

When they reached what passed as the centre of Pellestrina, Brunetti turned to his left and approached Signora Follini's store, while Vianello continued on ahead, intending to stop at the restaurant and see if the waiter could tell him where to find his brother.

Signora Follini was already standing behind the counter, talking to an old woman. Signora Follini glanced up when he came in and started to smile. But as Brunetti watched, he saw her suddenly remember the presence of the other woman and change the smile into a formal acknowledgement of the arrival of a stranger who had no claim to anything beyond civility.

'*Buon giorno*,' Brunetti said.

Signora Follini, today wearing an orange dress with large bands of ivory-coloured lace at neck and waist, returned his greeting but immediately turned her attention back to the old woman, who was watching Brunetti. She looked at him, eyes the clouded grey of advancing age, but no less keen for that. If she had teeth, she hadn't bothered to wear them that day. She was short, at least a head shorter than Signora Follini, and she was entirely dressed in black. Looking at her, Brunetti thought that the word 'swathed' would be more appropriate, for it was difficult to distinguish just what it was she wore. A long skirt came to well below her knees, and some sort of woollen coat was buttoned tightly over that. Wrapped around her shoulders and covering her head was a crocheted woollen scarf the ends of which hung down almost to her waist.

Her clothing declared her widowhood as indisputably as would a hand-held placard or a giant letter pinned to her breast. The South was full of women like this, shrouded in black and destined to pass, cloud-like, through the remaining years of their lives, the limits of their behaviour as strictly delineated as those of peasant women in Bengal or Peru. But that was the South, and this was Venice, where widows wore bright colours, went dancing if and with whom they pleased, married again if they so chose.

He felt her eyes on him, nodded, and said, 'Good morning, Signora.'

She ignored him and turned back to Signora Follini. 'And a package of candles and half a kilo of flour,' Brunetti thought she said, though her dialect was so strong he wasn't sure. Here he was, less than twenty kilometres from his own home, and he found it hard to understand the natives.

He moved towards the back of the store and started to examine the goods on the shelves. He picked up a can of Cirio tomatoes and, out of curiosity, turned it over to look at the sell-by date. It had expired two years before. He set the can carefully back into the ring of dust that had surrounded it and moved towards the soap powder.

He glanced back at the counter, but the widow was still there. He heard her talking to Signora Follini, but her voice was too low for him to hear what she was saying, not that he was sure he'd understand her if he could. A thin film lay on top of the irregularly stacked boxes of detergent; one had been chewed open at a corner, and a small mound of tiny white and blue beads had spilled out on to the shelf.

His watch told him he'd been inside the store for more than five minutes. Signora Follini had added nothing to the candles and flour, which sat on the counter in front of the old woman, but still they stood there and still they talked.

He retreated further into the back of the shop and directed his attention to a row of bottles of pickles and olives that stood at the height of his chest. One bottle of what appeared to be mushrooms caught his attention because of a small oval of white mould that had edged from beneath the lid and begun to make its way slowly down the side of the bottle. Next to it stood a tiny can that had no label. It sat there, looking curiously lost and useless, yet faintly menacing.

Brunetti heard the bell and turned towards the counter. The old woman was gone, and with her had disappeared the candles and flour. He walked towards the front of the store and said again, 'Buon giorno.'

She smiled in response, but the smile had little warmth; perhaps the old woman had taken some of it with her or had left behind a cool warning about how women with no visible husbands were meant to behave in the presence of strange men.

'How are you today, Signora?'

'Fine, thank you,' she answered with some formality. 'How can I help you?' On his previous visit, she would have asked this with the clear suggestion that what she would be willing to provide contained at least the promise of sensuality. This time, however, the list suggested by her voice went no further than dried peas, salt and a bottle of anchovies.

Brunetti gave her his warmest smile. 'I've come back to speak to you, Signora,' he began, wondering if this would cause her to respond. When it did not, he went on, 'I wanted to ask if you'd remembered anything else about the Bottins that might be useful to us.' Her face remained expressionless. 'You suggested, the last time we spoke, that you knew at least the son very well, and I wondered if you'd thought of anything else that might be important.'

She shook her head but still didn't speak.

'By now I suppose it's common knowledge that they were murdered,' he began and waited.

'I know,' she finally said.

'But what people don't know is that it was a particularly vicious crime, especially what was done to Marco.'

She nodded at this, to acknowledge either that she had heard him or that even this detail was now known to the people of Pellestrina.

'And so we need to learn as much about them as possible so that we can begin to get an idea of who would want to do this.' When she didn't respond, he asked, 'Do you understand, Signora?'

She looked up and met his eyes. Her mouth remained frozen in the smile the surgeons had given her, but Brunetti could not mistake the sadness in her eyes. 'No one would want to do Marco any harm. He was a good boy.'

She stopped here and glanced away from him, towards the empty back of the store.

'And his father?' Brunetti asked.

'I can't tell you anything,' she said in a tight voice. 'Nothing.'

Something in Brunetti responded to the nervousness in her voice. 'Nothing you tell me will be repeated, Signora.'

The immobility of her features made her expression impossible to read, but he thought he sensed her relax.

'They couldn't have wanted to kill Marco,' she said.

'They?' he asked.

The nervousness swept back. 'Whoever it was,' she said.

'What sort of man was he, Giulio?' Brunetti asked.

Her sculpted chin moved back and forth in absolute denial of any further information.

'But, Signora . . .' Brunetti began but was interrupted by the sound of the bell. He saw her eyes shoot in the direction of the door. She stepped back from the counter and said, 'As I've told you, Signore, you'll have to buy matches at the tobacco shop. I don't sell them.'

'Sorry, Signora. When I saw the candles you sold the old lady, I thought you'd be selling them, too,' he answered seamlessly, paying no attention to the sound of footsteps behind him.

Brunetti turned away from the woman and moved towards the door. As is the custom in small villages, he nodded in acknowledgement of the presence of the two men who stood there and, while paying no evident attention to them, registered every detail of their appearance. As he approached the door, they stepped to either side of it, a motion that filled Brunetti with a vague sense of menace, though the men made it clear that they took as little interest in him as he did in them.

The little bell tinkled as he opened the door, and when he stepped into the sunlight, his back gave an answering shiver as he heard the door close gently behind him.

He turned to the right, his mind absorbing the faces and forms of the two men. Though he recognized neither, Brunetti knew too well the type of men they were. They might have been related, so similar were the red, roughened complexions of their faces and so similar their thick, hardened bodies. But both of these things might just as easily have come from years of heavy work outside. The younger man had a narrow face, and dark hair slicked back with some sort of oily pomade. The older wore his in the same fashion, but as it was much thinner, it ended up looking as if it had been painted on to his skull, though a few greasy locks managed to dangle limply on the collar of his shirt. Both wore jeans that gave signs of heavy wear and the thick boots common to men who did heavy work.

The men had studied Brunetti with eyes framed by a multitude of small lines, the lines that came with years of life in the sun, and both had given him the sort of attention that is usually given to prey: motionless, watchful, eager to make a move. It was this sense of contained aggression that had set off alarms in Brunetti's body, regardless of the fact that the Signora was there as a witness, regardless of the fact that the men probably knew he was a policeman.

He walked down the narrow street and into the tobacco shop. It was as dim and grimy as Signora Follini's store, another place where failure had come to nest.

The man behind the counter raised his attention from the magazine he was reading and looked at him from behind thick glasses. 'Yes?' he asked.

'I'd like some matches,' Brunetti said, maintaining Signora Follini's story.

The man pulled open a drawer beneath the counter and asked, 'Box or booklet?'

'Box, please,' Brunetti said, reaching into his pocket for some small change.

The man set a small box of matches in front of Brunetti and asked for two hundred lire. As Brunetti placed the coins on the counter, the man asked, 'Cigarettes?'

'No,' Brunetti answered. 'I'm trying to stop. But I like to have matches in case I can't stand it any more and ask someone to give me one.'

The man smiled at that. 'Lot of people trying to stop,' he said. 'They don't want to, not really, most of them, but they think it's good for them, so they try.'

'And do they succeed?'

'Beh,' the man exclaimed in disgust. 'They manage it for a week or two, or a month, but sooner or later they're all back in here, buying cigarettes.'

'Doesn't say much for people's willpower, does it?' Brunetti asked.

The man picked up the coins and dropped

them one by one into the wooden cash drawer. 'People are going to do what they want to do, no matter what you tell them and no matter how bad they know it is for them to do it. Nothing can stop them; not fear or law or promises.' He saw Brunetti's expression and added, 'You spend a lifetime selling cigarettes, and that's one thing you learn. Nothing will ever stop them, not if they want to badly enough.'

11

The tobacconist's words lingered with Brunetti as he walked towards the restaurant: he wondered if they would some day apply to Vianello and the clams or whether the sergeant would turn out to be one of those rare men who have the strength of character to stop themselves from doing what they want to do. As for himself, Brunetti believed he was not particularly strong-willed and knew he often manipulated situations so that he could avoid having to make the decision to do something he didn't want to do.

Two years ago, when Paola had finally nagged him into having a complete physical exam, he had told the doctor not to bother with the tests for cholesterol and diabetes, leaving it to the doctor to infer that the tests were not necessary because he'd recently had them done. In truth, Brunetti had not wanted to know the results because he had not wanted to have to do whatever he would have to do if the results were bad. Whenever he thought of his deceit and the possible consequences to his family, he told himself he had never felt healthier in his life and to stop worrying about it.

And three years ago, when an Albanian suspect had been arrested for having beaten the two eleven-year-old prostitutes who helped to support him, Brunetti had done nothing to prevent his being assigned for questioning to a detective who had a daughter the same age and another whose fifteen-year-old daughter had been assaulted by another Albanian. Nor had he ever enquired as to just what happened during the examination, though the suspect had quickly confessed to the crimes.

Before he could examine his conscience further, he reached the restaurant and went in. From behind the counter, where he was making coffee for a few men standing at the bar, the owner acknowledged his arrival with a nod. 'Your officer is in the back,' he said. All of the men at the counter turned to look at Brunetti, and he felt the same intense stare he'd been given by the two men in the store. Ignoring it, he moved to the curtained doorway, pushed aside the strips of plastic, and went into the dining room.

Vianello sat at the same table, a bottle of

mineral water and a half-litre of white wine in front of him. As Brunetti pulled out the chair opposite him, Vianello leaned forward and poured some water, then some wine, into the glasses at Brunetti's place.

Brunetti drank down the glass of water, surprised at how thirsty he was, curious as to whether it could be a delayed response to the fear – he admitted that it was fear – he had felt when he turned his back on the two men. Looking across at Vianello, he asked, 'Well?'

'The waiter, Lorenzo Scarpa, hasn't been back to work since we were here. The boss says he called and said he had to go and take care of a friend, but he didn't say where the friend lived, and he didn't give any idea of how long he'd be gone.' Brunetti asked nothing about this, so Vianello continued. 'I went to his place – the boss gave me his address – but his neighbours can't remember seeing him for a few days, say they don't have any idea where he is.'

'And the brother, Sandro?'

'Surprisingly enough, he's still here. Well, he's been here. His boat is still out, left before dawn this morning and still isn't back.'

'What could that mean?'

'Anything, really,' Vianello said. 'That the fish are running and he doesn't want to stop or that he's had engine trouble. The boss here seemed to think it's nothing more than a run of good luck, lots of fish.'

Vianello sipped at his wine, then went on. 'Signora Bottin died of cancer five years ago. Her relatives have had nothing to do with Giulio or Marco since she died.'

'Why?' Brunetti asked.

'That house on Murano. They disputed her will, but as it had been left to her by her parents and Bottin agreed that it should go to the son entirely, there was really no case they could make for it.'

'And since then?'

'There's been no contact between them, it seems.'

'Where'd you learn this?'

'The owner of the bar. He seemed to think it was innocent enough to tell me at least this much.'

Brunetti wondered what new dispute would now result about ownership but asked, instead, 'And this Giacomini the waiter told us about?'

Vianello pulled out his notebook and flipped it open. 'Paolo Giacomini, another fisherman. The owner says he lives in Malamocco, but for some reason he keeps his boat here. He's known as a troublemaker, someone who likes to cause bad blood between people.'

'And the trouble between Scarpa and Bottin?'

'No one would tell me anything about it except that there was some sort of run-in between them a year or so ago. Either they collided or came close and got their nets tangled. Whatever it was, there's been bad feeling between them ever since.'

'We can try the police in Chioggia,' Brunetti suggested.

'Probably the best thing, if it happened there,' Vianello agreed. 'If that's where the *denuncia* was made, perhaps they can tell us something. I get the feeling that these people take care of things in their own way. And they've all taken a vow of silence where Bottin is concerned. No one can remember anything about him; certainly no one has a bad word to say about him.'

'Yet Signora Follini told me that, whatever happened, it happened because of him, not because of the son.'

'So now what do we do?' Vianello asked.

'First we have lunch,' Brunetti answered, 'then we go and see if we can find this Giacomini.'

The meal passed off pleasantly enough, in part because Brunetti made no comment upon Vianello's choices and in part because he restrained himself from having clams, though he did eat an enormous platter of *coda di rospo* which the owner assured him had been caught that morning. The owner had not succeeded in replacing Lorenzo Scarpa and had to wait on tables himself, so the meal took a long time to arrive, a situation worsened by the entrance of a string of Japanese tourists just as Brunetti and Vianello ordered.

Their guide seated them at two long tables against the walls, where they seemed quite happy to wait for their meal while smiling and bowing to one another, the guide, Brunetti and Vianello, and the owner. Their behaviour was so exquisitely restrained and polite that Brunetti was amazed that anyone should ever speak badly of them. When he and Vianello were finished, they paid their bill, again in cash, received no receipt and got to their feet. Automatically, Brunetti bowed in the direction of the Japanese, waited for Vianello to do the same and for the Japanese to respond, then led his sergeant out to the bar section, where they had coffee but refused grappa.

It had grown still warmer while they were inside, and they rejoiced in the heat of the day. It brought back the sense of boyish freedom they'd experienced when they set out that morning. Back at the police launch, they found no sign of Montisi, though a string of fish was hanging in the water from a stanchion on the other side of the boat.

Neither of them much minded having to wait, and they were happy enough to sit on a wooden bench that looked across the waters in the general direction of Venice, though all they could see was the water of the *laguna*, a few boats moving across it, and the topless, endless sky.

'Where do you think he's gone?' Brunetti asked.

'Montisi or Scarpa?'

'Montisi.'

'He's probably in some bar, learning more in five minutes than we have in two days.'

'Wouldn't surprise me in the least,' Brunetti said, removing his jacket and turning his face up to the sun. Vianello was prevented from doing the same only by the fact that he was wearing uniform.

After about ten minutes, Brunetti was awakened from a semi-doze by Vianello's voice, saying, 'Here he comes.'

He opened his eyes, looked to the right, and saw Montisi, wearing his dark uniform slacks and a white shirt with a large black stain on one shoulder, walking in their direction. When the pilot reached them, Brunetti moved to the left, making a space for him on the bench between them.

'And?' he asked when Montisi sat down.

'I decided to have trouble with the engine,' the pilot answered.

'Decided?' Vianello asked.

'That way I'd have to ask someone for help.'

'What did you do?'

'I sawed through one of the distributor wires with a file and left it hanging, then tried to start up. Couldn't. So I opened the engine again, saw what was wrong, and went into the village to see if someone would give me a piece of wire.'

'And?' Brunetti asked.

'And I found a man I know from the Army, when I did my military service. His son has a boat out here, and my friend takes care of the engines for him. He came along with me, saw the wire, went back to his workshop and found me a piece, then came back and helped me change it.'

'Did he realize what you'd done?' Vianello asked.

'Probably. I was hoping to get someone who didn't know much about engines, well, as much as I do. But Fidele probably saw what I'd done. Doesn't matter. I took him down to the bar to thank him and he was willing to tell me about them.'

'The Bottins?' Brunetti asked.

'Yes.'

'What did he say?'

Brunetti found it interesting, the way Montisi distanced himself from the information he'd managed to obtain. It was what Brunetti wanted or what Vianello wanted. It was probably no more than Montisi's way of remaining loyal to the other fisherman, the tribe he was so soon going to rejoin.

'Anything you're looking for, it was the father,' Montisi finally explained.

'Who told you that?' Vianello asked.

At the same time Brunetti asked, 'What did he do?'

Montisi answered both questions with the same shrug, then said, 'No one told me anything exact, but it was clear that no one liked him. Usually they pretend they do, at least they do when they're talking to foreigners like me. But not with Bottin. I figure it's something he did, but that's just a feeling. I don't have any idea what it could have been, but it was as if they didn't consider him one of them any more.'

'Because of the way he treated his wife?' Brunetti asked.

'No,' Montisi said with a sudden shake of his

head. 'She was from Murano, so she didn't count,' and with that, he dismissed her humanity as easily as the possibility.

There was a long silence. Three cormorants came whizzing past them and splashed down a good distance from shore. They swam around for a while, seemed to confer among themselves as to where the fish might be, then, so smoothly as hardly to disturb the surface of the water, disappeared below it, leaving no trace. Automatically, curious, Brunetti began to hold his breath when he saw them slip under the water, but he was forced to expel it and take three long breaths before the first of them popped up, corklike, quickly followed by the other two.

'Let's go over to Malamocco,' he said, getting to his feet.

The engine of the launch sprang instantly to life. Vianello cast off, and Montisi swung them out from the pier and in a broad circle back the way they had come. Hugging the narrow peninsula on his right, he headed towards Malamocco. As they approached the canal that led out into the Adriatic, Brunetti leaned forward to tap Montisi on the shoulder. The pilot turned to him, and Brunetti pointed off to the left, where he saw smoke billowing up in the far distance. 'What's that?' he asked.

Covering his eyes with his left hand, Montisi followed Brunetti's gesture and said, 'Marghera.'

Seeing nothing of interest, Montisi turned his attention back to the waters ahead. Suddenly, he switched the engine into neutral and then just as quickly into reverse, forcing the boat to glide to a halt. Brunetti, who had been trying to distinguish the source of the smoke, turned when he felt the abrupt change in the motor's rhythm.

'*Maria Vergine*,' escaped his lips as he saw an enormous ship looming, endlessly high, endlessly threatening, to their right. 'What is it?' he asked Montisi. Though they were a few hundred metres away, his perspective was still at an upward slant, and all he could see was the side of the hull, the Plimsoll line, and the left side of the glassed-in control deck, soaring as distant and high as a church tower.

'A tanker,' Montisi answered. He might as well have said, 'A rapist' or 'An arsonist', so fierce was his tone.

Their own engine silent, they were enveloped in the roar that issued from the tanker. The universe became noise, a force that battered against them as fiercely as the shock waves from an explosion. Involuntarily, all of them pressed their hands to their ears and kept them there until the tanker had passed them and was continuing up the Canale dei Petroli towards the factories on the mainland. The waves from its wake hit them then, and they were forced to grab at the railings to keep their balance as the launch bobbed up and down and back and forth, the three of them dancing like fools on the deck.

Both hands clenched on the railing in front of

him, Brunetti leaned forward and took a deep breath. His gaze fell to the waters below them, and he saw small, button-sized blobs on the surface. There were only a few, and he could not be sure that they had not been there before he saw the ship.

Montisi switched the engine back into life. Silent, they continued towards Malamocco.

12

The trip proved useless, as there was no sign of Giacomini at the address the owner of the restaurant had provided. It was too late in the day to continue to Chioggia, so Brunetti decided to contact the police by phone and told Montisi to take them back to the Questura.

Whether it was the sight of the tanker or the small dark blobs they had seen on the water, something had darkened their spirits, and they said little on the way back. The light continued to single out the myriad beauties of the city, especially to those who approached it, as people were meant to do, from the sea. It was late afternoon, and the sun still bore down on them; Vianello said something about having forgotten to put on sun screen. Brunetti ignored him.

As they pulled up to the Questura, Brunetti saw that Pucetti was on guard duty that afternoon, and the sight of the young officer gave him the idea. Pucetti saluted as they stepped off the boat. Brunetti told Vianello to call the Chioggia police to see if they had any details on the incident between Scarpa and Bottin and said he'd wait for him in his office but wanted to have a word with Pucetti first.

'Pucetti,' Brunetti began, 'how long are you assigned to guard duty?'

'All this week, sir. Then next week I have night patrol.'

'Would you be interested in a special assignment?'

The young man's face lit up. 'Oh, yes, sir.'

Brunetti appreciated his not complaining about guard duty: having to stand there all day with little to do but open the door or break up the occasional altercation between people waiting in long lines outside the various offices.

'Good, let me go and check the schedules,' Brunetti said and started to walk away. He had taken only two steps when he turned back towards Pucetti. 'Did you ever work as a waiter?'

'Yes, sir,' he answered. 'My brother-in-law has a pizzeria in Castello, and I work there sometimes on the weekends.' Again Pucetti pleased him by asking no questions.

'Good. I'll be back.'

He went immediately to Signorina Elettra's office, where he found her arranging a spray of forsythia in a blue Venini vase. 'Is that yours?' he asked, pointing to the vase.

'No, sir. It belongs to the Questura. The other one, the one I used to use, was stolen last week, so I had to replace it.'

'Stolen?' he asked. 'From the Questura?'

'Yes. One of the janitors left it in the washroom after he washed it out, and it disappeared.'

'From the Questura?'

'I'll be more careful with this one,' she said, slipping a curved branch into place. Brunetti had a friend who worked for Venini and so knew the cost of such a vase: no less than three million.

'How is it that the Questura came to buy this one?' he asked, careful of his phrasing.

'Office equipment,' she answered. She put the last branch in place and stepped aside to allow him to lift it for her. With a languid hand, she pointed to a spot on the windowsill, and Brunetti set it gently down just where she indicated.

'Is Pucetti smart enough for you?' he asked.

'That sweet young man with the moustache?' she asked in a voice that ignored the fact that Pucetti was probably no more than five years younger than she. 'The one with the Russian girlfriend?' she added.

'Yes. Is he bright enough for you?'

'To do what with?' she asked.

'To be out on Pellestrina.'

'Doing what?'

'Working in a restaurant but keeping an eye on you.'

'May I ask how you are going to bring this about?'

'The waiter who gave us the first information about Bottin has disappeared. He called the owner and gave him some story about having to go and take care of a sick friend, and there's been no sign of him since then. So they need a waiter.'

'What does Pucetti have to say about this?' she asked, sitting down behind her desk.

'I haven't asked him yet. I wanted to ask you first.'

'That's very kind of you, sir.'

'He'd be there to protect you, so I wanted to be sure you thought he was capable of doing that.'

She considered this for a moment and said, 'Yes, I think he'd be a good choice.' She glanced at the forsythia, then back at Brunetti. 'Shall I take care of scheduling him?'

'Yes,' Brunetti answered but then couldn't resist the temptation to ask, 'How will you do it?'

'He'll be put on something I think I'll call "Ancillary Duty".'

'What does that mean?'

'It means anything I want it to mean.'

'I see,' Brunetti said and then asked, 'What about Marotta? Isn't he in charge next week? Isn't it his decision?'

'Ah, Marotta,' she said with barely disguised contempt. 'He never wears a tie to work.' So much, thought Brunetti, for Marotta's chances of permanent promotion at the Venice Questura.

'While you're here, sir,' she said, pulling open a drawer and taking from it a few sheets of paper, 'let me give you this. It's everything I could find out about those people. And the autopsy report.'

He took the papers, and went back to his office. The autopsy, performed by a pathologist at the hospital whose name Brunetti did not recognize, stated that Giulio Bottin had died as the result of any one of three blows to his forehead and skull, the pattern of bone shattering consistent with the use of a cylindrical object of some sort, a metal pipe or pole, perhaps. His son had bled to death, the blade having sunk so deep as to nick the abdominal aorta. The absence of water in their lungs and the fact that Giulio Bottin would have taken some time to die made it unlikely that they had been killed soon before the sinking of the boat.

Brunetti had just finished reading the autopsy report when Vianello knocked and came in. 'I called Chioggia, sir,' the sergeant said, not bothering to sit down, 'but they had no details whatsoever.'

Brunetti set the papers aside. 'As you said, they don't seem to be the sort of people who expect the police to solve their problems for them.'

He half expected Vianello to ask if anyone did, any more, but the sergeant made no reply. Brunetti took this opportunity to tell Vianello about his plan to send Pucetti to Pellestrina.

'What about recommendations?' Vianello asked.

'Pucetti said he worked in his brother-in-law's pizzeria. He can call the place in Pellestrina and say he's heard they're looking for a waiter, then recommend Pucetti. All in the family.'

'What if someone recognizes him?' Vianello asked, echoing Brunetti's own fear.

'Not likely to happen, is it?' Brunetti asked by way of response, conscious as he did of how much he sounded like Signorina Elettra.

Reading the signs of Brunetti's reluctance, Vianello didn't object; excusing himself without asking for new orders, he went downstairs.

Brunetti returned to the papers Signorina Elettra had given him. If the Alessandro Scarpa Brunetti was curious about was in his thirties – which distinguished him from the other Alessandro Scarpa who lived on Pellestrina, who was eighty-seven – then he had been arrested three years before for threatening a man with a knife. The other man had, the next day, changed his story and retracted the accusation, so there was nothing in the police files against Scarpa, though the Maresciallo of Carabinieri on the Lido said that Scarpa was known to cause trouble when he drank.

No information could be gathered about anyone with the surname Giacomini.

Signora Follini, it turned out, was a horse of a different colour. Follini was not her married name, for Signora Follini, though she had often enjoyed the company of men, had yet to do so under benefit of clergy. Her given name was Luisa, and she had been born on Pellestrina fifty-two years before.

Her familiarity with the police, or perhaps it would be more exact to say theirs with her, began when she was nineteen, when she was arrested for soliciting. A first offender, she had been reprimanded and released, only to be arrested for the same offence at least three times during the next year. There was a long gap then, suggesting either that Luisa Follini had come to some accommodation with the local police or had moved from the area. She did not reappear in Pellestrina until twelve years ago, when she had been arrested under the still-stringent drug laws for possession, use and attempted sale of heroin as well as for prostitution.

Luckily for her, she had been accepted at a drug rehabilitation centre near Bologna, where she had spent three years, returning to Pellestrina, it seemed, cured of both her addiction to heroin and her occupation. Her parents had died during her absence, and she had taken over the small store they owned in the village, where she had remained until the present time.

Reading the report, Brunetti remembered that her dress had had long sleeves, and he wondered where the money for her surgery had come from and when she had had the operations done. Who had paid for them? The small store he had seen could in no way provide for the work evident in her face; nor, for that fact, could casual prostitution or the sale of heroin in a place as small as Pellestrina.

He thought back to the two occasions he had spoken with her. The first time, she had been flirtatious and wryly theatrical about the limitations of living in a place like Pellestrina. With the history she trailed behind her, she would surely know the full cost of that, he reflected. But she had given no sign of the nervous energy of the addict. Nor had her nervousness the second time seemed related to drugs: it had been the nervousness of fear, and it had peaked with the entrance of those two men.

He had no idea how late she would keep her store open. He pulled out the phone book and checked the listings for Pellestrina. Follini, Luisa was given. He dialled the number, and the phone was picked up on the third ring. She answered, giving her name.

'Signora,' he began, 'this is Commissario Brunetti. I spoke to you earlier.' He heard a soft click as the receiver was replaced.

He put the phone book back in the drawer, put the file to the left of his desk, and went downstairs to talk to Pucetti.

13

Pucetti could barely contain his delight at the assignment. At the mention of Signorina Elettra's name he smiled, and at Brunetti's explanation that it would be his chief duty to protect her, he seemed almost to glow. When the young officer asked whose idea it was to send her there, Brunetti hedged and answered, instead, that he hoped Pucetti's girlfriend would have no objection to the special assignment, that is, Ancillary Duty.

That night after dinner he told Paola about Pucetti, hoping she would agree that this would, if not assure, then at least increase Signorina Elettra's safety.

'What an odd couple they are,' Paola said.

'Who?'

'Signorina Elettra and Pucetti.'

'They're hardly a couple,' Brunetti protested.

'No, I know that. But I mean, as people; it's so odd that people like that, so bright, should be working for the police.'

Not a little indignant, Brunetti said, 'I work for the police, as well. I hope you haven't forgotten that.'

'Oh, don't be such a thin-skinned baby, Guido,' she said, putting her hand on his arm. 'You know exactly what I mean. You're a professional, with a law degree, and you joined the police when things were different, when it was a respectable thing to do with your life.'

'Does that mean it isn't any more?'

'No, I suppose it's still respectable,' she began, then, seeing his expression, hastily said, 'I mean of course it's a respectable choice; you know I mean that. But it's just that the best people, people like you, aren't joining it any more. In ten years, it will be filled with Pattas and Alvises, the ambition-maddened and the hopelessly stupid.'

'Which is which?' Brunetti asked.

She laughed at that. 'Well might you ask.' They were drinking verbena tisane out on the terrace, the children safely returned to their books. Four very plump clouds, pink with the reflected light of evening, formed a distant backdrop to the campanile of San Polo; the rest of the sky was clear and promised another day of glory.

She returned to the subject. 'Why do you

think it is that so few really worthwhile people join now?'

Instead of answering, he asked a question. 'It's the same for you, isn't it? What sort of new colleagues are you getting at the university?'

'God, we sound like Pliny the Elder, don't we, sitting around and grumbling about how disrespectful youth is and how everything is going to hell?'

'People have always said that. It's one of the few constants in the histories I read: every age sees the one before it as the golden age when men were virtuous, women pure, and children obedient.'

'Don't forget "respectful",' Paola suggested.

'The children or the women?'

'Both, I suppose.'

Neither of them spoke for a long time, not until the clouds had drifted to the south and served to frame the campanile of San Marco.

Brunetti broke the silence by asking, 'Who'd join now?' He let the question lie, and when Paola didn't bother to answer, he went on, 'It happens too often: we work to arrest them, then when we do, the lawyers get their hands on the case, or the judges, and they end up getting off. I've seen it happen dozens of times, and I'm seeing it happen more and more often. There's that woman who got married in Bologna last week. Two years ago she stabbed and killed her husband. Sentenced to nine years. But she's out on appeal after three months in jail, and now she's married again.'

Ordinarily, Paola would have made some ironic comment on the bravery of the new husband, but she waited to see if he was finished. When he went on, what he said shocked her. 'I could retire, you know.' Still she didn't say anything. 'I've got the years in service. Well, almost. I suppose what I mean is I could retire in two years.'

Paola asked, 'Is that what you want to do?'

He sipped at his tisane and found it had grown cold. He tipped the cold tea out into the large terracotta tub that held the oleander, poured a fresh cup, added honey, and said, 'Probably not. Not really. But it costs so much at times to watch what happens and not be able to do anything to stop it.' Brunetti leaned back in his chair and stretched his legs out in front of him, his cup held between both hands. 'I'm over-reacting, I know, to this thing with the woman getting married, but every once in a while I read something or something happens, and I just can't stand it.'

'Didn't the papers say he beat her?' Paola asked.

'I know someone in Bologna. He did the original questioning. She said nothing about that until she spoke to a lawyer. She'd been having an affair with the guy she married.'

'None of that was in the papers, so I suppose none of it was mentioned at her trial,' Paola said.

'No, there was no proof of the affair. But she killed the husband, maybe during an argument, as she said, and now she's married to the other guy, and nothing will happen to her.'

'Happily ever after?' Paola suggested.

'That's only a small case,' he began but instantly corrected himself, 'No, no one's murder is small. I mean it was a single case, and maybe there'd been an argument. But it happens all the time: men kill ten, twenty people, and then some clever lawyer, or more often, some incompetent judge, gets them out. And they don't hesitate a minute till they go back to doing what they do best, killing people.'

Paola, who had long experience of listening to him in these moments, had never heard Brunetti so distressed or angry about the conditions under which he worked.

'What would you do if you retired?'

'That's just it: I have no idea. It's too late to try to take the law exams; I'd probably have to go back to university and start all over again.'

'If there is one thing I recommend you don't do,' she interrupted, 'it is to think about going back to university.' Her shudder of horror at the thought was no less real for being consciously manufactured.

They considered the question for a while, but neither came up with anything. Finally Paola said, 'Didn't the noble Romans always go back to their farms and devote themselves to the improvement of the land and the writing of letters to friends in the city, lamenting the state of the Empire?'

'Umm,' Brunetti agreed. 'But I'm afraid I'm not noble.'

'And thank God you're not a Roman,' Paola added.

'Nor do we have a farm.'

'I suppose that means you can't retire,' she concluded and asked for another cup of tisane.

The weekend passed quietly. Brunetti had no clear idea of when Signorina Elettra planned to go out to Pellestrina. He thought of calling her at home, even looked up her number in the phone book, something he'd never done before. He found the listing, a low number in Castello that would put her home, he calculated, somewhere near Santa Maria Formosa. While he had the page open, he checked for other Zorzis and found at least two who lived within a few numbers of her address: family?

She had given him the number of her *telefonino*, but he'd left it in the office, and so short of calling her at home, he had no way of knowing what she was doing until Monday morning, when he would or would not see her at her desk at the Questura.

On Saturday evening, Pucetti called to tell him he was already on Pellestrina and already at work, though he had seen no sign of Signorina Elettra. His brother-in-law, Pucetti explained, after discovering that he and the owner of the restaurant in Pellestrina had many acquaintances in common, had secured Pucetti the chance to work at least until the owner could find out if Scarpa was coming back.

On Sunday afternoon Brunetti went into the room that had, over the course of years, been transformed from spare bedroom to junk room. On top of a wardrobe in one corner he found the hand-painted chest that had somehow come to him from his Uncle Claudio, the one who had always wanted to be a painter. Large enough to house a German Shepherd, the chest was entirely covered with brightly coloured flowers of confused species, assembled in gaudy promiscuity. For some reason it held maps, all thrown inside with much the same confusion as prevailed on the top and sides of the box.

Brunetti began by shifting them from one side to the other as he hunted for the map he wanted. Finally, when this proved futile, he began the slow, inescapable process of removing them one by one. The more he looked, the more it wasn't there. At last, after he had shifted most of the nations and continents of the world, he found the map of the *laguna* he had used, years ago, when he and his schoolfriends spent weekends and holidays exploring the weaving channels that surrounded the city.

He dropped the other maps back into the box and took the map of the *laguna* out on to the terrace. Careful of the long-dried tape that held parts of it together, he opened it slowly and stretched it out on the table. How tiny the islands looked, surrounded by the vast expanse of *palude*. For kilometres in every direction, the capillaries and veins of the channels spread, pumping water in and out twice a day, as regular as the moon itself. For a thousand years, those few canals at Chioggia, Malamocco and San Nicolò had served as aortas, keeping the waters clean, even at the height of the Serenissima's power, when hundreds of thousands of people had lived there, their waste added to the waters every day.

Brunetti caught himself before this thought could take its familiar course. He recalled what Paola had said two nights ago, of the disgruntled Roman, life blighted by displeasure with the present, ever longing for the better past he knew was lost, and he pulled his thoughts away from history and turned them to geography.

The immensity of the area depicted on the map reminded him how lost he was in it and how ignorant of how things were organized upon its waters, even in relation to the jurisdiction of crimes. If cases were given out, rather in the manner of party favours, to the first comer, then how could one expect to find consistent records of what had happened there?

He assumed that large fish were taken from the Adriatic; where then did the clams and shrimp come from? He had no idea what places in the *laguna* could legitimately be used for fishing, though he assumed that all of the shallow waters lying just off the coast of Marghera would be closed. Yet if what Montisi said, and Vianello believed, was true, then even that area was still fished.

He sometimes went to Rialto with Paola to buy fish and recalled the sign often placed on the gleaming skins of the fish on display: 'Nostrani,' as if the claim that the fish was 'Ours' somehow imbued it with health and goodness, washed it clean of even the thought of contamination. He'd seen the same sign on cherries, peaches, plums, and again, he realized, the same magic was meant to work: the fact that the fruit was Italian was enough to sweep it clean of all taint of chemical or pesticide and render it pure as mother's milk.

He'd once read a book that traced the history of what people ate, and so he knew that his ancestors, far from having enjoyed an Edenic diet both safe and healthy, had ingested vast quantities of chemicals and poisons with every bite and had risked tuberculosis, and worse, with every sip of milk.

Dissatisfied by his own dissatisfaction, he folded the map and took it back into the apartment. 'Paola,' he called towards the back of the apartment, 'let's go get a drink.'

The first thing he learned on Monday morning was that, despite his plans, he was in charge while Patta was gone. Marotta, it turned out, had been summoned back to Turin for a week to testify in a case. He had not been directly involved, had merely been in charge of a squad of detectives when two of them had made the arrest of six suspects in an arms trafficking case. It was highly unlikely that he would be called to testify, he probably could have refused to go, but as it meant a trip home at government expense as well as a living allowance for the time he was there, he accepted, leaving a note for Brunetti explaining that his presence was essential to the successful prosecution of the case and that he was sure Vice-Questore Patta would approve of his decision to designate Brunetti as his own acting commander.

Repeatedly he called down to Signorina Elettra's office during the course of the morning, but as it was her habit not to overburden the Questura with her presence when her superior was absent, he wasn't certain whether she had decided to sleep until noon or to go out to Pellestrina. At eleven, his phone rang, and he was greatly relieved to hear her voice.

'Where are you, Signorina?' he asked, rather than demanded.

'On the beach of Pellestrina, sir, the side that faces the sea. Did you know they'd removed the grounded ship?' When he didn't answer, she went on, 'I was surprised not to see it there. My cousin said they hauled it off last year. I miss it.'

'When did you get there, Signorina?'

'I came out before lunch on Saturday because I wanted to have as much time here as possible.'

'What did you tell your cousin?'

He heard the sharp cry of a seagull. 'That I was sorry I hadn't been out for so long but I wanted to get away from the city for a while,' she said, then paused and the gull had something else to say. When it was finished, she went on, 'I told Bruna I'd had *"una storia"* that ended badly and wanted to get away from anything that would remind me of him.' In a softer voice, she added, 'Well, that's true enough,' and Brunetti found himself immediately curious about who he was and why it had ended.

'How long did you tell her you'd be there?'

'Oh, I was vague about that; at least a week, probably more, depending on how I felt. But I already feel better; the sun's wonderful, and the air is completely different from the city. I could stay here for ever.'

The bureaucrat in him spoke before he could help it. 'I certainly hope you don't mean that.'

'Just a figure of speech, sir.'

'What are you going to do?'

'Walk on the beach and see who I meet. Go and have a coffee at the bar and see what's new. Talk to people. Go fishing.'

'Just a normal vacation on Pellestrina?' Brunetti asked.

'Exactly,' she said, to which the gull made no comment. With the promise to call him again, she broke the connection.

14

As she slipped the *telefonino* back into the left pocket of her jacket, Elettra Zorzi was glad she'd thought to bring the suede, instead of the wool. The pockets were deeper and thus more securely held the tiny Nokia, little bigger than a pack of cigarettes. And it was a better match for the navy blue slacks, though she wasn't really happy with the way it looked with the Topsiders she'd brought along to wear on the beach. She'd never liked the combination of leather and suede, wished now she'd bought that pair of fawn-coloured suede loafers she'd seen in the Fratelli Rossetti sale.

The gull called out again, but she ignored it. When it continued to squawk at her, she turned and walked directly at it until it took off and flew away down the beach in the direction of the Riserva of Ca' Roman. Like most Venetians, she tolerated gulls but loathed pigeons, which she viewed as a source of constant trouble, their nests blocking drainpipes and their constant droppings turning marble into meringue. She thought of the tourists she'd often seen in San Marco, pigeons hopping about on their heads and outstretched arms, and she shivered: flying rats.

She continued down the beach, away from the village, glad of the feel of the sun on her back, intent on nothing more than reaching San Pietro in Volta and having a coffee before turning back to Pellestrina. She lengthened her stride, aware at every step of how long she'd been sitting at a desk and how much her body rejoiced in this simple act of walking on the beach in the sun.

Her cousin Bruna, when she'd called last week, had not seemed at all surprised at her suggestion that she come out for a week or so. When she asked why Elettra was free at such short notice, she decided to tell at least part of the truth and explained that she and her boyfriend had planned for months to go to France for two weeks, but their sudden separation had ended those plans, leaving her with the impossibility of changing her request for vacation time. Bruna had shown no sign of taking offence at being only second choice and had insisted she come out immediately, to leave all thought of him behind in the city.

Though she'd been on Pellestrina only two days, it had pretty much worked. Her ex-boyfriend was a doctor, one of her sister's friends, and she'd probably known for months that he was wrong: too serious, too ambitious, and, she had to admit even this, too greedy. She had feared that being on her own again would be painful; instead, she had begun to realize, she felt rather like that gull: it hadn't liked the way it was treated, so it had taken flight and soared away.

She walked down to the water's edge and stooped to pull off her shoes and roll up the bottoms of her slacks. She could stand the water only for seconds before she danced back on to the sand, then flopped down and rubbed at one, then the other, foot. When they felt like feet again, she hooked two fingers into the backs of her shoes and walked along, barefoot, free, remembering what it was like to be happy.

Soon enough she ran out of sand and had to climb the steps to the top of the sea wall. Boats went about their boaty business to her right, and soon the small village of San Pietro in Volta appeared on her left.

At the bar, which occupied the ground floor of someone's house, she asked for a mineral water and a coffee, drank the water greedily, and sipped at her coffee. The man behind the bar, who was in his sixties, remembered her from other visits and asked when she had arrived. They fell into easy conversation, and soon he was talking about the recent murders, events in which she appeared to take little interest.

'Cut open, gutted like a fish,' he said. 'Pity. He was a nice boy. Amazing, really, when you think about his father.' Not enough time had passed for people to start to tell the whole truth about Bottin, she realized: he was still close enough to life to make people cautious about what they had to say of him.

'I didn't know them,' she said and glanced idly at the front page of *Il Gazzettino* that lay folded on the top of the counter.

'Marco went to school with my grand-daughter,' he said.

Elettra paid for the water and the coffee, said how wonderful it was to be out here again, and left. She used the sea wall to walk the entire way back to Pellestrina, and by the time she got there she was thirsty again, so she went into the front part of the restaurant for a glass of prosecco. And who should serve her but Pucetti himself, who paid her no more attention than he would any other attractive woman a few years older than he.

As she drank it, she listened to the men clustered at the bar. They too paid little attention to her, having slotted her into place as Bruna's cousin, the one who came out every summer, and thus a sort of honorary native.

The murders were mentioned, but only in passing, as just another example of the bad luck that afflicts all fishermen. More important, they discussed what to do about those bastards from

Chioggia who were coming over into their waters at night and ripping up the clam beds. One man suggested they tell the police; no one bothered to respond to a suggestion so patently stupid.

She went to the cash register and paid. The owner also remembered her as Bruna's cousin and welcomed her back. They chatted idly for a while, and when he too mentioned the recent murders, she said she was on vacation and didn't want to hear about such things, suggesting by her tone that people from the big city didn't really take much interest in the doings of provincials, however sanguinary they might be.

The rest of the day, and the next, passed quietly enough. She heard nothing new but was still careful to call Brunetti again and tell him that much, or that little. Remaining strong in her refusal to discuss the recent murders, she quickly adapted to the rhythm of Pellestrina, a village that led life at its own pace. The bulk of the population sailed off to work while it was still dark and returned only in the late morning or early afternoon. Many people went to bed not long after nightfall. She soon fell into a routine. Bruna took care of her grandchildren every day, while their mother taught in the local elementary school. To avoid the confusion brought into the house by the presence of two young children, Elettra spent most of her days outside, walking on the beach, occasionally taking the boat over to Chioggia for a few hours. But she always ended up having a coffee in the bar of the restaurant just at the time the men from the boats began to drift in.

Within days, she was an attractive fixture, and one that responded to any mention of the Bottins or their murder with silence. She realized from the first that they all disliked Giulio; only as time passed did she begin to sense that the objection to him went far beyond his penchant for violence. After all, these were men who made their living by killing, and though their victims were only fish, the job had rendered many of them casual about blood and gore and the taking of life. The savagery of Giulio's disposal seemed not to trouble them in the least; in fact, if they mentioned it at all, it was with something like grudging admiration. What they seemed to object to was his refusal to put the good of the hunting pack of Pellestrinotti ahead of all else. Any act of aggression or betrayal, so long as it was directed against the fishermen of Chioggia was completely justified, even praiseworthy. Giulio Bottin, however, had seemed capable of behaving in the same way towards his own kind, if it would work to his advantage, and this was something they would not forgive, not even after death, and not even after a death as horrible as his had been.

On the Wednesday afternoon, as she sat at a table in the front part of the bar, reading through *Il Gazzettino* and paying no attention, none at all, to the conversations around her, she was conscious of the arrival of someone new. She didn't look up until she had read a few more pages, and when she did, she saw a man a few years older than herself, the casual elegance of whose appearance made him stand out among the fishermen at the bar. He wore a pair of dark grey slacks and a pale yellow V-neck sweater over a shirt that went with his slacks perfectly. She was immediately intrigued by the colour of his sweater and by the fact that he appeared to be completely at ease with and accepted by these men. Most of them, she was sure, would die before they would wear yellow on anything other than a rain slicker.

He had dark hair and, from what she could see of his profile, dark eyes and brows. His skin was tanned or naturally bronzed; she couldn't tell which. He was taller than most of the other men, an impression heightened by the grace with which he carried himself. Any traditional idea of masculinity, especially in the company of these wind-hardened fishermen, would have been compromised, if not by the sweater, then by the way he inclined his head to listen to the men around him. In him, however, the total effect was of a masculinity so certain of itself as not to be bothered by such trifles of dress or behaviour.

Elettra consciously returned her eyes to the newspaper and her attention to the man. He was, it turned out, somehow related to one of the fishermen. More drinks were ordered, and Elettra found herself approaching the sports pages, something not even her devotion to duty could cause her to read. She closed the paper and got to her feet. As she walked towards the cash register, one of the men, a relative – she had no idea how – of Bruna's husband, called her over to meet the new arrival.

'Elettra, this is Carlo; he's a fisherman, one of us.' With two thick fingers, the man plucked at the fine wool of Carlo's sweater and asked, 'He doesn't look it, does he?' The general laughter which greeted this was easy and comfortable, and Carlo joined in with good grace.

Carlo turned to her and smiled, held out his hand and took hers.

'Another stranger?' he asked.

She smiled at the idea. 'If you're not born here, I suppose you're always a stranger,' she answered.

His chin tilted to one side and he glanced at her more closely. 'Do I know you?' he asked.

'I don't think so,' she answered, momentarily confused into thinking that perhaps she knew him, as well. But she was sure she would have remembered him.

'No, I haven't met you,' he said with a smile that was even warmer than the one he'd given on taking her hand. 'I would have remembered.'

This echo of her own thought disconcerted her. She nodded to him and then to the other men at the bar, muttered something about going back to her cousin's, paid for her coffee, and escaped into the sunlight.

Her doctor had been handsome; as she walked home, she confessed to herself that she had a weakness for male beauty. This Carlo was not only handsome, but, from the little she had seen of him, simpatico as well. She told herself sternly that she was out here on police business. Though he didn't live on Pellestrina, there was nothing that excluded Carlo from possible connection with the murder of Giulio and Marco Bottin. She smiled at that; soon she'd be like the members of the uniformed branch, seeing everyone, everywhere, as a probable suspect, even before there was any evidence that a crime had been committed.

She put all thought of the handsome Carlo behind her and went back towards Bruna's home. On the way, she used her *telefonino* to call Commissario Brunetti at the Questura and tell him that she had nothing to report save that it was the general opinion among the fishermen that, with the change of moon, the anchovies would start to run.

15

Brunetti, left behind while Signorina Elettra disported herself in the sun and walked on the beach, without learning anything at all about the murders, was having as little success as she. He had called Luisa Follini's number again, but a man answered, and this time it was Brunetti who hung up without speaking. It was instinct that had made him call her, some atavistic response to the menace radiating from the two men who had come into the store, and it was this same instinct that made him decide to send Vianello to stop in and have a word with her after he made another attempt to find Giacomini.

Following Brunetti's orders, Vianello went out to Malamocco again, where he managed to find Enrico Giacomini without difficulty. The fisherman recalled the fight between Scarpa and Bottin and said it had been provoked by Scarpa, who had accused Bottin of having a big mouth. Vianello pressed Giacomini and asked if he knew what Scarpa had been talking about, but the fisherman said he could think of nothing, but he said it in such a way as to give the sergeant, no mean judge of situations for all his apparent stolidity, a sense that here he was treading on some Pellestrina secret. Even as he asked the other man if he were sure he had no idea what Scarpa had intended, Vianello was overcome with a sense of the absurdity of his attempt to unearth information from one fisherman about another. Their definition of loyalty was not one that encompassed the police; in fact, it probably failed to encompass all of humanity aside from the small part of it fishing in the waters of the *laguna* and the Adriatic.

Both irritated at Giacomini's obvious evasions and curious to learn more about what had taken place between Bottin and Scarpa, Vianello asked Montisi to take him down to Pellestrina. Leaving Montisi with the boat, he went first to Signora Follini's shop – but it was lunchtime, and the shop was closed. Brunetti had warned him not to call attention to Signora Follini, so Vianello walked past it without paying any apparent attention.

He turned left and towards the address he had been given for Sandro Scarpa, the originator of the remark that had triggered Bottin's anger.

But Scarpa, who was not at all happy to be pulled away from his lunch by the police, said the fight with Bottin had been provoked by the dead man, and anyone who said anything else was lying. No, he couldn't remember exactly what it was Bottin had said, nor could he recall why it had so angered him. Besides, he added, it hadn't been much of a fight, not really. These things happened, he implied, when it was late at night and men had been drinking: they meant nothing, and no one ever thought about them again.

With no warning, Vianello asked him if he knew where his brother was; Scarpa said he thought he'd gone to Vicenza to see a friend about something. He did not ask Vianello to leave, only his lunch was growing cold in the kitchen and there was nothing more to say about Bottin. Vianello saw no reason to prolong this conversation and so went to the restaurant to have a glass of wine in the bar.

When he walked in, he was briefly disoriented and wondered if he was somehow already back at the Questura, for behind the bar he saw Pucetti, and sitting at a table to the left, reading *Il Gazzettino* with the attention he had previously known her to devote only to *Vogue*, sat Signorina Elettra. Both glanced up when he came in. Both reacted to the sight of his uniform, and he hoped the men standing at the bar saw how they did: even the faces of men he'd repeatedly arrested had seldom shown such suspicion and dislike.

After a long pause, Pucetti drifted over, asked him what he wanted and then was a long time bringing the glass of prosecco. When he did bring it, it was sour and warm. Vianello took a sip, set the glass sharply on the counter, paid, and left.

After another few minutes, seeing the sports page approach once again, Signorina Elettra folded the newspaper, paid for her coffee, nodded to a few of the men at the bar, and went out into the sun. She had gone only a few metres when she heard, from behind her, a voice she recognized instantly. 'Going back to your cousin's house?' he asked.

She turned and saw him, hesitated a moment, then returned the smile he offered her. 'Yes, I suppose so.' When she saw his confusion, she explained, 'She took the kids up to the Lido to buy shoes for the summer, and they won't be back until after lunch.'

'So you have the chance to eat in peace for a change?' he asked with another, broader smile.

'No, they're really very good. And besides, they do have first right to the house and to Bruna.'

'So you're free,' he asked, more interested in that than in discussing the behavior of the children.

'I suppose so,' she answered, then, realizing how very ungracious that sounded, changed it to, 'Yes, I am.'

'Good. I hoped to talk you into a picnic on the beach. There's a place on the jetty where the tide has pulled away some of the boulders, so there's no wind at all.'

'Picnic?' she asked, seeing that his hands were empty.

He raised them and hooked his thumbs into what she had thought were braces. 'In here,' he said, turning halfway round and showing her a small black backpack, just large enough to hold a picnic lunch for two.

Her smile was involuntary. 'Good,' she said. 'What did you pack?'

'Surprises,' he answered, and this time she noticed the way his smile always began at his mouth and then crept up into his eyes.

'Good. I just hope one of them is mortadella.'

'Mortadella?' he asked. 'How did you know? I love it, but I never think anyone else does, so I never bring any. It's such peasant food: I can't imagine anyone like you eating it.'

'Oh, but I do,' she said with real enthusiasm, ignoring his compliment, at least for the moment. 'It's true, isn't it? no one feels comfortable eating it any more. They want, oh, I don't know, caviare or lobster tails, or . . .'

'When what they're really lusting for,' he broke in, 'is a *panino* with mortadella and so much mayonnaise it drips out of the sandwich and down their face.' Casually, as though picnics were a habit between them, he linked his arm in hers and turned away towards the sea wall and the beach.

When they reached the jetty, Carlo jumped up on to the first of the giant boulders, then turned and reached down to help her up. When she was beside him, he took her arm in his, and she was pleased to notice that he didn't point to every uneven rock or surface as though she were incapable of seeing them. More than halfway along, he paused, leaned down, and studied the rocks below. He told her to wait, then jumped down on to an enormous boulder that jutted out at a perilous angle. He stretched out his hand, and she jumped down beside him. There was an immense hole in the side of the jetty where some of the boulders had been ripped away by a storm: the resulting cave was just large enough for the two of them. It was empty of cigarette ends or discarded food wrappings, proof that it was effectively hidden from detection by the Pellestrinotti.

The floor of the cave was a carpet of white sand, and some quirk of tide or pressure had left a flat-topped block jutting from the back wall. It served perfectly as a table; quickly Carlo covered it with the things he pulled from his pack. Like Indians, they sat cross-legged on the sandy floor to eat, the sun slanting, the waves slapping on the rocks below.

Even without mortadella, the picnic was perfect, Elettra judged. Not only because of the thick sandwiches of prosciutto, each slice of bread heavily buttered, and the chilled bottle of Chardonnay, and not because of the strawberries that followed, each to be dipped in mascarpone in open defiance of all dietary sanity. She judged the picnic to be perfect because of the company: Carlo listened to her as though they were old friends, talked to her as though he'd known her for years, and all of those happy ones.

He asked what she did, and she said she worked in a bank: very boring, but a safe job to have in times like these, with unemployment skyrocketing all about them. When she asked, he said he was a fisherman and left it at that. It was only by careful questioning that she got him to tell her that he had abandoned his studies when his father died two years ago, returning to Burano to be with his mother. She liked the way he spoke about it, as if entirely unconscious of how naturally he had assumed the responsibility for his mother.

As they spoke about their families and their hopes, Elettra slowly became conscious of a growing undercurrent of excitement, though nothing either of them said or did could be judged to have produced it. The more she listened to him, the more she felt that this was a voice she'd listened to before and, she became aware, would very much like to hear again.

When the sandwiches were finished, the wine drunk, the last of the mascarpone licked from greedy fingers, she noticed that he carefully picked up the empty wrappings and the napkins they'd used in place of plates and stuffed them in the empty backpack. He saw her watching what he was doing and said, grinning, 'I hate it when the beaches are covered with junk.' With a self-conscious shrug he pulled up one side of his mouth in a grimace she had already come to recognize and like. 'I suppose it's stupid to bother, but it seems little enough effort.'

She leaned forward and put her napkin into the pack on top of his. As she did so, her breast brushed against his arm, and she was shocked by the power of her response, one that had nothing at all to do with remembered pleasures but stunned her with the promise of future ones. He shot her a look almost stupid with surprise, but when she pretended to have been unconscious of the contact, he turned his attention to the backpack and pulled the strings tight.

After this, though she pretended to be interested in a large boat on the horizon that was visible from the opening in the rocks, she was conscious of his watching her. She sensed, rather than saw, his self-critical grimace, and then he asked, 'Coffee?'

She smiled and nodded, but she was never to know whether his question filled her with relief or disappointment.

16

Brunetti, far from sitting by the waves and dipping fresh strawberries into mascarpone, found himself trapped in his office and buried under the waves of paper generated by the organs of the state. He had thought that, during Patta's absence and Marotta's withdrawal, it would fall to him to make decisions that would affect the way justice was pursued in Venice. Even if he could see to nothing more than assigning incompetent officers to work on minor cases such as complaints about over-loud televisions, thus freeing the better ones to work on more serious crimes, he would at least be working for the general good. But he had no time for things even as simple as this. In the absence of what he now realized must be the daily filtering done by Signorina Elettra, papers flooded into his office and soaked up all of his working hours. It seemed that the Ministry of the Interior was capable of producing volumes of regulations and announcements every day, making determinations on subjects as diverse as the necessity of providing a translator when foreign suspects were questioned or the height of the heels on the shoes of female officers. His eyes passed over them all; it would be untrue to say he read them, for that act implies at least a minimum of comprehension, and Brunetti quickly passed beyond that possibility into a numbed state where he read words and words and set the pages aside with no idea of what those words signified.

He could not stop his imagination from drifting off to Pellestrina. He found time to speak to Vianello but was disappointed to hear how little the other man had learned. He was intrigued, however, when Vianello mentioned the strong sense he'd had when speaking to the people on Pellestrina that they all considered Bottin not to be one of them, for this confirmed a suspicion Brunetti had formed, he no longer remembered why. When Brunetti gave Vianello's remarks further thought, he found it even stranger. It was unusual in his experience for members of a community as tightly closed as that of Pellestrina to voice collective disapproval of one of their own. The secret of their survival had always lain in maintaining a united front against strangers, and no force was as alien as the police. He was struck by the repeated disparity between what was said about Giulio and what was said about Marco. Everyone mourned the boy's death, but no one on Pellestrina seemed to shed any tears for Giulio Bottin. What was even stranger was how careless they had been in making this known.

The rising tide of paper swept these thoughts from Brunetti's mind for the next two days. On Friday he had a call from Marotta, who told him he'd be back from Turin on Monday. Brunetti did not ask if he had testified in the trial; he cared only that the other commissario take his turn at dealing with the papers.

He and Paola were invited to dinner with friends on Saturday evening, so when the phone rang just before eight, just as he was knotting his tie, he was tempted not to answer it.

Paola called down the hallway, 'Shall I get it?'

'No, I will,' he said, but he said it reluctantly, wishing one of the children were there to answer it for him, lie, say they'd just gone out. Or say their father had decided to move to Patagonia and herd sheep.

'Brunetti,' he answered.

'It's Pucetti, sir,' the young officer said. 'I'm in a phone booth by the dock. A boat just came in. A body's been fished up.'

'Who is it?'

'No idea, sir.'

'Man or woman?' he asked, heart cold at the thought of Signorina Elettra.

'I don't know that either, sir. One of the fishermen came in a minute ago and told the men at the bar what happened, so we all came out here to get a look.' Brunetti heard noises in the distance, and then the receiver was replaced.

He put his own phone down and went back towards the bedroom. Paola, glancing up, saw the expression on his face. She wore a black dress, tight around the hips and cut very low at the back, a dress he thought he'd never seen before. She was just putting on her second earring but let her hands fall to her sides when she saw him. 'Well, I didn't much want to go, anyway,' she said, tossing the earring back into the drawer of their dresser, the top one, the one she used to hold jewellery and, for some reason he had never fathomed, the bottles of vitamins she took. Casually, like someone asking for a half-dozen eggs, she said, 'I'll call Mariella.'

He knew men who kept secrets from their wives. He knew one married man who kept two mistresses and had kept them for more than a decade. He knew men who had managed to lose their businesses and homes before their wives had any idea they gambled. For a moment he contemplated the possibility that Paola had sold her soul to the devil in exchange for the mystic power to read his mind. No, she was too smart to make that bad a bargain.

'Or do you want to call the Questura first?' she asked.

He started to explain what it was but stopped

himself, as if silence would keep Signorina Elettra safe. 'I'll use the *telefonino*,' he said and took it from the dresser where he had left it in anticipation of a peaceful evening with friends. Paola went down to the living room to make her call, and he punched in the familiar number of the Questura. He asked that a boat collect him and take him out to Pellestrina. He pushed the little blue button, dialled Vianello's number and, careful to remember the instructions he'd been given when issued the phone, pushed the blue button again.

Vianello's wife answered. When she heard who it was she made no attempt at pleasantry, but said she'd get Lorenzo. The radar of policemen's wives knew when an evening was ruined: some were gracious, others were not.

'Yes, sir?' the sergeant asked.

'Pucetti just called. From a public phone. They've fished up a body.'

'I'll be at the Giardini stop,' Vianello said and hung up.

He was there fifteen minutes later, but he was not in uniform, nor did he do more than raise his hand in acknowledgement to Brunetti when the boat slowed without stopping to allow him to step on board. Vianello assumed he'd been told everything Brunetti knew, so he didn't waste time asking questions, nor did he voice Signorina Elettra's name.

'Nadia?' Brunetti asked in the shorthand of long association.

'Her parents were taking us to dinner.'

'Anything special?'

'Our anniversary,' Vianello answered.

Instead of apologizing, Brunetti asked, 'How many?'

'Fifteen.'

The launch swung to the right, taking them down towards Malamocco and Pellestrina. 'I called for a scene of crime team to come out,' Brunetti said. 'But the pilot'll have to go around and collect them, so I doubt they'll be out any time soon.'

'How do we explain getting there so quickly?' Vianello asked.

'I can say someone called us.'

'I hope no one saw Pucetti making the call, then.'

Brunetti, who almost never remembered to carry his, asked, 'Why wasn't he given a *telefonino*?'

'Most of the young ones have their own, sir.'

'Does he?'

'I don't know. But I suppose not, if he called you from a public phone.'

'Stupid thing to do,' Brunetti said, aware as he spoke that he was transforming the fear he felt for Signorina Elettra into anger at the young officer for provoking his fear in the first place.

Brunetti's *telefonino* rang. When he answered it, the operator at the Questura said that a call had just come in, a man saying that a woman's body had been pulled up in the nets of a boat and had been taken to the dock at Pellestrina.

'Did he give his name?' Brunetti asked.

'No, sir.'

'Did he say he'd found the body?'

'No, sir. All he said was that a boat had come in with a body, not that he'd had anything to do with it.'

Brunetti thanked him and hung up. He turned to Vianello. 'It's a woman.' The sergeant didn't say anything, so Brunetti asked, 'If all those boats have radios and phones, why didn't they call us?'

'Most people don't much want to get involved with us.'

'If they've got a woman's body in their fishing nets, it doesn't seem to me there's any way they can help getting involved with us,' Brunetti said, transferring a bit of his anger to Vianello.

'People don't think of those things, I'm afraid. Perhaps most of all when they've got a woman's body in their nets.'

Knowing the sergeant was right and sorry he'd spoken so sharply, Brunetti said, 'Of course, of course.'

The lights of Malamocco swept by, then the Alberoni, and then there was nothing but the long straight sweep towards Pellestrina. Soon, ahead of them they saw the scattered lights of the houses and the straight line of lights on the dock along which the town was built. Strangely enough, there was no evidence that anything extraordinary had taken place, for there were only a few people visible on the *riva*. Surely, even the Pellestrinotti could not have been so quickly hardened to death.

The pilot, who had not been out to Pellestrina during this investigation, started to pull the launch into the empty place in the line of fishing boats. Brunetti jumped up the steps and put a hand on his shoulder, saying, 'No, not here. Down at the end.'

Instantly, the pilot reversed the engines, and the boat slowed, then started to pull back from the *riva*. 'Over there, to the right,' Brunetti told him, and the pilot brought the boat gently up to the dock. Vianello tossed the mooring rope to a man who approached them, and as soon as he had tied it round the metal stanchion, Brunetti and Vianello jumped from the boat.

'Where is she?' Brunetti asked, leaving it to the boat's markings to explain who they were.

'Over here,' the man said, turning back towards the small group of people who stood in the dim light cast by the street lamps. As Brunetti and Vianello approached, the group separated, creating a passage towards what lay on the pavement.

Her feet lay in a pool of light, her head in darkness, but when Brunetti saw the blonde hair, he knew who it was. Fighting down a surge of relief, he drew closer. At first he thought her eyes were closed, that some gentle soul had pressed them closed for her, but then he saw that they were gone. He remembered that one of the policemen had explained the decision to bring up the bodies of the Bottins because there were crabs down below. He had read books in which the stomachs of people in situations like this were said to heave, but what Brunetti felt registered in his heart, which pounded wildly for a few seconds and did not grow steady until he looked away from the woman's face, out over the calm waters of the *laguna*.

Vianello had the presence of mind to ask, 'Who found her?'

A short, stocky man stepped forward from the shadows. 'I did,' he said, careful to keep his eyes on Vianello rather than on the silent woman over whom all of this was being said.

'Where did you find her? And when?' Vianello asked.

The man pointed in the general direction of the mainland, off to the north. 'Out there, about two hundred metres offshore, right at the mouth of the Canale di Ca' Roman.'

When he failed to answer Vianello's second question, Brunetti repeated it. 'When?'

The man glanced down at his watch. 'About an hour ago. I brought her up in my net, but it took me a long time to get her alongside the boat.' He looked back and forth between Brunetti and Vianello, as if searching to see which of them would be more likely to believe what he said. 'I was alone in my *sandolo*, and I was afraid I'd capsize if I pulled her in.' He stopped.

'So what did you do?'

'I towed her,' he said, obviously troubled by

having to confess this. 'It was the only way to get her here.'

'Did you recognize her?' Brunetti asked.

He nodded.

Glad not to have to look at Signora Follini, Brunetti let his eyes rove around the faces of the people above her, but Signorina Elettra was not among them. If they looked down at the body, their faces disappeared in the shadows cast by the overhead lights, but most of them preferred not to. 'When did any of you see her last?' he asked.

No one answered.

He caught the eye of the one woman standing in the group. 'You, Signora,' he said, keeping his voice soft, merely inquisitive, no trace of authority in it. 'Can you remember when you last saw Signora Follini?'

The woman stared back at him with frightened eyes, then glanced to right and left. Finally she said, all in a rush, 'A week ago. Maybe five days. I went to the store for toilet paper.' Suddenly aware of what she had said in front of all these men, she covered her mouth with her hand, looked down, then quickly up again.

'Perhaps we could move away from here,' Brunetti suggested, moving back towards the bright windows of the houses. A man approached from the direction of the village carrying a blanket. As he drew close to the body, Brunetti forced himself to say, 'You'd better not do that. The body shouldn't be touched.'

'It's for respect, sir,' the man insisted, though he didn't look down at her. 'She shouldn't be left like that.' He held the blanket draped over one arm, a gesture that conveyed a curious sense of formality.

'I'm sorry, but I think it's better,' Brunetti said, giving no hint of how deeply he sympathized with the man's desire. His refusal to let the man cover Signora Follini lost him whatever sympathy he might have gained by moving the crowd away from the body.

Sensing this, Vianello moved a few steps further towards the village, put his hand lightly on the arm of the woman, and said, 'Is your husband here, Signora? Perhaps he could take you home.'

The woman shook her head, freed her arm from his hand, but slowly and with no hint of having taken or wanting to give offence, and walked away towards the houses, leaving the matter to the men.

Vianello moved closer to the man who had stood next to the woman. 'Can you remember when you saw Signora Follini last, Signore?'

'Some time this week, perhaps Wednesday. My wife sent me to get mineral water.'

'Do you remember who else might have been in the store when you were there?'

The man hesitated a moment before he answered. Both Brunetti and Vianello noticed this; neither gave any sign that they had.

'No.'

Vianello didn't ask for an explanation.

Instead, he turned back to the crowd. 'Can anyone else tell me when they saw her?'

One man said, 'Tuesday. In the morning. She was opening the store. I was on my way to the bar.'

Another volunteered, 'My wife bought the newspaper on Wednesday.'

When no one else spoke, Vianello asked, 'Does anyone remember seeing her after Wednesday?' None of them answered. Vianello pulled his notebook from his back pocket, opened it, and said, 'Could I ask you to give me your names?'

'What for?' demanded the man with the blanket.

'We're going to have to speak to everyone in the village,' Vianello began reasonably, as if taking no notice of the question or the tone in which it had been asked, 'so if I can get your names, we won't have to bother any of you again.'

Though not fully persuaded by this, the men nevertheless gave him their names and, when asked, their addresses. Then they filed slowly away, moving in and out of the circles of light, leaving the pavement to the two policemen and, at a distance, to the woman who lay silent, her blank eyes raised to the stars.

17

Before he spoke, Brunetti moved even farther away from the body of the dead woman. 'When I was in the store with her last week, two men came in. It was obvious they made her nervous. When I called her, I think it was Monday, she hung up as soon as she heard my name. When I called again, later in the week, a man answered, and I hung up without saying anything. Probably stupid.' He thought of what he'd learned about her, that she had been an addict for so many years and had stopped, come home, and gone to work in her parents' store. 'I liked her. She had a sense of humour. And she was tough.' The subject of these observations lay behind them, deaf now to the opinion of others.

'Sounds like you mean that as a compliment,' Vianello said.

Without hesitation, Brunetti answered, 'I do.'

After a pause, Vianello asked, 'And she didn't have any illusions about life in Pellestrina, did she?'

Brunetti looked over at the low houses of the village. A light went out in a downstairs window of one of them, and then in another. Was it because the residents of Pellestrina hoped to get what sleep they could before the fishing fleet set sail or was it to darken their rooms, the better to enable them to see what was going on outside? 'I don't think any of them have any illusions about living here.'

If either of them thought about going to the bar to have a drink while they waited for the scene of crime team, neither suggested it. Brunetti glanced back at the police launch and saw the pilot, sitting in a pool of light on the mushroom-shaped top of the metal stanchion, smoking a cigarette, but he didn't move off in that direction. It seemed little enough to remain with Signora Follini until the others arrived to transform her into a crime victim, a statistic.

The second police launch brought not only the four men of the team but a young doctor from the hospital who worked as a substitute when neither Rizzardi nor Guerriero was available. Brunetti had been at two crime scenes when he had been sent to declare the victim dead, and both times the doctor had behaved in a way that Brunetti did not like, dismissive of the solemnity of the moment. Only five years out of medical school, Dottor Venturi had apparently spent his time acquiring the arrogance, rather than the compassion, of his profession. He had also carefully copied the meticulous dress of his superior, Rizzardi, though the result always seemed slightly ridiculous on his short, stubby body.

The boat pulled in and moored beside theirs; the doctor jumped heavily down and walked towards the forms he knew to be Brunetti and Vianello, but he made no acknowledgement of their presence. He wore a dark charcoal grey suit with just the faintest of dark vertical stripes, a pattern which emphasized, rather than disguised, his rotundity.

He looked down at Signora Follini's body for a moment, then pulled the handkerchief from his breast pocket and dropped it on the wet pavement beside her before kneeling carefully on it. He picked up her hand without bothering to look at her face, felt her wrist, then let it slap wetly back on the pavement. 'She's dead,' he said to no one in particular. He glanced up at Brunetti and Vianello to see how they would respond.

When neither of them spoke, Venturi repeated, 'I said she was dead.'

Brunetti looked away from the *laguna* then and glanced down at the young doctor. He wanted to know the cause of her death, but he did not want to watch this young man touch her again, so he simply nodded in acknowledgement and turned back to his contemplation of the distant lights visible on the water.

Vianello signalled to the men who had drawn up behind the doctor as he knelt over the body. Venturi started to get to his feet, but the toe of his right foot slipped on the wet pavement and he stopped himself from falling prone only by putting both palms flat down in front of him. Quickly he scrambled to his feet. He moved away from the body, careful to keep his dirty hands away from his sides, turned to one of the photographers, and said, 'Would you get me my handkerchief?'

The photographer, a man of about Brunetti's age, was busy setting up his tripod. He pulled one of the legs out, screwed it in place, looked over at the doctor and said, 'I didn't drop it,' and turned his attention to the second leg.

Venturi opened his mouth to reprimand the technician, thought better of it, and headed off in the direction of the launch, leaving his hand-kerchief on the ground beside the body. Brunetti watched as he walked away, hands held horizontal, and was struck by how much like a penguin he looked. The empty boat bobbed out in the water, at least a metre from the edge of the pier. Neither of the pilots was anywhere to be seen. Rather than haul the boat closer by means of its mooring rope or attempt the broad leap from the pier to the deck, Venturi walked along the pier and sat on a wooden park bench. Brunetti suddenly noticed the heavy evening mist that had settled in, and was glad of it.

He walked back to Signora Follini and knelt

beside her, welcoming the momentary distraction of the dampness that began to soak into the knees of his trousers. She wore a low-cut angora sweater, the pile of the fabric swirled into chaotic ridges and whirls by the water in which she had floated. Though he was no pathologist, Brunetti was familiar with the signs of violent death, but he saw none here. The skin of her throat was untouched, as was the fabric of her sweater. With the fingers of his right hand, he lifted the hem of her sweater, exposing her stomach. Seeing nothing but the stretch marks of age, he turned his eyes away and covered her again.

The various technicians busied themselves while Vianello and Brunetti waited. As they stood there idly, Brunetti saw the man with the blanket approach again. He went up to Vianello and said, nodding in the direction of the technicians, 'When they're finished, can you cover her?'

Vianello agreed and took the blanket the man offered.

'I don't need it back, so don't worry about that,' the man said, then walked away from the pier and disappeared into the darkness at the mouth of a small alley that ran between the houses. Time passed. Occasionally, the darkness was punctured by flashes from the technician's camera. Vianello waited until the crime team had finished and started to assemble their equipment, then he walked over to Signora Follini, flung the blanket open in the air and let it fall over her, careful to cover her face and her eyes.

'Rizzardi would have told us something,' Vianello said as he rejoined Brunetti.

'Rizzardi would have picked up his own handkerchief,' Brunetti answered.

'Does it matter that we won't know what killed her until the autopsy?' Vianello asked.

Brunetti tilted his chin in the direction of the houses of Pellestrina, most of them fully dark by now. 'Do you think any of them is going to help us, even when we do know?'

'It seems some of them liked her,' Vianello said with cautious optimism.

'They liked Marco Bottin, too,' was Brunetti's rejoinder.

Because of the presence in the village of Signorina Elettra and Pucetti, Brunetti judged it better to delay until the next day the questioning that would have to be done. That might give the two of them, moving casually among the residents, the opportunity to hear things which would be forgotten or ignored by the time the police began the formal inquiry into the death of Signora Follini.

Brunetti signalled to the technicians and they unrolled a stretcher. The blanket barely shifted as they lifted Signora Follini and carried her over to the launch.

On the way back to Venice, Brunetti stood on deck, thinking of the jokes he and Vianello had made about Signora Follini, though at the time neither of them had had any idea of how practised her attentions had been. He took some comfort in the thought that, had she heard their jokes, she might have been amused by them, but the realization that she was now far beyond any possibility of sensing his regret merely added to his remorse.

He was home long after midnight but found Paola, as he had hoped, waiting for him. She was sitting in bed, reading, but she closed the book and set it on the table then removed her glasses before she spoke. 'What happened?'

Brunetti hung his jacket in the closet, pulled off his tie and draped it over the back of a chair. 'Signora Follini. Someone pulled her out of the *laguna*,' he said as he started to unbutton his shirt. He sat, more tired than he had realized, on the chair beside the bed and bent down to untie his shoes. 'Someone tossed her in the water and left her to drown, I think.'

'Because of the other killings?' she asked.

'It would have to be.'

'Is she still out there?' Paola asked. For a moment, Brunetti thought she must mean Luisa Follini, whose body was by now lying in the chill company of the other dead at the Ospedale Civile, but then he realized she must mean Signorina Elettra.

'I'll tell her to come back,' he said. Before Paola could comment, he padded down to the bathroom, where he was careful to avoid looking at himself in the mirror as he brushed his teeth.

Some time later, when he slipped under the

covers beside her, Paola picked up just where things had been left. 'Will she listen to you?'

'She always listens to me.'

'So does Chiara,' Paola said but left it at that.

He turned towards her and draped his arm over her stomach. He felt her move, and the light in the room went out. She shifted and slipped her arm around him until his head rested comfortably in the hollow just under her shoulder. He lay in the arms of his wife and thought of another woman, but because he told himself he was thinking of her safety, he made no effort to resist the thought.

After a long time, so long that both of them should have been asleep, Paola said, 'You better do something about this.'

He made a noise, and then more time passed, and then they both slept.

The next morning, even before he left home, he called the morgue and asked the attendant who had been assigned to do the autopsy on the woman brought in from Pellestrina the night before.

'Dottor Rizzardi.'

'Good. When?'

There was a pause, and Brunetti heard the sound of a page being turned. 'There were two people who died in Castello. Probably fumes from their water heater. But I can put her up first. He should be done by eleven.'

'Thanks,' said Brunetti. 'Tell him I'll call, would you?'

'Certainly, Commissario,' the attendant said and put the phone down.

Brunetti was keen to know when Signora Follini had died, and only Rizzardi could tell him that. Some time after Wednesday, unless he found someone who said they'd seen her later than that.

And where? He found the map of the *laguna* and studied the narrow length of Pellestrina. At the southern end was the mouth of the canal where she had been found, about three kilometres from the village, just beyond the protected area of the Riserva of Ca' Roman. He folded the map and slipped it into the inside pocket of his jacket. Only one of the pilots could tell him what he wanted to know about tides and currents and the way things drifted in the water.

At the Questura, he went first to the room used by the officers and there found Montisi, who often opted to work the quieter Sunday shift. The pilot was sitting in the strangely empty officers' room, looking idly at a ragged copy of *Il Gazzetta dello Sport* in a manner that suggested he would be just as interested in staring at the wall. Brunetti spread the map on top of the newspaper, repeated what the fisherman said about where he found Signora Follini, and asked the pilot to explain what could have happened to have brought her there.

After studying the map for a while, Montisi asked, 'How bad was she?'

She was dead, Brunetti thought. How much

worse could things be for her? 'I don't understand.'

'You saw her body, didn't you?' the pilot asked patiently.

'Yes.'

'How much damage had been done?'

'Her eyes were gone.'

Montisi nodded, as if he'd expected this. 'How about her arms and legs? Did it look like she'd been dragged on the bottom?'

Brunetti, with some reluctance, cast his memory back to the last he'd seen of Signora Follini. 'She was wearing a sweater and slacks, so I couldn't see her arms or legs. But I didn't notice any damage to her hands or face. Aside from the eyes.'

Montisi grunted and bent over the map. 'They brought her in about eight, didn't they?'

'That's when the call reached me.' Brunetti was surprised to realize that, even with the pilot, he didn't mention that the call had come from Pucetti. Perhaps this was the beginning of real paranoia.

'You don't have any idea of when she went in?'

'No.'

Montisi pushed himself up from the desk and went over to a glass-fronted bookcase, a relic from former days. He pulled open the door and took down a thin, paper-covered book, flipped it open, ran his forefinger down a page, turned it, did the same with the next, and then the next. He found what he was searching for, studied it, then shut the book and put it back in the case.

When he returned to the desk, he said, 'I need to know how long she was in the water. She could have drifted out there from just about anywhere: Chioggia, Pellestrina, even from one of the other channels if she was dumped over the side.' He paused, then added, 'The tide was running strong last night because of the full moon, and it was running out when they found her, so she was headed out to sea. That would make it more unlikely that she'd be found.'

'I won't know when she died until later this morning, after I talk to Rizzardi,' Brunetti said.

Montisi indicated that he had heard. 'If she was in the water for a long time, then whoever did it probably just tossed her in, not planning much of anything. But if she wasn't dead a long time, then they threw her in some place where they knew the tide would pull her out into the Adriatic. If she got caught in the bottom of the channel, then there wouldn't have been much of her left when she got there: the tides are strong, and she'd be moving quickly. A lot of her would have been pulled off by the stones down there.'

Montisi saw the look his superior gave him. 'It's not my doing, sir. It's just the way the tides work.'

Brunetti thanked him for the information, made no comment on Montisi's casual assumption that she had been murdered, and went back up to his own office to wait for it to be time to call Rizzardi.

The doctor, however, called him first to tell

him that the cause of death was simple drowning, in salt water.

'Could someone have drowned her?' he asked.

Rizzardi's answer took a moment to come. 'Possibly. All they'd have to do is push her in from a boat or take her into the water and hold her down. There were no recent signs that she had been tied up.'

Before Brunetti could ask about that, the pathologist added, 'From a gynaecological point of view, she was interesting.'

'Why?'

'There are signs that, at one time or another, she'd had most of the major venereal diseases, and there are signs of at least one abortion.'

'She was an addict for years,' Brunetti said. Rizzardi grunted, as though that fact were so obvious as barely to merit mention. 'And, it seems, a prostitute.'

'That's what I would have guessed,' Rizzardi observed with a neutrality that reminded Brunetti of how much he liked the doctor, and why.

Brunetti went back to the question he had not been able to ask. 'You said there were no recent signs that she had been tied up. What does that mean?'

There was a long hesitation but at last the pathologist said, 'There are signs of binding on the upper arms and ankles. So I'd guess that whoever she was with most recently, if she had a steady man, was interested in rough stuff.'

'What do you mean, "rough stuff?" Rape?'

'No,' Rizzardi's answer was immediate.

'Then what else? What else can it be?'

'If sex is rough, it's not necessarily rape,' Rizzardi said with sufficient asperity to leave Brunetti waiting for a terse, 'Commissario' at the end of the sentence.

'Then what's rape?' Brunetti asked.

'If either partner is unwilling, then it's rape.'

'Either?'

Rizzardi's voice softened, 'We live in different times, Guido. The days are gone when rape was something that happened only between a violent man and an innocent woman.'

Brunetti, father of a teenage daughter, was curious to hear what Dottor Rizzardi had to say on the subject, but he couldn't see how this would advance his investigation and so he let it go and asked, 'When did it happen?'

'I'd guess it was two days ago, some time Friday night.'

'Why?'

'Just believe me, Guido. This isn't television, where I have to talk about the contents of her stomach or the amount of oxygen in her blood. Two days ago,' he repeated, 'probably in the evening, after ten or so. Just believe me and believe it will stand up in court.'

'If it ever gets to court,' Brunetti said absently, a remark not necessarily intended for the pathologist.

'Well, that's your job. I just tell you what the physical evidence tells me. You've got to figure out why and how and who.'

'Would that it were so easy,' Brunetti said.

Rizzardi chose not to discuss the relative demands of their separate professions and ended the call, leaving Brunetti to go out to Pellestrina to begin to try to answer those questions.

18

Even though it was Sunday, Brunetti saw no reason why he and Vianello should not go out to Pellestrina in the hope of discovering something that might contribute to an understanding of Signora Follini's death. Montisi was not at all unwilling to take them out, insisting that the news in the paper bored him; since he didn't like soccer much he would just as soon not waste his time reading about the day's matches.

As they stood on the deck of the launch at the Giardini stop, motor idling, waiting for Vianello to show up, Brunetti returned to Montisi's remark and asked, 'What sports do you like, then?'

'Me?' Montisi asked, a delaying tactic Brunetti recognized from long familiarity with witnesses who found a question uncomfortable.

'Yes.'

'Do you mean to play or to watch, sir?' Montisi asked evasively.

By now more curious about the reason for Montisi's reluctance than to know the answer to the question, Brunetti said, 'Either.'

'Well, I don't play sports, not at my age,' Montisi said in a manner that suggested no further information would be forthcoming.

'But to watch?' Brunetti asked.

Montisi looked off down the long, tree-lined *viale* that led to Corso Garibaldi, eager for a sign of Vianello. Brunetti watched the people walking by. After a long time, Montisi said, 'Well, sir, it's not like I know anything about it or I go to any special trouble to watch it, but I like to look at the sheepdog trials, on television. From Scotland, you know.' When Brunetti said nothing, Montisi added, 'And New Zealand.'

'Not much coverage in the *Gazzettino*, I'd imagine,' Brunetti observed.

'No,' the pilot answered, then, looking off towards the arch at the end of the *viale*, said, 'There's Vianello,' relief audible in his voice.

The sergeant, today in uniform, waved as he approached and then jumped on deck. Montisi pulled away from the *riva* and headed towards the now familiar canal that led towards Pellestrina's peaceful observance of the Lord's Day.

The fact that religion is a thing of the past and no

longer exerts any real influence on the behaviour of the people of Italy has in no way affected their churchgoing habits, especially in the smaller villages. In fact, some sort of algebraic equation might well be made to connect the smallness of a parish and the proportion of people who attend Mass. It is those gross heathens, the Romans and the Milanese, who do not attend, the millions among whom they live keeping them safe from the eye and tongue of local comment. The Pellestrinotti, however, are conscientious in their attendance at Mass, regular attendance allowing them to keep track of the doings of their neighbours without seeming to pry, for anything that has happened, especially anything that could call into question either virtue or honesty, is sure to be discussed on the steps of the church on Sunday morning.

It was there that Brunetti and Vianello awaited them, and awaited events, just before twelve, as the eleven o'clock Mass was ending and the villagers of Pellestrina were enjoined one final time to 'go in peace'.

Religion, Brunetti reflected, as he stood on the steps, though he had never realized this until Paola had pointed it out to him, always made him uncomfortable. Paola had had what he considered the good fortune to be raised, more or less, entirely free of religion, as neither of her parents had ever bothered attending church functions, at least not those where religious observance of any sort was the reason for attendance. Their social position often required them to attend ceremonies such as the investiture of bishops or cardinals, even the coronation, if that is the proper noun, of the current Pope. But these were ceremonies which had to do not with faith but with power, which quality Paola had always insisted was the real business of the Church.

Because she was as devoid of faith as she was of the habit of religious observance, she had no grudge against religion, not at all, and viewed the peculiar ways in which people chose to observe its rules with anthropological distance. Brunetti, on the other hand, had been raised by a mother who believed, and though he had ceased to do so well before his adolescence, he nonetheless carried within him the memory of faith, though faith deceived. He knew his attitude to religion was adversarial, if not antagonistic; however much he tried to fight this, he could not escape it or the guilt it caused him. As Paola never ceased to remind him, 'I'd rather be a pagan suckled on a creed outworn . . .'

All of this crowded into his head as he stood on the steps of the church, waiting to see who would emerge and what new information they would bring him. An organ pealed out, the purity of its tone speaking more to the quality of the sound system inside the church than to the talent of the organist. The doors swung open, the music swelled and cascaded down the steps, quickly followed by the first members of the congregation. Seeing them, Brunetti was struck, not for the first time, by how haunted the faces of people emerging from church were.

Had they been a herd of animals, a flock of sheep jumping over a low stile into a new field, their sudden apprehension of a foreign presence could not have been more evident, nor could the wave of uneasiness that rippled from the front to the back of the group as each new member became aware of the potential threat that awaited them on the steps. Had Vianello not been in uniform, Brunetti had no doubt that many of them would have pretended not to have seen the two men. As it was, some of them still made a great business of not noticing them, though Vianello's white uniform hat was as glaringly evident as the halo on any of the saints left behind them in the church.

Brunetti, making an attempt not to appear to be doing so, studied the faces of the people who walked past him. At first, he thought he was noticing the effect of their conscious efforts to look both innocent and ignorant, but then he realized that what he was seeing were the effects of a restrictive geography: many of them looked alike. The men were all short, their heads round, eyes close together. Their generally muscular build he attributed to the work most of them did, as must be the case with the sun-scored and deeply lined faces of all of them, even the youngest. The women showed more diversity of feature, though a common thickness seemed to have settled on the bodies of any of them over the age of thirty.

This morning no one paused on the steps of the church to talk to their neighbours. Instead, the entire congregation responded to some common, urgent summons to their homes. To say they fled is to exaggerate. To say they moved away quickly and nervously is not.

As the last of them moved off, Brunetti turned to Vianello, hoping to lighten his sense of discomfiture by asking if they should blame their failure on the sergeant's uniform. Before he could speak, however, he saw Signorina Elettra emerge from the bar that stood to the left of the church. That is, he saw her emerge from the bar briefly and then step partly back inside. She came out again, more slowly this time, and as she walked away from the door, he saw the reason for the delay: a young man held her hand and stood in the doorway, calling back to someone inside the bar. Whatever it was he said, it caused a shout of laughter from more than one voice, at which Signorina Elettra yanked his arm, finally pulling him from the doorway.

The young man stepped towards her and with what seemed the ease of long familiarity put his arm around her shoulder and pulled her close. There was an utter lack of coquettishness in the way she responded, wrapping her left arm around his waist and falling into step beside him, moving towards the two policemen they had not yet seen. Considerably taller than she, the man leaned his head down and said something; Elettra glanced up at his face and answered with a smile Brunetti had never seen her use before. The man bent and kissed the top of her head, causing them to stop for an instant. When he lifted his head, he saw Brunetti and Vianello on the steps of the church and came to a sudden halt.

Signorina Elettra, surprised, looked up at the young man's face, then followed the path of his eyes. The exclamation that emerged from her open mouth was drowned by the first peal of the church bells above them. She recovered her composure long before the twelfth bell struck, by which time she had redirected her attention, momentarily distracted by the unexpected sight of a policeman on the steps of the church, to the serious business of lunch with her new friend.

After an hour of attempting to interview the people of Pellestrina, Brunetti decided it would be futile until they had all finished their lunch. He and Vianello therefore retreated to the restaurant and had a sober meal which neither of them enjoyed, despite the freshness of the food and the crispness of the wine. They decided to split up, hoping that the sympathy Vianello had established when he spoke to people would be sufficient to overcome the inevitable response to his uniform.

At the first two houses, Brunetti was told that they did not know Signora Follini at all well, one of the men even going so far as to say that he took his wife down to the Lido in the car once a week: at the local store the prices were far too high and many of the items on sale no longer fresh. The man was an embarrassingly bad liar, a fact which his wife tried to ignore by carefully arranging and rearranging four porcelain figurines which bore a vague resemblance to dachshunds. Brunetti thanked them both, and left.

No one answered the door at the next two houses; the response might as easily have been the result of choice as absence. The third door, however, was opened almost before he finished knocking, presenting Brunetti with every policeman's dream: the watchful neighbour. He knew her from a single glance at her tight lips, recognized the type in her eager eyes and forward-leaning posture. The fact that she did not rub her palms together did not detract from the overall impression of satisfaction conveyed by her avid smile: here at last was someone who would share her shock and horror at the terrible deeds, commissions and omissions of which her neighbours were guilty.

Her hair was coiled in a thin bun at the back of her head, recalcitrant wisps held down by a scented greasy pomade. Though her face was thin, her body was rounded, with no visible waist. Over a black dress that was slowly turning green with age and repeated washing, she wore a soiled apron which, years ago, might once have been covered with flowers.

'Good afternoon, Signora,' he began, but before he could give his name, she interrupted him.

'I know who you are and why you're here. It's

about time you came to talk to me.' She tried to express disapproval, but it was impossible for her to suppress her satisfaction at his arrival.

'I'm sorry, Signora,' he began, 'but I wanted to see what the others had to say before talking to you.'

'Come in, come in,' she said, turning and leading him towards the back of the house. He followed her down a long, damp hallway, at the end of which light came from an open doorway into the kitchen. Here there was no change in temperature, no comforting warmth to compensate for the seaside dankness of the corridor, and no pleasant scents of cooking to cut through the oppressive smell of mould, wool, and something feral and animal he couldn't recognize.

She directed him to a seat at the table and, without offering him anything to drink, sat down opposite.

Brunetti took a small notebook from the side pocket of his jacket, opened it, and uncapped his pen. 'Your name, Signora?' he asked, careful to speak Italian and not Veneziano, knowing that the more formal and official this interview could be made to seem, the greater would be her pleasure and sense of gratification at finally having made the authorities aware of the many things she had nursed to her bosom all these thankless years.

'Boscarini,' she said. 'Clemenza.' He made no comment and wrote silently.

'And you've lived here how long, Signora Boscarini?'

'All my life,' she answered, equally careful to speak Italian but not finding it at all easy. 'Sixty-three years.'

Emotions or experiences he couldn't imagine made her look at least ten years older than that, but Brunetti did nothing more than make another note. 'Your husband, Signora?' Brunetti asked, knowing that she would be compli-mented by the assumption that she must have one, insulted to be asked if she did.

'Dead. Thirty-four years ago. In a storm.' Brunetti made a note of the importance of this fact. He looked up again and decided not to ask about children.

'Have you had the same neighbours all this time, Signora?'

'Yes. Except for the Rugolettos three doors down,' she said, giving an angry toss of her chin to the left. 'They moved in twelve years ago, from Burano, when her grandfather died and left them the house. She's dirty, the wife,' she said in dismissive contempt and then, to make sure he understood why, added, 'Buranesi.'

Brunetti grunted in acknowledgement, then, wasting no time, asked, 'Did you know Signora Follini?'

She smiled at this, hardly able to contain her pleasure, then quickly smothered the expres-sion. Brunetti heard a small noise and glanced across at her. It took him an instant to realize that she was actually licking her lips repeatedly, as if freeing them at last to tell the awful truth. 'Yes,' she finally said. 'I knew her, and I knew her parents. Good people, hard working. She killed them. Killed them as if she'd taken a knife and driven it into her poor mother's heart.'

Brunetti, looking down at his notebook to hide his face, made encouraging noises and continued to write.

Again she paused, made the licking noise, then went on. 'She was a whore and a drug addict and brought disease and disgrace on her family. I'm not surprised that she's dead or that she died the way she did. I'm just surprised that it took so long.' She was silent for a moment, and then added, in a voice so unctuous Brunetti closed his eyes, 'God have mercy on her soul.'

Allowing the deity sufficient time to register the request, Brunetti then asked, 'You said she was a prostitute, Signora? While she was here? Was she still?'

'She was a whore when she was a child and a young woman. Once a woman does that sort of thing, she's defiled, and she never loses the taste for it.' Her voice reflected both certainty and disgust. 'So she must have been doing it now. That's obvious.'

Brunetti turned a page, mastered his expression, and looked up with an encouraging smile. 'Do you know anyone who might have been her client?' He saw her begin to answer, then think of the consequences of false accusation and close her mouth.

'Or suspect anyone, Signora?' When she still hesitated, he shut the notebook, placed it on the table, capped his pen and placed it on top. 'It's often just as important for us, Signora, to have a sense of what's going on, even if we don't have proof. It's enough to start us on the right road, to know where to begin to look.' She said nothing, so he went on, 'And it's only the most courageous and virtuous citizens who can help us, Signora, especially in an age when most people are all too willing to close their eyes to immorality and the sort of behaviour that corrupts society by destroying the unity of the family.' He had been tempted to refer to 'sacred unity', but thought it might be excessive and so contented himself with the lesser nonsense. It sufficed, however, for Signora Boscarini.

'Stefano Silvestri.' The name slithered off her lips: the man who had been so careful to explain that he took his wife to the larger stores on the Lido once a week. 'He was always in the store, like a dog sniffing at a bitch to see if she was ready for him.'

Brunetti received this information with his accepting noise but made no motion towards his notebook. As if encouraged by that act of discretion, she went on: 'She tried to make it look like she wasn't interested, made fun of him whenever anyone was around, but I know what she was up to. We all did. She led him on.' Brunetti listened calmly, trying to recall if this woman had been on the steps of the church and wondering what going to Mass might mean for someone like her.

'Can you think of any other man or men who might have been involved with her?' he asked.

'There was talk,' she began, all too eager to let him know. 'Another married man,' she began, lips wet and eager. 'A fisherman.' For a moment, he thought she was going to name him, but he saw her consider the consequences, and she said only, 'I'm sure there were many more.' When Brunetti remained silent in the face of this slander, she said, 'It's because she provoked them.'

'Of course,' he permitted himself to say. Which would be worse, he wondered: death at sea or another thirty-four years with this woman? He sensed that she was willing to tell him nothing more, assuming that what she had given him was information and not mere spite and jealousy, he got to his feet and picked up his notebook and pen. Slipping them into his pocket, he said, 'Thank you for your help, Signora. I assure you that everything you've said will be kept in the strictest confidence. And, speaking personally, I would like to remark that it is rare for a witness to be so willing to give us this sort of information.' It was a small shot, and it seemed to pass her by, but it was still a shot and it made him feel better. With every expression of politeness, he took his leave, glad to escape from her house, her words, and the sound of that flicking, reptilian tongue.

As they had agreed, he and Vianello met at the bar at five. Each ordered coffee, and when the barman moved off after setting the small cups down in front of them, Brunetti asked, 'Well?'

'There was someone. A man,' Vianello said.

Brunetti tore open two packets of sugar and poured them into his coffee, stirred it and drank it in one long sip. 'Who?' Vianello, he noticed, still drank his coffee without sugar, a habit his own grandmother had believed 'thinned the blood', whatever that meant.

'No idea. And it was only one man who said anything, something about the way Signora Follini was always up before dawn, even though the store didn't open until eight. It wasn't actually what he said so much as the way he said it, and the look his wife gave him when he did.'

That was all Vianello had, and it didn't seem like very much. It could have been Stefano Silvestri, though Brunetti hardly thought his wife was the sort who would allow her husband to be anywhere before dawn other than lying beside her or working his nets.

'I saw Signorina Elettra,' Vianello added.

Brunetti forced himself to pause before asking, 'Where?'

'Walking towards the beach.'

Brunetti refused to ask and after what seemed a long time, Vianello added, 'She was with the same man.'

'Do you know who he is?'

Vianello shook his head. 'I suppose the best way to find out would be to ask Montisi to ask his friend.'

Brunetti didn't like the idea, didn't like the chance of doing anything that would call attention to Signorina Elettra in any way. 'No, better to ask Pucetti.'

'If he ever comes back to work,' Vianello said, casting his eyes towards the far end of the bar, where the owner was deep in conversation with two men.

'Where's he living?'

'In one of the houses. Cousin of the owner or something.'

'Can we get in touch with him?'

'No. He didn't want to bring his *telefonino*; said he was afraid someone might call and leave a message that would compromise him.'

'We could have issued him one, then none of his friends would know the number,' Brunetti said with undisguised irritation.

'Didn't want that, either. Said you never know.'

'Never know what?' Brunetti demanded.

'He didn't say. But I imagine he thinks someone at the Questura might mention that he'd been issued a phone for use on some special assignment, or someone might make a call to it, or someone might be listening to all of our calls.'

'Isn't that a bit paranoid?' Brunetti asked, though he had himself, more than once, contemplated the third possibility.

'I think it's always safer to assume that everything you say is overheard.'

'That's no way to live,' Brunetti said hotly, believing this.

Vianello shrugged. 'So what shall we do?'

Brunetti remembered Rizzardi's comments

about 'rough sex'. 'I'd like to find out who she was seeing.' He caught Vianello's glance and added, 'Signora Follini, that is.'

'I still think the best way is to ask Montisi to ask his friend. These people aren't going to tell us anything, at least not directly.'

'I had a woman tell me that Signora Follini was still tempting the local men to sin,' Brunetti said, disgust mingled with amusement.

'Presumably one of the ones who was tempted was either her husband or the man next door.'

'Two doors down.'

'Same thing.'

Brunetti decided to return to the boat to ask Montisi to speak to his friend. That proved unnecessary, as the pilot, whom they ran into upon leaving the bar, had been invited to the man's home for lunch, and then they had spent the rest of the afternoon sipping grappa and talking about their old days in the Army. After they'd relived the Albanian campaign and toasted the three Venetians who had not returned with them, their talk turned to their current lives. Montisi had been very careful to set the record straight about where his loyalties might lie, declaring his intention of retiring from the police as soon as he could.

As the three policemen walked slowly towards the boat, Montisi explained that it had proven relatively straightforward, and he had emerged, the bottle of grappa almost finished, with the name of Luisa Follini's lover.

'Vittorio Spadini,' he said, not without pride in his achievement. 'He's from Burano. A fisherman. Married, three children, the sons are fishermen and the daughter's married to one.'

'And?' Brunetti asked.

Perhaps as a result of the grappa or perhaps because of the recent talk of retiring, Montisi answered, 'And that's probably more than you and Vianello would get if you stayed here a week.' Surprised to hear himself speak like this, he added, 'Sir', but the time between the answer and the title had been prolonged.

Silence fell, broken only when Montisi added, 'But he's not fishing much any more. He lost his boat about two years ago.'

Brunetti thought of Signora Boscarini's husband and asked, 'In a storm?'

Montisi dismissed the idea with a quick shake of his head. 'No, worse. Taxes.' Before Brunetti could ask how taxes could be worse than a storm, Montisi explained. 'The Guardia di Finanza hit him with a bill for three years' false declarations of what he earned. He tried to fight it for a year, but in the end he lost. You always do. They took his boat.'

Vianello broke in to ask, 'Why is that worse than a storm?'

'Insurance,' Montisi answered. 'Nothing can insure you against those bastards from the Finanza.'

'How much was it worth?' Brunetti asked, again made aware of just how little he knew about this world of boats and the men who went to sea in them.

'They wanted five hundred million. That was fines and what they calculated he owed them, but no one has that much cash, so he had to sell the boat.'

'My God, are they worth that much?' Brunetti asked.

Montisi gave him a puzzled glance. 'If they're as big as his was, they're worth much more; they can cost a billion.'

Vianello broke in. 'If they wanted five hundred million for three years, that probably means he cheated them out of twice that, three times.'

'Easily,' Montisi agreed, not without a hint of pride at the cleverness of the men who fished the *laguna*. 'Ezio told me Spadini thought he'd win. His lawyer told him to fight the case, but he probably did that just to make his own bill bigger. In the end, Spadini had no choice: they came and took it. If he had come up with enough cash to pay the fine, too many questions would have been asked,' he said, leaving the others to assume that the money was there, hidden in secret investments or accounts, like so much of the wealth of Italy. He glanced at Vianello and added, 'Someone told me that the judge was one of the Greens.'

Vianello shot him a glance but said nothing.

Montisi went on, 'That he had a grudge against all of the *vongolari* because of what they do to the *laguna*.'

At this, Vianello finally said, his voice dangerously tight, 'Paolo, cases like this, about taxes, don't come up before judges.' Before Montisi could answer, he added, 'Whether they belong to the Greens or not.' Then, turning to Brunetti but obviously aiming his remarks at Montisi, Vianello added, 'Next we're probably going to be told about the way the Greens take vipers up in helicopters and drop them in the mountains to repopulate the species.' Then to Montisi he said, his voice more aggressive than Brunetti could ever remember it, 'Come on, Paolo, aren't you going to tell us how friends of yours have found dead vipers in bottles up in the mountains or how they've seen people tossing them out of helicopters?'

Montisi looked at the sergeant but didn't bother to answer, his silence resonant with his conviction of the futility of attempting to reason with fanatics. Brunetti had, over the course of the years, heard many people speak of these mysterious, malevolent helicopters, piloted by mad ecologists bent on restoring some perverted idea of 'nature', but it had never occurred to him that anyone could actually believe in them.

They had reached, not just an impasse, but the boat. Montisi turned away from them and busied himself with the mooring ropes. Vianello, perhaps in an attempt to soften the effect of his remarks, went to the back and began to untie the second rope. Brunetti left them to it, busy with calculations of the surprising sums that had just been referred to. When Montisi had the rope coiled, Brunetti followed him aboard and called to him as the pilot went up the steps towards the wheel, 'You'd have to catch a lot of fish to afford a boat like that.'

'Clams,' Montisi instantly corrected him. 'That's where the money is. No one's going to take a shot at you over fish, but if they catch you digging up their clams and ruining their beds, then there's no telling what they'll do.'

'Is that what he did, ruin the beds?' Brunetti asked.

'I told you it's what they all do,' Montisi answered. 'They'll dig anywhere, and every year there are fewer clams. So the price goes up.' He looked from Brunetti to Vianello, who was standing on the dock, listening. With a brusque beckoning gesture, the pilot waved towards the sergeant and said, 'Come on, Lorenzo.' Vianello tossed his end of the rope around one of the stanchions on the side of the boat and jumped on board.

'But if he's lost his boat,' Brunetti said, pretending to ignore the successful conclusion of peace negotiations, and bringing the conversation back from the general to the particular, 'what does he do now?'

'Fidele said he's working for one of his sons, runs one of his boats for him,' Montisi said, pulling out dials on the panel in front of him. 'It's a much smaller boat, and there's only two of them on it.'

'Must be difficult for him,' Vianello interrupted, 'not being the owner any more.'

Montisi shrugged. 'Depends on the son, I suppose.'

'And Signora Follini?' Brunetti asked, again bringing the conversation back to his immediate concern.

'It had been going on for about two years,' Montisi said. 'Ever since he lost the boat.' Feeling that this wasn't sufficient explanation, Montisi went on. 'He doesn't have to get to sea so early any more, only when he wants to.'

'And the wife?' Vianello asked.

All of Italy and all of its history and culture went into the shrug with which Montisi dismissed this question. 'She's got a home, and he pays the rent. They've got three children, all married and on their own. What has she got to complain about?' Anything else he might have said was lost in the sound of the engine, which sprang to life at his command.

Not wanting to discuss this, Brunetti was content that they should return to the city, to their own homes and to their own children.

19

Brunetti had been in his office for less than an hour the following morning when he answered the phone to hear Signorina Elettra's voice.

'Where are you?' he asked brusquely, then moderated his tone and added, 'I mean how are you?'

Her long silence suggested how she felt about being questioned in this manner. When she did answer, however, there was no sign of resentment in her voice. 'I'm on the beach. And I'm fine.'

The far-off cries of the gulls spoke to the truth of the first, the lightness in her voice to the second.

'Signorina,' he began with little preparation and less thought, 'you've been there more than a week now. I think it's time you began to think about coming back.'

'Oh, no, sir, I don't think that's a good idea at all.'

'But I do,' he insisted. 'I think you should say your farewells to your family and report for work tomorrow.'

'It's the beginning of the week, sir. I'd planned to stay until at least the weekend.'

'Well, I think it would be better if you came back. There's a lot of work that's piled up since you left.'

'Please, sir. I'm sure it's nothing one of the other secretaries couldn't handle.'

'I need to get some information,' Brunetti said, realizing how close his voice came to pleading. 'Things I don't want the secretaries to know about.'

'Vianello can handle the computer well enough now to get you what you want.'

'It's the Guardia di Finanza,' Brunetti said, playing what he thought would be a trump card. 'I need information from them and I doubt that Vianello would be able to get it.'

'What sort of information, sir?' He heard noises in the background: gulls, a horn of some sort, a car engine starting, and he remembered how narrow the beach of Pellestrina was and how close to the road.

'I need to know about tax evasion.'

'Read the newspaper, sir,' she said, laughing at her own joke. When there was no response, she said, the laughter gone and her voice less rich for that, 'You can call their main office and ask. There's a *maresciallo* there, Resto, who can tell you everything you need to know. Just tell him I told you to call.'

He had known her long enough to recognize the polite inflexibility he was dealing with. 'I think it would be better if you handled it, Signorina.'

All pleasantness dropped from her voice as she said, 'If you keep this up, sir, I'll be forced to take a week of real vacation, and I'd rather not do that because it would take a lot of time to adjust the timetables.'

He wanted to cut it short and simply ask her who the man was he had seen her with yesterday, but their relationship had ill prepared him for such a question, especially in the tone he knew he would be incapable of preventing himself from using. He was her superior, but that hardly gave him the authority to act in *loco parentis*. Because the difference in their positions precluded the intimacy of friendship, he could not ask her to tell him what was going on between her and the handsome young man he had seen her with. He could not think of a way to express concern that would not sound like jealousy, and he could not explain, even to himself, which it was he actually felt.

'Then tell me if you've learned anything,' he said in a voice he forced himself to make less stern, hoping that this would be viewed as compromise rather than the defeat it so clearly was.

'I've learned to tell *un sandolo* from *un puparin*, and I've learned to spot a school of fish on a sonar screen,' she said.

He avoided the lure of sarcasm and asked, voice bland, 'And about the murders?'

'Nothing,' she admitted. 'I'm not from here, so no one talks about them in front of me, at least not to say more than the sort of things people say.' She sounded wistful at the confession that the Pellestrinotti did not treat her like one of their own, and he wondered about the lure of the place, or the people, that could cause this response. Yet he would not ask.

'What about Pucetti? Has he learned anything?'

'Not that I know, sir. I see him in the bar when he makes me a coffee, but he's given no sign that he has anything to tell me. I don't see that there's any sense in keeping him out here any longer.'

She was not alone in that sentiment: Brunetti had already had three questions about Pucetti from Lieutenant Scarpa, Patta's assistant, who had noticed the absence of the young officer's name from the regular duty roster. With the ease of long habit, Brunetti had lied and told Scarpa that he had assigned the young officer to the investigation of suspected drug shipments at the airport. There was no reason for his lie beyond his instinctive suspicion of the lieutenant and his desire that no one at all should learn of Pucetti's presence, nor that of Signorina Elettra, on Pellestrina.

'The same goes for you, Signorina,' he said,

aiming at lightness and humour. 'When are you coming back?'

'I told you, sir. I want to stay a bit longer.'

Above the cries of the gulls, a man's voice called out, 'Elettra.' He heard her sudden intake of breath, and then she said into the phone, *'Ti chiamerò. Ciao Silvia,'* and then she was gone, leaving Brunetti strangely unsettled that, in order finally to use the familiar *tu* with him, she had had to call him Silvia.

Signorina Elettra had no trouble whatsoever in addressing Carlo as *tu*. In fact, there were times when she thought that the grammatical intimacy did little justice to the sense of ease and familiarity she felt with him. Not only had something about him seemed familiar when they first met; it had continued to grow as she listened to him talk and came to know him better. They both loved mortadella, but they also loved, of all improbable things, Asterix and Bracio di Ferro, sugarless coffee and *Bambi*, and both confessed that they had cried when they learned of the death of Moana Pozzi, going on to say they'd never felt so proud to be Italian as when they saw the spontaneous outpouring of sympathy for the death of a porno star.

They'd spent hours talking during this week, and it had pained her, in the face of his openness, to maintain the lie that she was working for a bank. He'd expanded on his brief history of his life and told her he'd studied economics in Milano before abandoning his studies and returning home when his father died two years ago. There was, as neither of them needed to be told, no suitable work for a man who still had to pass two exams before finishing his degree in economics. She admired his honesty in telling her that he had no choice but to become a fisherman, and she delighted in hearing the pride with which he spoke of his gratitude to his uncle for having offered him a job.

The work on the boat was so heavy and exhausting that he had twice fallen asleep in her company, once while they sat in their cave on the beach and once as he sat beside her in the bar. She didn't mind either time, as it gave her the chance to study the small hollow just in front of his ear and the way his face relaxed and grew younger as he slept. She often told him he was too thin, and he replied that it was the work that did it. Though he ate like a wolf, and she had seen proof of this at every meal, she saw no trace of fat on his body. When he moved, he seemed to be composed of flexing lines and muscles; the sight of his bronzed forearm had once brought her close to tears, so beautiful did she find it.

When she gave it thought, she reminded herself that she was out on Pellestrina in order to listen to what people had to say about murder, not to fall into the orbit of a young man, no matter how beautiful he might be. She was there in the hope of picking up some piece of information that might be of use to the police, not to find herself enmeshed by a man who, if only by virtue of his occupation, could well be one of the people she should be gathering information about.

All of this fled her mind as Carlo's arm found its already familiar place on her shoulder, his left hand curving around behind her to come to rest on her arm. She'd already grown accustomed to the way his hand registered his emotions, fingers tightening on her arm when he wanted to emphasize something he said or tapping out a quick rhythm whenever he was preparing to make a joke. Though a number of men had touched her arm, few had managed to touch her heart the way he did. One night, when she'd gone out on the boat with him and his uncle, she'd seen his hands glistening in the light of the full moon, covered with fish guts, scales and blood, his face distant and intense with the need to shovel them from the nets into the refrigerated hold below decks. He'd looked up and seen her watching him and had immediately turned himself into Frankenstein's monster, arms raised in front of him, fingers quivering menacingly as he tromped, stiff-kneed, towards her.

She squealed. There is no more delicate word: she squealed in delighted horror and backed up against the rail of the boat. The monster approached, and as he reached her, his hands moved past her head, careful not to touch her hair, and Carlo's smiling mouth came down softly on her own, lingering there until his uncle shouted from the tiller, 'She's not a fish, Carlo. Get back to work.'

But today, here on the beach, there was no thought of work. His hand tightened on her arm; a gull squawked and took flight as he pulled her, not roughly but not gently, towards him. Their kiss was long and their bodies grew, if possible, closer together. He pulled away from her, moved his hand up and placed it gently on the back of her head, pressing her face into the angle of his shoulder. His hand moved and began gently running up and down, up and down her back then stopped, fingers splayed, at her belt.

Elettra made a sound, part sigh, like a soprano about to begin an important aria. The tips, only the tips, of his last two fingers slipped below her belt. Her mouth opened and she pressed it against his collarbone, then suddenly she bit at it through the heavy wool of his sweater.

She moved back from him then, grabbed blindly for his hand, and moved off, quickly, leading him down the beach and towards the entrance to the cave in the jetty.

20

Brunetti, less troubled by his passions, but still smarting from being called Silvia, considered the lies he had just told Signorina Elettra. There was no information he wanted from the Guardia di Finanza, and it was true that Vianello had indeed arrived at a point where he could summon up a remarkable amount of information from the computer. The name of the Finanza stuck in his mind, however, reminding him of something else he'd read or been told about them; as always, it had been something unpleasant.

He got up and stood by his window, his attention drawn down into Campo San Lorenzo, where someone – perhaps the old men who lived in the nursing home there – had constructed multi-storeyed shelters for the stray cats who had haunted the *campo* for years. He wondered what generation of cat he looked at today, how they were descended from the cats who'd been there when he'd first come to the Questura, more than a decade ago.

The name crept into his mind with all the grace and limberness of one of those cats: Vittorio Spadini, the man said to be Luisa Follini's lover. He'd had his boat confiscated by the Finanza, when was it, two years ago? Spadini lived on Burano; it was a fine spring day, a perfect day to go out to Burano for lunch. Brunetti left word with the guard at the door that, if anyone asked for him, he was to say that the Commissario had a dental appointment and would be back after lunch.

He got off the vaporetto at Mazzorbo and turned to his left, eager for the walk to the centre of Burano, already anticipating lunch at da Romano, where he hadn't eaten for years. The sun warmed him and his stride lengthened, his body happy to be in the sun, breathing in the iodine-laden air. Dogs romped on the new grass, and old ladies sat in the sun, glad for the added chance at life that springtime promised them. An enormous black dog rose up from beside his master, who sat calmly reading the *Gazzettino*, and lumbered towards Brunetti. He bent down and offered the back of his hand, which the dog licked happily. Then, tired of Brunetti, he loped back and flopped down again beside his owner.

Even before he reached the Burano boat

station, Brunetti had begun to notice the presence of people, far more than seemed normal for a weekday morning in late spring. When he got to the first of the stalls selling 'original Burano lace', most of which he had always thought was imported from Indonesia, he found his way forward blocked by pastel-coloured bodies. He began to skirt around them, confused by how unaware they seemed that other people wanted to walk to actual destinations rather than mill around and regroup idly in the middle of the pavement.

He turned from the piazza into Via Galuppi and headed for da Romano; he was sure he could reserve a place for one o'clock: a single person was always welcome in a restaurant. At worst, he might have to wait a quarter-hour, but on a day like this it would be a joy to sit at a table in one of the bars that lined the street, sip a prosecco, perhaps read the paper.

The small tables in front of the restaurant were all occupied; at many of them, three people sat at tables designed for two. He passed through the door and into the restaurant, but before he could speak, one of the waiters, hurrying past with a platter of seafood antipasto, saw him and called out, '*Siamo al completo.*'

For a moment, it occurred to Brunetti to argue and try to find a place, but when he glanced around inside he abandoned the idea and left. Two other restaurants were similarly full, though it was just after twelve, far too early for a civilized person to want to eat.

Brunetti had lunch in a bar, standing at the counter and eating toast filled with flabby ham and a slice of cheese that tasted as if it had spent most of its life in plastic. The prosecco was bitter and almost completely flat; even the coffee was bad. Disgusted with his meal and angered by the disappointment of his hopes, he walked dispiritedly down to a small park, bent on sitting in the sun to allow his mood to lighten. He sat on the first bench he saw, put his head back and turned his face to the sun. After a few minutes, his attention was drawn by a furious barking, and he opened his eyes to see again the enormous black dog, which he now recognized as a Newfoundland.

The dog dashed madly across the grass, aiming at a small blonde girl who stood at the foot of the ladder of a long children's slide. Seeing the dog approaching, the little girl grabbed the sides of the ladder and began to scramble up. The dog's owner stood at the other side of the park, its leash hanging helplessly from his hand, calling after the dog.

Barking wildly, the dog reached the slide. The girl, at the top, screamed in terror, her voice high and piercing. Suddenly the dog launched itself up the ladder, astonishing Brunetti, who watched helplessly as it reached the top. The girl dropped on to the top of the metal slide and sailed down; the dog plunged after her, front legs stiff.

The little girl sprawled into the sand at the bottom of the slide, and Brunetti leaped to his feet and started to run in her direction, his hand reaching helplessly for the gun he had, again, forgotten to wear. He closed his right hand into a fist and ran on.

The dog landed just to the left of the little girl, who opened her arms and embraced its enormous head. Its barks were drowned by her shrill laughter, and then all noise stopped as the dog set itself to trying to lick her face off.

Brunetti stopped, almost pitching headlong on to the grass. He looked across at the dog's owner, who waved once and started towards him. The little girl got to her feet and ran around to the ladder, the dog following joyously in her wake. Again he followed her up to the top and then down the slide, and at the bottom they fell into the same pink-tongued tableau. Before the owner could reach him, Brunetti turned and walked away, heading for Campo Vigner, the address the phone book listed for Vittorio Spadini.

The house on the right of Spadini's was bright red, the one to the left as bright a blue. The Spadini house, however, was a pale pink, bleached clean by years of rain and sun. Brunetti noticed other signs: a curtain falling from the rod at one of the windows, the right side of a shutter all but eaten through by rot. The Buranesi were, if nothing else, a house-proud people, and so it surprised him to see such patent signs of neglect.

He rang the bell, waited a moment, and rang it again. No one answered, so after a time he went to the red house and rang the bell there. It was opened by a round woman, or at least his first glance suggested that she was round. Short, even shorter than Chiara, she must have weighed more than a hundred kilos, most of which had decided to settle between her breasts and her knees. Her head was round and her face was round; even her little eyes, squeezed tight by the flesh surrounding them, were round.

'Good afternoon, Signora,' he said. 'I'm looking for Signor Spadini.'

'So are a lot of people,' she said with a laugh that set most of her body shaking loosely.

'I beg your pardon.'

'His wife's looking for him, and his sons are looking for him, and I suppose, if my husband thought there was any chance of getting the money he lent him back, he'd be looking for him, too.' Again, she laughed and again she shook.

Brunetti, unsettled by the strange dissonance between what she had to say and the way she chose to say it, asked, 'When was the last time anyone saw him?'

'Oh, last week some time.' Then, explaining the casualness with which she said this, she explained, 'He does this all the time, disappears and doesn't come home until he's spent all his money and has to go to work again.'

'As a fisherman?'

'Of course,' she said, this time not laughing; in fact, her face expressed confusion that this stranger at her door could think there was anything else a man from Burano could do to earn his living.

'And his wife?'

'She works,' the woman explained. Then, seeing that Brunetti was about to ask for an explanation, added, 'a cleaner at the elementary school'.

As if it had suddenly occurred to her that this man, clearly not a Buranesi, though he did speak Veneziano, had not explained the reason for his curiosity, she asked, 'Why do you want to see him?'

Brunetti smiled easily and, he hoped, wryly. 'I suppose I'm in the same position as your husband, Signora. I lent him some money.' He sighed, shook his head, and spread his hands in a display of mingled disappointment and resignation. 'Any idea where I might find him?'

She laughed again, this time at the absurdity of his errand. 'No, not until he decides to come back. He's a forest bird, Vittorio: he arrives and disappears when he wants to, and there's no catching him, no matter how much you might want to.'

For a moment, Brunetti toyed with the idea of giving her his home number and asking her to call if Spadini returned, but he thought better of it, thanked her for her help, and added, 'I hope your husband has better luck.'

All of her shook again at the unlikeliness of this; she smiled, and closed the door, leaving Brunetti to make his way through the milling crowds towards the vaporetto and back to Venice.

Back at the Questura, he was astonished to find Pucetti, in uniform, standing outside the Ufficio Straniero, keeping an eye on the people who stood in line, waiting for their papers to be processed.

'What are you doing here?' he asked the equally surprised officer.

'I called in this morning and asked for you, sir,' Pucetti said, ignoring the people who stood behind him. 'But I was put through to Lieutenant Scarpa. I think he'd left orders that he was to speak to me whenever I called. He said he had direct orders from the Vice-Questore that I was to report here instantly, in uniform. I tried to tell him I was on a special assignment, but he said it would be grounds for dismissal if I refused to obey.' Pucetti had the courage not to look away and spoke directly to Brunetti. 'I didn't think I could refuse a direct order, sir. So I came back.'

'Have you seen him?' Brunetti asked, keeping a tight rein on his anger.

'Scarpa?'

'Yes,' Brunetti answered, refusing to correct Pucetti for omitting the lieutenant's title. 'What did he say?'

'He asked me where I'd been, and I told him I'd been ordered not to speak about it to anyone.'

'Did he ask who gave you the order?'

'Yes, sir.' Pucetti's voice was calm. 'I told him

you did, and he said he'd speak to you about it.'

'Anything else?'

'No, sir. That's all he said.'

Though Brunetti had himself considered summoning Pucetti back to Venice, he could not stand the fact that Scarpa had gone over his head.

'I'm sorry sir,' Pucetti said, then turned away for a moment to stare at a heavily bearded man whose voice was raised in protest at the man behind him in the line. A look from Pucetti sufficed to quiet them both, and he turned back to Brunetti.

'Did you have the chance to speak to Signorina Elettra?' Brunetti asked casually.

'Once or twice, sir, when she came in for a coffee, but there were always people there, so we just played our roles and talked about the weather or the fishing.'

'That young man,' Brunetti began. 'Do you have any idea who he is?' It didn't occur to Brunetti that he left it to Pucetti to infer which man he meant, nor did he consider the significance of the fact that Pucetti knew exactly whom he intended.

'He's the nephew of one of the fishermen out there.'

'What's his name?'

'Who, the man or his uncle?'

'The man. What's his name?' Brunetti realized how eager he sounded, so he slipped one hand into the pocket of his jacket and shifted his weight, to stand in a more relaxed posture. 'If you know, that is,' he added lamely.

'Targhetta,' Pucetti answered, with no indication that he found Brunetti's interest at all out of the ordinary. 'Carlo.'

Brunetti was about to ask more about the young man and what he was doing on Pellestrina when he sensed Pucetti's increasing curiosity as to his interest in Signorina Elettra's personal life. 'Good, thank you, Pucetti. You can put yourself back on the usual duty roster,' he said, quite forgetting that they had been using the same roster for two weeks now in the absence of Signorina Elettra to oversee the rotation of staff.

Back in his office, he did allow for her absence and phoned the office of the Guardia di Finanza himself, asking for Maresciallo Resto.

The Maresciallo, he was told, was momentarily out of the office, and would he like to speak to someone else? His refusal was instantaneous and automatic, and when he hung up he was assailed by the full significance of his response. Even in something like this, an ordinary phone call from one agency of the state to another, he was unwilling to reveal the reason for his call to anyone, regardless of their rank or position, unless that person were vouched for by someone he knew and trusted. What saddened him was not so much the fact that the people he dealt with might be in the pay of the Mafia or unreliable for some other reason, as the fact that distrust was an instinct, one so strong as to preclude *a priori* any chance of cooperation among the fragmented forces of public order. And Maresciallo

Resto, he realized, had earned his trust only by having earned Signorina Elettra's. This reflection brought him back to Pellestrina, the now-identified young man, and thoughts of Signorina Elettra. He dwelt upon those for a quarter of an hour and then called the Finanza again.

'Resto,' a light voice answered.

'Maresciallo,' Brunetti began, 'this is Commissario Guido Brunetti, at the Questura. I'm calling to ask you for some information.'

'Are you Elettra's boss?' the man asked, surprising Brunetti not by the question but by the casual use of her first name.

'Yes.'

'Good. Then ask anything.' Brunetti waited, though he waited in vain, for the usual encomia to Signorina Elettra's many virtues.

'I'm curious about a case you handled two years ago. A fishing boat was sequestered from a fisherman on Burano, Vittorio Spadini.' He waited for Resto to comment, but the other man was silent, and so Brunetti went on. 'I'd like to know whatever you can tell me about the case, or about him.'

'Is this about the murders?' Resto asked, surprising him with the question.

'Why do you ask?'

Resto gave a small laugh. 'There've been three deaths on Pellestrina in the last ten days, two of them fishermen, and now the police call and ask me about a fisherman. I'd have to be a *Carabiniere* not to wonder about the connection.'

It was said as a joke, but it was not a joke.

'He's said to have been involved with one of the victims,' Brunetti offered by way of explanation.

'Have you questioned him?'

'There's no sign of him. A neighbour says he's not around.'

Resto paused, then said, 'Wait a minute while I get the file.' He was gone for a short time, then came back, picked up the phone, and said, 'The file's down in the archive. I'll call you back,' and hung up.

So Resto also wanted to be sure who he was talking to, Brunetti realized, suspecting that the Maresciallo had the file in his hand but thought it wisest to call the Questura and ask for Brunetti.

When the phone rang a moment later, he answered with his name and, as nothing was to be gained by provoking the man, resisted the temptation to ask Resto if he were sure now with whom he was dealing.

Brunetti heard pages being turned, and then Resto said, 'We started the investigation in June, two years ago. We put a flag up at his bank and put a tap on his phone and his accountant's phone and fax. We kept track of how much he sold at the fish market, then checked to see how much of that he declared.'

'What else?' Brunetti prodded.

'And we ran the usual checks on him.'

'Which are?' Brunetti asked.

'I'd rather not say,' Resto answered. 'But we eventually realized he was selling clams and fish for a value of almost a billion lire a year and declaring an income of less than a hundred million.'

'And?' Brunetti asked into the next silence.

'And we kept an eye on him for a few months. And then we landed him.'

'Like a fish?'

'Exactly. Like a fish. But he turned into a clam once we had him. Nothing. No money, no idea where he's got it. If he's got it.'

'How long do you think he was earning this much?'

'No way of knowing. Could have been five years. Or more.'

'And you've no idea where he's got it hidden?'

'He could have spent it.'

Brunetti, who had seen the state of Spadini's house, doubted that, but he didn't offer this information. He considered what he'd heard, then asked, 'What put you on to him?'

'One-one-seven.'

'Excuse me?' Brunetti said.

'The number, the one for anonymous *denuncie*.'

Brunetti had heard, for years, about this number, 117, set up to allow citizens to make anonymous accusations of tax evasion. Though he had heard the story, he had never quite believed in it and had persisted in thinking of 117 as yet another urban myth. But here was a maresciallo of the very Finanza itself, telling him it was true: the number existed and it had been used to launch the investigation of Vittorio Spadini, one that led to the loss of his boat.

'What sort of record is kept of these calls?'

'I'm afraid I can't discuss that with you, Commissario,' Resto said, neither regret nor reluctance audible in his voice.

'I see,' Brunetti answered. 'Were criminal charges pressed against him at the time?'

'No. It was judged better to fine him.'

'How much was the fine?'

'Five hundred million lire,' Resto said. 'At the end, that is. It was higher at the beginning, but then it was reduced.'

'Why?'

'We examined his assets, and all he had was the boat and two small bank accounts.'

'Yet you knew he was making half a billion a year?'

'We had reason to believe that, yes. But it was decided that, in the absence of equity on his part, we would settle for the lesser sum.'

'Which represented?'

'His boat, and the money in both of those accounts.'

'And his house?'

'The house is his wife's. She brought it to the marriage, and so we had no right to it.'

'Have you any idea where the money's gone?'

'None. But there are rumours that he gambles.'

'Unluckily, it would seem,' Brunetti observed.

'Everyone who gambles gambles unluckily.'

Brunetti gave this the laugh it deserved, then asked, 'And since then?'

'I've no idea,' Resto answered. 'He's not been

reported to us since then, so there's nothing else I can tell you about him.'

Brunetti asked, 'Did you meet him?'

'Yes.'

'And?'

Without hesitation, Resto said, 'And he's a very unpleasant man. Not because of what he did. Everyone cheats. We expect that. But there was a kind of frenzy in his resistance to us I've rarely seen before. I don't think it had anything to do with the money he lost, though I could be wrong.'

'If not the money, then what?'

'Losing. Or being defeated,' Resto suggested. 'I've never seen a man so angry at having been caught, though it was impossible we wouldn't catch him, he'd been so stupid.' It sounded as though it was Spadini's carelessness he disapproved of, not his dishonesty.

'Would you say he's violent?' Brunetti asked.

'Does that mean do I think he's capable of those murders?'

'Yes.'

'I don't know. I suppose many people are, though they don't realize it until they get into the right situation. Or the wrong one,' Resto added quickly. 'Maybe. Maybe not.' When Brunetti said nothing, Resto said, 'I'm sorry not to be able to answer that for you, but I just don't know.'

'That's all right,' Brunetti said. 'Thank you for what you could tell me.'

'Let me know what happens, will you?' Resto said, surprising Brunetti with his request.

'Of course. Why?'

'Oh, just curious,' Resto said, disguising something, though Brunetti couldn't tell what. With a mutual exchange of pleasantries, the two men took their leave of each other.

21

Brunetti found his family seated around the table when he came in, almost-empty dishes of lasagne before them. Chiara got up and kissed him, Raffi said, '*Ciao, Papà*' before returning to his pasta, and Paola smiled in his direction. She went to the stove, bent and opened the oven, pulled from it a plate with a large rectangle of lasagne in the centre, and set it at his place.

He went to the bathroom, washed his hands, and came back, aware of how hungry he was and how happy to be home with them.

'You look like you were in the sun today,' Paola said, pouring him a glass of Cabernet.

He took a sip. 'Is this the stuff that student of yours makes?' he asked, raising the glass and studying the colour.

'Yes. Do you like it?'

'Yes. How much did we buy?'

'Two cases.'

'Good,' he said and started to eat his pasta.

'You look like you were in the sun today,' Paola repeated.

Chewing, he swallowed, and said, 'I was out on Burano.'

'*Papà*, can I go out with you the next time you go?' Chiara interrupted.

'Chiara, I'm talking to your father,' Paola said.

'Can't I talk to him at the same time?' she asked with every evidence of offended pride.

'When I'm finished.'

'But we're talking about the same thing, aren't we?' Chiara asked, smart enough to remove any sound of resentment from her voice.

Paola looked at her plate then set her fork very carefully beside her unfinished lasagne.

'I asked your father,' she began, and Brunetti was aware of her referring to him as 'your father'. Beneath that linguistic distance, he suspected, lay some other.

Chiara started to speak, but Raffi gave her a sharp kick under the table, and her head swung towards him. He pressed his lips together and narrowed his eyes at her, and she stopped.

Silence fell, then lay, on the table. 'Yes,' Brunetti said, clearing his throat and then continuing. 'I went out to Burano to talk to someone, but he wasn't there. I tried to eat at da Romano, but there were no tables.' He finished his lasagne and looked across at Paola. 'Is there any more? It's delicious,' he added.

'What else is there, *Mamma*?' Chiara demanded, appetite overcoming Raffi's warning.

'Beef stew with peppers,' Paola said.

'The one with potatoes?' Raffi asked, his voice rich with feigned enthusiasm.

'Yes,' Paola said, getting to her feet and starting to stack the plates. The lasagne, to Brunetti's diappointment, proved to be much like the Messiah: there was no second coming.

With Paola busy at the stove, Chiara waved a hand to get Brunetti's attention, then tilted her head to one side, gaped her mouth open and stuck out her tongue. She crossed her eyes and tilted her head to the other side, then turned it into a metronome, shaking it quickly back and forth, her tongue lolling slackly from her mouth.

From her place at the stove, where she was busy serving the stew, Paola said, 'If you think this beef will give you Mad Cow Disease, Chiara, perhaps you'd prefer not to eat any.'

Instantly, Chiara's head was motionless, her hands folded neatly in front of her. 'Oh, no, *Mamma*,' she said with oily piety, 'I'm very hungry, and you know it's one of my favourites.'

'Everything's your favourite,' Raffi said.

She stuck her tongue out again, but this time her head remained motionless.

Paola turned back to the table, placing a dish in front of Chiara, then Raffi. She set another in front of Brunetti and then served herself. She sat down.

'What did you do at school today?' Brunetti asked the children jointly, hoping that one of them would answer. As he ate, his attention drifted from the chunks of stewed beef to the cubes of carrot, the small slices of onion. Raffi was saying something about his Greek instructor. When he paused, Brunetti looked across at Paola and asked, 'Did you put Barbera in this?'

She nodded, and he smiled, pleased he'd got it right. 'Wonderful,' he said, spearing another piece of beef. Raffi concluded his story about the Greek teacher, and Chiara cleared the table. 'Little plates,' Paola told her when she was done.

Paola went to the counter and removed the round top from the porcelain cake dish she had inherited from her Great-Aunt Ugolina in Parma. Inside it, as Brunetti had hardly dared hope, was her apple cake, the one with lemon and orange juice and enough Grand Marnier to permeate the whole thing and linger on the tongue for ever.

'Your mother is a saint,' he said to the children.

'A saint,' repeated Raffi.

'A saint,' intoned Chiara as an investment towards a second helping.

After dinner, Brunetti took a bottle of Calvados, intent on maintaining the apple theme introduced by the cake, and went out on to the terrace. He set the bottle down, then went back into the kitchen for two glasses and, he hoped, his wife. When he suggested to Chiara that she do the dishes, she made no objection.

'Come on,' he said to Paola and returned to the terrace.

He poured the two glasses, sat, put his feet up on the railing, and looked off at the clouds drifting in the far distance. When Paola sat down in the other chair, he nodded towards the clouds and asked, 'You think it'll rain?'

'I hope so. I read today that there are fires in the mountains up above Belluno.'

'Arson?' he asked.

'Probably,' she answered. 'How else can they build on it?' It was a peculiarity of the law that undeveloped land upon which the construction of houses was forbidden lost that protection as soon as the trees on it ceased to exist. And what more efficient means of removing trees than fire?

Neither of them much wanted to follow up this subject, and so Brunetti asked, 'What's wrong?'

One of the things Brunetti had always loved about Paola was what he persisted, in the face of all her objections to the term, in thinking of as the masculinity of her mind, and so she did not bother to feign confusion. Instead, she said, 'I find your interest in Elettra strange. And I suppose if I were to think about it a bit longer, I'd probably find it offensive.'

It was Brunetti who echoed, innocently, 'Offensive?'

'Only if I thought about it much longer. At the moment, I find it only strange, worthy of comment, unusual.'

'Why?' he asked, setting his glass on the table and pouring some more Calvados.

She turned and looked at him, her face a study in open confusion. But she did not repeat his question; she attempted to answer it. 'Because you have thought about little except her for the last week, and because I assume your trip to Burano today had something to do with her.'

Other qualities he had always admired in Paola were the fact that she was not a snoop and that jealousy was not part of her makeup. 'Are you jealous?' he asked before he had time to think.

Her mouth dropped open and she stared at him with eyes that might as well have been stuck out on stalks, so absolute was her attention. She turned away from him and said, addressing her remarks to the campanile of San Polo, 'He wants to know if I'm jealous.' When the campanile did not respond, she turned her eyes in the direction of San Marco.

As they sat, the silence lengthening between them, the tension of the scene drifted away as if the mere mention of the word 'jealousy' had sufficed to chase it off.

The half-hour struck, and Brunetti finally said, 'There's no need for it, you know, Paola. There's nothing I want from her.'

'You want her safety.'

'That's for her, not from her,' he insisted.

She turned towards him then and asked, without any trace of her usual fierceness, 'You really believe this, don't you, that you don't want anything from her?'

'Of course,' he insisted.

She turned away from him again, studying the clouds, higher now and moving off towards the mainland.

'What's wrong?' he finally asked into her expanding silence.

'Nothing's really wrong. It's just that we're at one of those points where the difference between men and women becomes evident.'

'What difference?' he asked.

'The capacity of self-deceit,' she said, but corrected herself and said, 'Or rather, the things about which we choose to deceive ourselves.'

'Like what?' he asked, striving for neutrality.

'Men deceive themselves about what they do themselves, but women choose to deceive themselves about what other people do.'

'Men, presumably?' he asked.

'Yes.'

If she had been a chemist reading the periodic table of the elements, she could not have sounded more certain.

He finished his Calvados but did not pour any more. A long time passed in silence, during which he considered what she had said. 'Sounds like men get a better deal,' he finally replied.

'When don't they?'

By the next morning, Brunetti had transformed Paola's observation that he had thought about little except Signorina Elettra during the last week, which was true, into an assertion that she had reason for jealousy, which was hardly the same thing. Fully persuaded that Paola had no cause for jealousy, his concern for Signorina Elettra continued uppermost in his mind, blunting his ordinary instinct to be suspicious of and curious about everyone involved in a case. Odd tinglings, if they could be called that, thus went unanswered, and some of the finer threads leading out from the investigation remained unfollowed.

Marotta returned and took over the handling of the Questura. Because murder was such a rare occurrence in Venice, and because Marotta was an ambitious man, he asked for the files on the Bottin murders and, after having read them, said he would take charge of the case himself.

When he failed to find the number of Signorina Elettra's *telefonino*, Brunetti spent a half-hour at the computer, attempting to get into the records at TELECOM, only to give up and ask Vianello if he could obtain the number. When he had it, he thanked the sergeant and went up to his own office to make the call. It rang eight times, then a voice came on, telling him the user of the phone had turned it off but he could, if he chose, leave a voice message. He was about to give his name when he remembered the look she'd given the young man for whom he now had a name and, instead, calling her Elettra and using the intimate *tu*, said it was Guido and asked her to call him at work.

He called down to Vianello and asked him to have another look with the computer, this time for anything he could find out about a certain Carlo Targhetta, perhaps resident on Pellestrina. Vianello's voice was a study in neutrality as he repeated the name, which made it clear to Brunetti that the sergeant had spoken to Pucetti and knew full well who the young man was.

He took a blank piece of paper from his drawer and wrote the name Bottin in the centre, then the name Follini off on the left. Spadini's name was next, at the bottom. He drew a line connecting Spadini and Follini. To the right of Spadini's name, he wrote that of Sandro Scarpa, the waiter's brother, said to have had a fight with Bottin, whose name he connected to Scarpa's. Below that he wrote the name of the missing waiter. And then he sat and looked at these names, as if waiting for them to move around on the paper or for new lines to point out interesting connections among them. Nothing appeared. He picked up the pen again and wrote Carlo Targhetta's name, sticking it into an inconspicuous corner and conscious that he wrote it in smaller letters than those he'd used for the other names.

Still nothing happened. He opened the front drawer, slipped the paper inside, and went downstairs to see what Vianello had discovered.

Vianello, in the meantime, had been larking around in the files of the various agencies of government in an attempt to see if Carlo

Targhetta had done his military service or if he had ever had any trouble with the police. Quite the opposite, it seemed, or so he told Brunetti when he came into Signorina Elettra's office, where the sergeant was using the computer.

'He was in the Guardia di Finanza,' Vianello said, surprised at the news.

'And now he's a fisherman,' Brunetti added.

'And probably earning a hell of a lot more doing that,' remarked Vianello.

Though this was hardly in question, it did seem a strange career change, and both of them wondered what could have prompted it. 'When did he stop?' Brunetti asked.

Vianello pressed a few keys, studied the screen, pressed some more, and then said, 'About two years ago.'

Both of them thought of it, but Brunetti was the first to mention the coincidence. 'About the same time that Spadini lost his boat.'

'Uh huh,' Vianello agreed and hit a key that wiped the screen clean. 'I'll see if I can find out why he left,' he said and summoned up a fresh screenful of information. For a number of seconds, new letters and numbers flashed across the screen, chasing one another into and out of existence. After what seemed like an inordinately long time, Vianello said, 'They're not saying, sir.'

Brunetti leaned down over the screen and started to read. Much of it was numbers and incomprehensible symbols, but near the bottom he read, 'Internal use only, see relevant file,' after which there followed a long string of numbers and letters, presumably the file in which the reason for Carlo Targhetta's departure was to be found.

Vianello tapped his finger on the final phrase and asked, 'You think this means something, sir?'

'Everything has to mean something, doesn't it, really?' Brunetti offered by way of response, though he was curious as to just what this might mean. 'You know anyone?' he asked Vianello, using the centuries-old Venetian shorthand: friend? relative? old classmate? someone who owes a favour?

'Nadia's godmother, sir,' Vianello said after a moment's reflection. 'She's married to a man who used to be a colonel.'

'They weren't invited to your anniversary dinner, were they?' Brunetti asked.

Vianello smiled at the reminder of the favour Brunetti now owed him. 'No, they weren't. He retired about three years ago, but he'd still have access to anything he wanted.'

'Is Nadia very close to them?' Brunetti asked.

Vianello's smile was sharklike. 'Like a daughter, sir.' He reached for the phone. 'I'll see what he can find out.'

Brunetti assumed from the brevity of Vianello's opening salvo that he had reached the retired Colonel directly. He heard him explain his request. When Vianello, after a short pause, said only 'June two years ago,' Brunetti assumed that the Colonel had not bothered to ask why the sergeant wanted the information. When Brunetti heard Vianello say, 'Good, then I'll call you tomorrow morning,' he left and went back to his own office.

22

The following morning, Brunetti left for work before Paola was awake, thus avoiding the need to answer any questions about the progress of the investigation. Because Signorina Elettra had not answered his call or at least had not phoned him at the Questura the day before, he could allow himself to think she had obeyed him and returned from Pellestrina. Consequently, he toyed with the idea, as he walked to work, that he might arrive at the Questura to find her at her desk, dressed for spring, happy to be back and even happier to see him.

His thought, however, was not father to her deed, and there was no sign of her in her office. Her computer sat silent, its screen blank, but he went upstairs before that could be made to serve as an omen of any sort.

Stopping in the officers' room on the way up, he found Vianello at his desk, a disassembled pistol spread in a mess in front of him. The metal parts lay scattered on an open copy of *Gazzetta dello Sport*, their dull menace in sharp contrast to the pink paper, like a ballet dancer wearing brass knuckles.

'What's going on?' Brunetti asked.

The sergeant looked up and smiled. 'It's Alvise's, sir. He started to take it apart to clean it this morning, but he couldn't remember how to put it back together.'

'Where is he?' Brunetti asked, looking around.

'He went to get a coffee.'

'And left it here?'

'Yes.'

'What are you doing?'

'I thought I'd put it back together for him, sir, and just leave it on his desk.'

Brunetti gave this the thought it deserved and said, 'Yes, I think that's best.'

Ignoring the gun, Vianello said, 'The Colonel called back.'

'And?'

'And he's not saying.'

'Which means?'

'It probably means he'd say if they'd told him but they won't tell him.'

'Why do you say that?'

Vianello considered how best to begin, finally saying, 'He was a colonel, so he's used to being obeyed by almost everybody. I think what happened is that they refused to tell him why

Targhetta left, but he's ashamed to admit that, so he says that he's not allowed to reveal the information.' He paused, then added, 'It's his way of saving face, makes it sound like it's his decision.'

'You sure?'

'No,' the sergeant answered, 'but it's the explanation that makes most sense.' There was another long pause and he added, 'Besides, he owes me a number of favours. He'd do it if he could.'

Brunetti considered this for some time then, realizing that Vianello must have been thinking about it for even longer, asked, 'What do you think?'

'I'd guess they caught Targhetta at something but couldn't prove it or didn't want to risk the consequences of arresting him or charging him. So they just quietly let him go.'

'And put that in his file?'

'Uh huh,' Vianello agreed, turning his attention to the pistol. Quickly, with expert fingers, he began to pick up the scattered parts and slip them into place. Within seconds, the pistol was reassembled, returned to cold lethality.

Setting it aside, Vianello said, 'I wish she were here.'

'Who?'

'Signorina Elettra,' Vianello answered. For some reason, it pleased Brunetti that he did not speak of her familiarly.

'Yes, that would be useful, wouldn't it?' Stymied, suddenly aware of how practically dependent upon her he had become in recent years, Brunetti asked, 'Is there anyone else?'

'I've been thinking about that since he called,' Vianello said. 'There's only one person I can think of who might be able to do it.'

'Who?'

'You're not going to like it, sir,' the sergeant said.

To Brunetti, that could mean only one thing; that is, one person. 'I told you I'd prefer not to have anything to do with Galardi,' Brunetti said. Stefano Galardi, the owner and president of a software company, had gone to school with Vianello, but he had long since left behind him all memory of having grown up in Castello in a house with no heat and no hot water and had soared off into the empyrean reaches of cyberwealth. He had scaled the social and monetary ladder and was accepted, indeed welcomed, at every table in the city, except perhaps at the table of Guido Brunetti, where he had, six years before, made very obvious and very drunken advances to Paola until told to leave by her very angry and very sober husband.

Because Galardi was persuaded that Vianello had, almost twenty years ago, saved him from drowning after a particularly riotous Redentore party, he had served, before the advent of Signorina Elettra, as a means to obtain certain kinds of electronic information. Not the least of Brunetti's pleasures in Signorina Elettra's prowess was the fact that it freed him of any obligation to Galardi.

Neither of them said anything for a long time, until Brunetti said, 'All right. Call him.' He left the room, not wanting to be present when Vianello did.

His curiosity was satisfied two hours later, when Vianello came in and, unasked, took the seat opposite his superior. 'It took him this long to find the right way in,' he said.

'And?'

'My guess was right. They caught him tampering with evidence in a case and threw him out.'

'What evidence? And what case?'

Vianello began with the first question. 'The only thing he could give me was the translation of the code.' He saw Brunetti's confusion and said, 'Remember that list of numbers and letters at the bottom of the report?'

'Yes.'

'He found out what that means.' Vianello went ahead without forcing Brunetti to ask him. 'They use it, he told me, in any case where a member of the Finanza either overlooks or hides evidence or in some way attempts to affect the outcome of an investigation.'

'By doing what?' Brunetti asked.

'The same things we do,' answered a shameless Vianello. 'Look the other way when we see our grocer not giving a *ricevuta fiscale*. Not remember seeing the start of any fight between a police officer and a civilian. Things like that.'

Ignoring Vianello's second example, Brunetti asked, 'In his case, what did he do? Specifically.'

'He couldn't find out. It's not in the file.' Vianello allowed Brunetti a moment to digest the significance of this and then added, 'But the case was Spadini's. The name's not there, but the code number for one of the cases Targhetta was working on then is the same as the one listed for Spadini.'

Brunetti considered this. Life had taught him to be profoundly suspicious of coincidence, and it had similarly taught him to view any seemingly random conjunction of events or persons as coincidence and thus be suspicious of that, as well. 'Pucetti?' Brunetti asked.

Vianello shook his head. 'I asked him, sir, but he knows nothing at all about Targhetta, just saw him a few times in the bar.'

'With Elettra?'

'He didn't say, sir.' Brunetti didn't notice how evasive Vianello's answer was.

Brunetti considered various possibilities, including going out to Pellestrina himself. After a time he asked Vianello, 'Do you think Montisi's friend would tell him anything if he called?'

'Only way to know is to ask Montisi,' Vianello said with a smile. 'He's off duty today. You could call him at home.'

This was quickly done, and Montisi agreed to speak to his friend. He called back ten minutes later to say his friend wasn't home and wouldn't be back until that evening.

That left Brunetti and Vianello nothing to do but stew and worry. The sergeant, preferring to worry in his own office, went downstairs.

Brunetti thought of the favours he owed and was owed in return as a pack of playing cards grown greasy and torn with much use. You tell me this, and I'll tell you that; you give me this, and I'll pay you back with that. You write a letter of recommendation for my cousin, and I'll see that your application for a mooring for your boat is put on the pile for consideration this week. Sitting at his desk, staring off into space, he mentally pulled out the deck and began to rifle through the cards. He found one, set it aside, and went on. He shuffled through some more, considered selecting another one, but put it back and continued through till the end. Then he went back to the original card and contemplated it, trying to remember when he had last touched it. He hadn't, but Paola had, devoting a few days to coaching the man's daughter before her final literature exams at the university. The girl had passed, with honours, certainly more than enough justification for Brunetti to play the card.

Her father, Aurelio Costantini, had been quietly retired from the Guardia di Finanza a decade ago after being acquitted of charges of association with the Mafia. The charges were true, but the proofs were inadequate, and so the General had quietly been put out to pasture on full pension, there to reap the benefit of his many years of dutiful – and double – service.

Brunetti called him at home and explained the situation. In a manner graceful yet direct, he added that it had nothing to do with the Mafia. The General, mindful perhaps that his daughter had applied to Ca' Foscari for a teaching position, could not have been more eager to help and said he'd call Brunetti before lunch.

A man of his word, the General called back well before noon, saying that he was on his way to meet a friend who still worked for the Finanza, and if Brunetti would meet him for a drink in about an hour, he'd give him a copy of Targhetta's entire internal dossier.

Brunetti dialled his home number and, relieved to be able to speak to the answering machine, left a message saying he wouldn't be home for lunch but would return at the normal time that evening. The General was a courtly, white-haired man with the upright carriage of a cavalry officer and the elided R so common to the upper classes and those who aspired to them. He sipped at a prosecco while Brunetti, who had seen the size of the folder the General laid on the counter in front of them, quickly ate two sandwiches by way of lunch. They discussed, as people in the city had for the last three months, the weather, both expressing intense hope for rain; nothing else would clean the Augean stables that the narrowest *calli* had become.

On his way back to the Questura, Brunetti mused upon the oddness of his own behaviour regarding the two men who had supplied him with the evidence he carried under his arm: Galardi had done nothing but behave in the way drunks are in the habit of behaving, and Brunetti would have nothing to do with him; General Costantini, about whose guilt no doubt existed, had corrupted the state by selling its secrets to the Mafia, yet Brunetti would meet him in public, smile, ask him for favours, and never think of questioning him about the ties he might still have to the Guardia di Finanza.

The instant he was back in his office, opening the file, all such Jesuitical thoughts disappeared as he dedicated himself to an examination of the personnel file of Carlo Targhetta. Thirty-two, Targhetta had been a member of the Finanza for ten years before 'deciding to leave', as the file put it. Venetian by birth, he had done service in Catania, Bari and Genoa before being stationed in Venice three years ago, a year before the incident that led to his departure. His file was full of praise from all of his commanding officers, who spoke of his 'devotion to duty' and 'intense loyalty'.

From what Brunetti could make of the euphemistic language in the file, at the time of his resignation, Targhetta had been serving as an operator assigned to answering anonymous calls that came in to report cases of tax evasion. He had made an error in reporting one of the calls: the Finanza maintained it was one of commission, while Targhetta insisted it had been one of omission. The Guardia di Finanza had eliminated the necessity of deciding which by offering Targhetta the opportunity to leave the service, an offer he had accepted, though he left without a pension.

Enclosed was a cassette tape, labelled with a date that Brunetti took to be the day of the call that had precipitated events. Stapled to the inside of the folder was a pile of papers headed with the same date: a glance suggested it was a transcript of the calls. He took the tape down to one of the rooms where recordings were made of interrogations. He slipped the tape into the recorder and pushed 'Play'. He opened the file.

There followed a long call, transcribed on the first page, in which a woman said she wanted to report her husband, a butcher, for not fully declaring his income. Her accent was pure Giudecca, and the way she spoke of her husband suggested decades of resentment. All doubt of her motivation disappeared when she lost control and began screaming that this would settle him and *quella puttana di Lucia Mazotti*. Some of her wilder accusations were noted only by a modest line of asterisks.

The next calls were from old women who said they had not been given *ricevute fiscali* by their newsagents, only to be told, with great patience on Targhetta's part, Brunetti had to admit, that newsagents didn't have to give receipts. Targhetta was careful to thank both of them for doing their civic duty, though the weariness with which he did so was clear, at least to Brunetti.

'Guardia di Finanza,' Brunetti listened to Targhetta's by now familiar voice say.

'Is this the right number to call?' a man's voice asked in heavy Veneziano.

Brunetti had noticed, in the previous calls, that Targhetta always answered in Italian, but if his caller spoke in Veneziano, he slipped into dialect to make them feel more comfortable. He did so now, asking, 'What did you want to call about, sir?'

'About someone who isn't paying taxes.'

'Yes, this is the right number.'

'Good, then I want you to take his name.'

'Yes, sir?' Targetta asked and paused for the response.

'Spadini, Vittorio Spadini. From Burano.'

There was a longer pause, then Targhetta said, without any trace of a Venetian accent, his voice far more formal and official, 'Could you tell me more about this, sir?'

'That bastard Spadini's fishing up millions every day,' the man said, voice tight with malice or anger. 'And he never pays a lira in taxes. It's all black, so it's never taxed. Everything he earns is black.'

In the past, Targhetta had asked for more information about the person being accused: where they lived, what sort of business they had. This time, instead, he asked, 'Could you give me your name, sir?' He had never done that before.

'I thought this line was supposed to be anonymous?' the caller said, immediately suspicious.

'It usually is, sir, but in a case of something like this – you did talk of millions, didn't you? – we prefer to be a bit more certain about just who is making the *denuncia*.'

'Well, I'm not going to give you my name,' the man said hotly. 'But you better take down that bastard's name. All you've got to do is go to the fish warehouse in Chioggia when he unloads, and you'll see how much he's caught, and you'll see who's buying it.'

'I'm afraid we can't do that unless I have your name, sir.'

'You don't need my name, you bastard. It's Spadini you should be after.' With that, the man slammed down the phone.

There was a brief silence, and then he heard Targhetta say, 'Guardia di Finanza'.

Brunetti switched off the tape recorder and looked down at the transcript. There, clearly typed out in the manner of a play script, were all of the calls, the characters' names given as 'Finanziere Targhetta' and 'Cittadino.'

He flipped through the remaining pages and saw that there were three more calls. He switched the tape back on and, following the script, listened to all of them, through to the end of both transcript and tape.

He read the last page again and turned it over, expecting to find the blank inside cover of the file. Instead he found, written by hand, a small group of separate sheets held together by a paper clip. Each had spaces at the top for date, time, name of the accused, and at the bottom a small space for the initials of the officer taking the call. He counted them and found only six. He read the name of the butcher, of the two newsagents, and the names given during the three final calls, but there was no record of the call about Spadini. Seven calls on the tape and seven calls in the transcript, but only six calls listed on the separate invoices, each of them carefully initialled 'CT' at the bottom.

He pushed 'REWIND' and, starting and stopping, eventually found the beginning of the call that did not appear on the transcript. He played it through, listening attentively to the voice of the caller. His mother would have identified the accent instantly; if it had been from anywhere on the main island, she probably could have told him which *sestiere* the man came from. The best Brunetti could determine was that it came from one of the islands, perhaps from Pellestrina. He played the tape again and listened to the surprise in Targhetta's voice when he heard Spadini's name. He had been unable to disguise it, and it was then that he had begun to discourage the caller: there was no other way to describe his manner on the tape. The more the caller attempted to provide information, the more insistently did Targhetta tell him that he was obliged to give his name, a demand that was sure to drive off any witness, especially one dealing with the Guardia di Finanza.

He realized how wise the Finanza was to record the calls. So this was how the watchers were watched. Targhetta, unaware that the call was being recorded, would only have to neglect to fill out the form to believe that he had removed all trace of the call. When confronted with the recording of the missing call, if that was the way the Finanza did things, all he would have to do is say the form must have been lost. Obviously, they had not believed him, for how else could his sudden departure from the service after ten years be explained?

But could someone who had worked for the Finanza for a decade have been so stupid as not to realize that the calls were recorded? Brunetti knew, from long experience, that even when phone calls were recorded, they were not necessarily listened to again. Targhetta may well have put his trust in bureaucratic incompetence and hoped that his lapse would pass unnoticed, or, from the sound of his voice, he may have been so surprised that he had responded instinctively and tried to silence the caller without any thought of the consequences.

There remained only one piece of the puzzle or, thought Brunetti as he pulled out the paper on which he'd drawn lines between the names of the people involved, only one line to draw: the one connecting Targhetta and Spadini. That was easy: geometry had long ago taught him that a straight line was the shortest distance between two points. But that did not get him any closer to understanding the connection: that would depend upon his penetrating the silence of the Pellestrinotti.

23

As soon as he decided that he needed to speak to Targhetta, Brunetti spent some time debating whether to call Paola and tell her he was going out to Pellestrina. He didn't want her to question his motives, nor was he much inclined to examine them himself. Better, then, just to have Montisi take him out and have done with it.

He didn't want to take Vianello, though he did not bother to analyse his motives for that decision. He did, however, rewind the tape, stick it in his pocket, and stop in the officers' room to borrow a small battery-powered tape recorder, just on the off chance that he might find someone on Pellestrina who would be willing to listen to it and perhaps identify the voice of the caller.

The day had turned cooler, and there were dark clouds to the north, enough to give him reason to hope that rain might finally be on the way. He remained below deck in the cabin on the way out, reading through yesterday's newspaper and a boating magazine one of the pilots had left behind. By the time they reached Pellestrina, he had learned a great deal about 55 horsepower motors, but nothing further about Carlo Targhetta or Vittorio Spadini.

As they were pulling in, he went upstairs and joined Montisi in the cabin.

Glancing back towards the city, Montisi said, 'I don't like this.'

'What, coming out here?' Brunetti asked.

'No, the feel of the day.'

'What does that mean?' Brunetti asked, suddenly impatient with sailors and their lore.

'The way the air feels. And the wind. It feels like *bora*.'

The newspaper had forecast fair weather and rising temperatures. Brunetti told him this but Montisi snorted in disgust. 'Just feel it,' he insisted. 'That's *bora*. We shouldn't be out here.'

Brunetti looked ahead of them and saw bright sun dancing on still water. He stepped out of the cabin as the boat pulled up to the dock. The air was still, and when Montisi killed the motor, not a sound disturbed the peaceful silence of the day.

Brunetti jumped off and moored the boat, feeling quite proud of being able to do so. He left Montisi to find other old sailors to discuss the weather with and went to the village and the restaurant where his investigation had begun.

When he entered, there was a moment's pause in the conversation, but then it jump-started itself as everyone attempted to fill the silence created by the arrival of a commissario of police. Brunetti went to the counter and asked for a glass of white wine, looking around him while he waited for it, not smiling but not looking as if he had any particular reason to be there.

He nodded to the barman when he brought the wine and held up a hand to prevent his turning away. 'Do you know Carlo Targhetta?' he asked, deciding to waste no more time in futile attempts to outwit the Pellestrinotti.

The barman tilted his chin to one side to give every indication that he was considering the question, then said, 'No, sir. Never heard of him.'

Before Brunetti could turn to the old man standing beside him at the counter, the barman announced, in a voice loud enough to be heard by everyone in the room, 'Anyone here know someone called Carlo Targhetta?'

A chorus repeated the same response, 'No, sir. Never heard of him.' With that, normal conversation resumed, though Brunetti registered the quick exchange of complicit smiles.

He directed his attention to his wine and reached idly for that day's *Gazzettino*, lying folded on the bar. He flipped it to the front page and started to read the headlines. Gradually, he felt the room's attention wander away from him, especially at the entrance of a beefy-faced man who came in saying that it had started to rain.

He spread the paper on the bar. With his left hand, he pulled the tape recorder from his pocket and slipped it under the newspaper. He'd run the tape back to the place where the caller had accused Spadini directly of a crime and his voice had grown heated and loud. He lifted the corner to look at the recorder. He thumbed the VOLUME dial, set his right forefinger on the PLAY button, and let the paper fall back into place. Keeping his finger on the button, he raised his glass and took a sip, his attention seemingly devoted entirely to the newspaper.

Three men went outside to see about the rain, and the men left in the bar grew quiet, waiting for them to come back and report.

Brunetti pressed PLAY. 'That bastard Spadini's fishing up millions every day. And he never pays a lira in taxes. It's all black. Everything he earns is black.'

The glass of wine fell from the hand of the old man standing beside him and shattered on the floor. '*Maria Santissima*,' he exclaimed. 'It's Bottin. He's not dead.'

His voice drowned out the next exchange on the tape, but the entire bar heard Targhetta say, '. . . we prefer to be a bit more certain about just who is making the *denuncia*.'

'*Oh, Dio*,' said the old man, reaching a feeble

hand towards the counter and propping his weight on it. 'It's Carlo.'

Brunetti slipped his hand under the newspaper and pushed the STOP button. The loud click rang out in the silence, wounding it but not altering it. The old man was silent, though his lips continued to move in muttered prayer or protest.

The door opened and the three men came back, their shoulders dark and their heads wet with the rain. Joyously, like children let out of school early, they cried out, 'It's raining, it's raining,' then fell silent when they sensed the charged atmosphere in the room.

'What's wrong?' one of them asked, putting the question to no one in particular.

Brunetti said, in an entirely normal voice, 'They told me about Bottin and Spadini.'

The man he addressed looked around the bar for confirmation and found it in the averted eyes and continuing silence. He shook his arms, spraying water around him, then went to the bar and said, 'Give me a grappa, Piero.'

The barman set it down in front of him without speaking.

Talk gradually resumed, but quietly. Brunetti signalled to the waiter and pointed to the old man beside him. He brought a glass of white wine for the old man, who took it and drank it down like water, replacing the glass loudly on the bar. Brunetti nodded, and the waiter refilled it. Turning to face him, Brunetti asked, 'Targhetta?'

'His nephew,' the old man said and swallowed the second glass.

'Spadini's?'

The man looked at Brunetti and held his glass out to the waiter, who filled it again. Instead of drinking it, the old man set it on the bar and stared into it. He had the rheumy eyes of the habitual drinker, the man who woke up to wine and went to sleep with it on his tongue.

'Where's Targhetta now?' Brunetti asked, folding the paper, as if this were the least interesting question he could think of.

'Fishing, probably, with his uncle. I saw them at the dock a half-hour ago.' His lips puckered in a fisherman's disapproval, and Brunetti waited for him, like Montisi, to say something about the *bora* and not liking the feel of the air, but instead he said, 'Probably took that woman again. Bad luck, having a woman on a boat.'

Brunetti's hand tightened on the paper. 'What woman?' he forced himself to ask in a neutral voice.

'That one he's been fucking. The one from Venice.'

'Ah,' Brunetti said, forcing his hand to release the paper and pick up his glass of wine. He took a sip, nodded his approval at the old man and then at the waiter. He made himself look at the newspaper again, as if utterly uninterested in this woman from Venice and what Carlo was doing to her, concerned only with yesterday's soccer results.

Light flashed at the windows, and after a

moment thunder followed, so loud as to set the bottles at the back of the bar rattling. The door opened and another man slipped in, wet as an otter. When he paused at the open door, all sound inside the bar was drowned by the sound of the rain, battering down, exploding from the gutters. Another flash of light streamed in, and everyone in the bar braced themselves for the explosion that must follow. When it came it lingered for long seconds and, just as it began to roll away, was replaced by the fierce shriek of the *bora*, sweeping down from the north. Even inside the bar, they were aware of the sudden drop in temperature.

'Where would they be?' Brunetti asked the old man.

He drank the wine and gave Brunetti an inquisitive look. Brunetti nodded at the waiter, and again the glass was filled. Before he touched it, the old man said, 'They haven't been out long. Probably try to get away from this.' With his chin, he indicated the door and, beyond it, the lightning, wind and rain that had turned the day to chaos.

'How?' Brunetti asked, reining in his rising fear and careful to make it sound as if he was only mildly curious about the ways of the *laguna* and the men who fished upon its waters.

The old man turned his attention to the man to his right, the first to come in from the rain. 'Marco,' he asked, 'where would Vittorio go?'

Brunetti was conscious of the strained silence as all of the fishermen waited to see who would be the next to follow the old man in breaking ranks by talking to the policeman.

The man questioned looked down into his glass, and some instinct prevented Brunetti from signalling the waiter to fill it. Instead, he stood quietly and waited for an answer.

The man addressed as Marco looked at the old man. After all, it was he who had asked the question. If the policeman heard the answer, it wasn't his fault. 'I think he'd try for Chioggia.'

A man at a far table said, in quite an ordinary voice,'He'd never make it, not with the *bora*, and not with the tide behind it. If he went anywhere near the Porto di Chioggia, he'd be taken out to sea.' No one objected, no one spoke; the only sounds were of the rain and wind, now a single, overwhelming noise.

From another table, a man's voice said, 'Vittorio's a bastard, but he'll know what to do.'

Another half-rose to his feet and flung out his hand in the direction of the door. 'No one knows what to do in that.' His angry tones were immediately answered by another bolt of lightning, closer now, swiftly followed by a cascade of thunder.

When the sound diminished to the mere pounding of rain, a man near the door said, 'If it gets worse, he'd probably try to run ashore down at the Riserva.' Brunetti had spent a good deal of time studying the map, having things on it pointed out to him by Montisi, so he knew this had to be the Riserva di Ca' Roman, a barren oblong of sandy soil that hung like a

268

pendant drop from the southern end of the long, thin finger of Pellestrina.

'Run aground?' Brunetti asked him.

The man began to answer, but his voice was lost in a tremendous crash of thunder that seemed to shake the entire building. When silence finally returned, he tried again. 'There's no place to dock, but he could probably run his boat up on to the beach.'

'Why not come back here?'

The old man shook his head wearily, either at the impossibility of such a feat in weather like this or at the ignorance of a person who would have to ask it. 'No chance. If he tried to turn in the canal, the wind and tide could turn him over. Only thing he can do is try to run on to Ca' Roman. Back in '27,' he began, making it sound as though he'd seen that storm, too, 'that's what happened to Elio Magrini. Flipped him over like a turtle. They never found him, and what was left of the boat wasn't worth salvaging.' He raised his glass, perhaps to the memory of Elio Magrini, and emptied it in a single long swallow.

During all of this, Brunetti had been considering possibilities: with the wind coming from the north-west and the retreating tide pushed along by it, the narrow spit of land that led down to Ca' Roman would be awash, perhaps already completely under water. He and Montisi could get there only by boat, and if what the old man said was true, that would mean running the police launch aground.

'You really think she's gone out with him? In this?' Brunetti asked in his best man of the world voice.

The puff of wind the old man shot out of his compressed lips expressed disgust, not only at the foolishness of Signorina Elettra, but at that of all women. Adding nothing, the old man pushed himself away from the bar and went to sit at one of the tables.

Brunetti placed a few thousand lire on the bar, put the tape recorder back in his pocket, and started for the door. Just before he reached it, it banged open from outside, but no one came in: only wind and rain battered it repeatedly against the wall. Brunetti stepped out into the rain, careful to pull the door shut behind him.

He was instantly wet; it happened so quickly that he had no time to worry about it or to think about protecting himself from the rain. One moment he was dry, the next soaked through, his shoes filled with water, as though he'd stepped into a lake. He set off back towards the pier and, perhaps, Montisi. After a few seconds he had to raise a hand above his eyes to block the power of the wind that drove rain into them, blinding him. His progress was slowed by the added weight of water that bore him down, pulling at his shoes and jacket.

Once he stepped out from the shelter of the buildings that lined the *laguna* side of the road, the wind pounded at him, as if trying to batter him to the ground. Luckily, a row of street lights ran along the pier, and in the dim light they managed to cast through the sudden darkness of the day, he made his way towards the launch. He moved ahead slowly, or he might have fallen when his foot hit the metal stanchion to which the boat was moored.

He grabbed at its mushroom top with both hands, leaned towards the vague shape he thought was the boat, and called Montisi's name. When there was no response, he bent and felt for the mooring line, but when he found it, it was slack in his grasp, for the wind had driven the boat tight against the side of the pier. He stepped on to the boat and, blinded by a sudden gust of rain, stumbled against the door of the cabin.

Montisi opened the door, popped his head outside, and seeing that it was Brunetti, pulled him in. There, sheltered from the rain, Brunetti realized that the noise of it crashing into the pavement and on to the water had deafened him to all other sounds. It took him a moment to adjust to the relative silence of the cabin.

'Can you move in this?' he called to Montisi, his voice raised unnecessarily against the sound of the rain.

'What do you mean, "move"?' the pilot asked, unwilling to believe the obvious.

'Down towards Ca' Roman.'

'That's crazy. We can't go out in this.' As if to prove him right, a sheet of rain pounded against the starboard windows of the cabin, drowning out voices and thought. 'We have to wait until it's over to go back.' The wind had risen, so Montisi had to shout.

'I'm not talking about going back.'

Montisi, afraid he'd misunderstood, asked, 'What?'

'Elettra's with them. On Spadini's boat. Someone said they were going out fishing.'

Montisi's face grew stiff with surprise, or fear. 'I saw them. At least I saw a boat, a fishing boat. It went past about twenty minutes ago. Two men, and someone leaning over the other side, pulling a rope up from the water. You think it's her?'

Brunetti nodded: it was easier than speech.

'They're crazy to go out in this,' Montisi said.

'Someone said they'd head towards Ca' Roman and try to run ashore there.'

'That's crazy, too,' Montisi shouted. Then, 'Who told you this?'

'One of the fishermen.'

'From here?'

'Yes.'

Montisi closed his eyes as if to study the map of the land and the channels running beside it. Farther down, the land was bisected by the Porto di Chioggia, a kilometre wide, but still narrow enough to allow fierce rip tides to run through, especially when there were heavy winds to drive them. On a day like this, it would be suicide to try to cross it in a boat as light as the police launch. Even a fishing boat the size of the one he'd seen would have trouble. Before the Porto, however, there was the last point of land, home to nesting birds and the crumbling ruins of a fort. Yet even if someone were to run aground there, waves might still pull the boat off, swirling it into the water to be swept around the tip of the island and out to sea.

Montisi opened his eyes and looked at Brunetti. 'Are you sure?'

'What? That she's on board?'

This was Montisi, gruff, often irascible Montisi, asking the question.

'I'm not sure. A man in the bar said she was on the pier with them.'

'It couldn't be anyone else,' Montisi said, more to himself than to Brunetti. He pushed past Brunetti and opened the door to the cabin. He stepped outside for a moment, closed his eyes and held his palms up in front of him, like an Indian listening for the voice of one of his gods. Eyes still closed, he turned his head to one side, then the other, searching for something Brunetti couldn't hear.

He stepped back into the cabin and commanded, 'Go out and get two life jackets.' Brunetti sprang to obey. He was back with the jackets in an instant, no wetter than before. He watched Montisi to see how he tied it around his body and then did the same.

'All right,' Montisi said. 'There's going to be a pause in the wind, and then it will get worse.' Brunetti had no idea how Montisi knew this, but it never occurred to him that it was less than pure truth. His voice raised, Montisi went on, 'I'm going to take us down there. If we run aground in the channel, I should be able to back us off, at least until the wind gets worse. When we get down to Ca' Roman, you'll have to use the spotlight to look for them or for the boat. If they've run aground, I'll try to take us in next to them.'

'And if they're not there?' Brunetti asked.

'Then I'll try to bring us round and get us back here.'

For a moment, remembering the story of Elio Magrini, Brunetti was tempted to ask the pilot if they should risk this, but he stopped himself and, instead, ran his cupped hands over his face and head to stop the water from dripping into his eyes.

Montisi switched the motor into life, turned on the lights and the windscreen wipers, neither of which seemed to make much difference against the growing darkness and cascading rain. Remembering in time, Brunetti ran out into the storm to uncoil the mooring rope and loop it loosely around a stanchion on the railing of the boat. He went back into the cabin and stood behind Montisi. Idly, he wiped with the sodden sleeve of his jacket at the humidity condensed on the windows of the cabin, but as soon as he wiped them clear, they immediately turned opaque, and he was forced to keep wiping them.

Montisi flipped another switch, and a current of air flowed across the inside of the windscreen, removing the film of humidity. Slowly, he moved the boat away from the pier.

The boat lurched to the left as though slapped by an enormous hand, slamming Brunetti against the side of the cabin. Montisi tightened his grip on the tiller and leaned his weight to the right, fighting against the force of the wind.

Dirty grey froth banged against the windscreen; the door to the cabin slammed open and then shut. Again and again, the wind forced them to the left. Montisi hit another switch, and a powerful spotlight on the prow made a feeble attempt to penetrate the chaotic darkness in front of them. As soon as it punched a hole and they could see a few metres ahead, another wave or spray of foam roared in to wipe out the space.

One side of the cabin door crashed open against Brunetti's back, but the blow was buffeted by his life jacket, and he hardly registered it. Nor was he much aware of the temperature, which continued to drop as the *bora* roared over them. The boat jumped to the left again, and again Montisi pulled it back into what might have been the centre of the channel. From behind them, out on the back deck, they heard an enormous crash, and a piece of wood smashed through the starboard window of the cabin, grazing Brunetti's hand before landing at their feet.

He had to put his mouth close to Montisi's ear to shout, 'What was it?'

'I don't know. Something from the water.' Brunetti glanced down at it but it was nothing more than a bottle-sized piece of rotten wood.

He flipped it out of the way with an impatient foot, but no sooner had he done so than a sudden gust of wind rolled it back towards him. Rain flooded through the broken window, soaking Montisi and lowering the temperature of the cabin even more.

'Oh Dio, oh Dio,' he heard Montisi begin to mutter. The pilot suddenly swung the wheel to the left and then as quickly to the right, but not before both of them felt a heavy thud against the port side of the boat.

Brunetti froze, waiting to see if the boat began to founder or sink lower in the water. Realizing that Montisi could have no clearer idea than he of what had happened, he didn't bother him with a question. There were two smaller thumps, but the boat continued to move forward, though the wind seemed to grow more intense, always pounding at them from the right.

Out of nowhere, a shape loomed up on the left, and Montisi almost fell on to the wheel, trying to put his whole weight into pulling it to the right. The shape moved out of sight, but then, from behind them, there was an enormous, pounding crash, as powerful as the thunder had been, and the boat spun off, but heavily, as though it were suddenly as sodden as Brunetti's clothing.

Montisi swung the tiller to the left, and even Brunetti could sense how slow the boat was to respond. 'What happened?'

'We hit something. I think it was a boat,'

Montisi answered, still pulling at the wheel. He pushed the throttle forward, and Brunetti heard the engine respond, though the boat seemed to move no faster.

'What are you doing?'

'I've got to run us in,' Montisi said, leaning forward, straining to see what was in front of them.

'Where?'

'Ca' Roman, I hope,' Montisi said. 'I don't think we've passed it.'

'If we have?' Brunetti asked.

By way of answer, all Montisi did was shake his head, but Brunetti didn't know if this was to deny the possibility or the consequences.

Montisi hit the throttle again, and though this increased the sound of the engine, it had no effect on their speed. A wave crashed over the side of their bow, and over the deck, hurling water up the wall of the cabin. Through the broken window it poured in over both of them.

'There, there, there!' Montisi shouted. Brunetti bent forward to stare out of the wind-screen but could see nothing but an unbroken grey wall in front of them. Montisi turned to look at him for a second. 'Don't go outside until we hit. When we do, climb up on the deck. Don't go over the side. Get to the front and jump as far forward as you can. If you land in water, keep going forward, and when you get out of the water, keep going.'

'Where are we?' Brunetti demanded, though the answer would not mean anything to him.

There was a tremendous crash. The boat stopped as though it had run headlong into a wall, and both men were thrown to the floor. The boat tilted over on its right side, and water flooded in through the shattered window. Brunetti pushed himself to his feet and grabbed at Montisi, who had a long gash on the side of his head and responded slowly, moving like a man under water. Another wave broke through the window and poured down on them.

Brunetti reached down to help the pilot, who was already pushing himself upright, though this was hard to do on the steeply slanting deck. 'I'm all right,' Montisi said.

One side of the cabin door hung from a single hinge, and Brunetti had to kick it open. When he pulled Montisi outside, water surged at them from everywhere. Remembering what Montisi had told him, he pulled and pushed the pilot up on to the raised deck in front of the cabin, then hauled himself up afterwards.

Pushing Montisi in front of him, Brunetti held him steady with one hand as waves raged at the stricken boat, rocking the deck back and forth under their feet. Step by step they moved drunkenly towards the prow and the single searchlight that cut the darkness in front of them. They reached the railing, and Montisi, without an instant's hesitation or a backward glance, leaped heavily from the prow of the boat, disappearing into the greyness.

A wave knocked Brunetti to his knees; he grabbed the base of the spotlight to hold himself steady as another and stronger wave battered at him from behind, sending him sprawling. He pulled himself to his knees, then to his feet, and moved again to the point of the prow. At the moment when he shifted his balance to spring forward, an enormous wave swept up from behind him, catapulting him, head over heels, into the howling darkness.

24

Had Montisi and Brunetti approached Pellestrina earlier, as they passed the dock of San Pietro in Volta they would have seen a glowing Signorina Elettra, dressed in navy blue linen slacks, standing on the deck of a large fishing boat, waiting impatiently to set off, while Carlo and the man she had always heard called Zio Vittorio waited as the double fuel tanks were filled. She was vaguely conscious, to the degree that she could be conscious of anything other than Carlo when she was with him, of a low bank of clouds lying off behind the dimly seen towers of the distant city. But when she turned towards the waters of the Adriatic, invisible beyond the low houses of Pellestrina and the sea wall that protected them from those waters, she saw only fluffy, careless clouds and a sky of such transparent blue as to add to her already considerable joy. When Vittorio pulled his boat away from the gas station just above San Vito, the police launch was already moored to the dock in Pellestrina, and by the time the fishing boat passed the launch, heading south, Brunetti was already inside the bar, having his first sip of wine.

It would be an exaggeration to say that Signorina Elettra was afraid of Zio Vittorio, but it would also be less than true to say that she was comfortable in his presence. Her response to him was somewhere in between, but because he was Carlo's uncle, she usually managed to ignore the uneasiness he created in her. Zio Vittorio had always been perfectly friendly with her, always seemed glad to find her in Carlo's house and at his table. Perhaps it would come close to explaining her feelings to say that, when she spoke to Vittorio, she was always left with the suspicion that he was secretly enjoying the thought of where else in Carlo's house she had been.

He was not a tall man, Zio Vittorio, hardly taller than she, and had the same muscular frame as his nephew. Because he had spent most of his life at sea, his face was tanned mahogany, making the grey eyes which were said to resemble those of his sister, Carlo's mother, seem all the lighter in contrast. He wore his thinning hair slicked straight back from his face, long at the base of his head, and kept it in place with a pomade that smelled of cinnamon and metal filings. His teeth were perfect: one night after dinner he had cracked open walnuts with them, smiling at her when she failed to disguise her shock at this.

He must have been sixty, an age which, to Elettra, automatically consigned him to a genderless void in which any sort of expressed interest in sex was embarrassing, even worse than that. Yet the consciousness of sex and sexual activity always seemed to lurk behind even his most innocent remarks, as though he were incapable of conceiving a universe in which men and women could relate to one another in any other way. Somewhere, beneath the tremor that still filled her when she thought of Carlo, this vague unease lurked, though she had become adept at ignoring it, especially on a day like this, when the sky to the east boded so well.

The heavy boat pulled out into the channel and started to move south, back past Pellestrina and towards the narrow opening of the Porto di Chioggia, through which they would pass into the open sea. There was no thought of fishing that day: his uncle had told Carlo he wanted to take the boat to sea to test a rebuilt motor that had just been installed. It had sounded perfectly fine when they set out, but just as the boat grew level with the Ottagono di Caroman, Vittorio called back to them that something was wrong. Only seconds later both Carlo and Elettra felt a sudden change in the rhythm of the motor: it began to hiccup, and the boat jerked reluctantly ahead instead of proceeding steadily.

Carlo walked forward, saying, 'What is it?'

The older man flicked the starter switch off, then on, then off again. In the momentary calm, he answered, 'Dirt in the fuel line, I'd say.' He switched on the motor again, and this time it jumped to life and throbbed with the steady rhythm they were accustomed to.

'Sounds fine to me,' Carlo said.

'Hmm,' his uncle murmured, seeming to listen to Carlo but really intent on the sound of the engine. He placed the palm of his left hand flat on the control panel and shoved the throttle forward with his right. The volume increased, but suddenly the engine gave a single dyspeptic burp and then a series of choking noises until it stopped entirely.

Carlo, as he knew to his cost, was neither a real fisherman nor a mechanic, though he had learned to do much of the work of the first. In a case like this, he deferred absolutely to his uncle's greater experience and wisdom and so waited to be told what to do. The boat slowed, then stopped dead in the water.

Vittorio told Carlo to stay where he was and turn the engine on when he told him to, then went to the centre of the back deck and disappeared down the hatchway to the engine room. After a few minutes, he shouted up to Carlo, telling him to switch on the engine. The starter gave a dry click and failed to engage, so he turned it off and waited. Minutes passed.

Signorina Elettra came to the door to ask what was wrong, but he smiled at her and said everything was fine, then waved her to the back of the boat, out of the way.

Vittorio called out again, and this time when Carlo turned on the engine it caught on the first try and responded to each small increase or decrease of the throttle. Vittorio came out of the hatchway and back into the cabin, saying, 'Fuel line, like I thought. All I had to do was . . .' but he was interrupted by the sound of his *telefonino*. As he reached for it, he signalled for Carlo to leave the cabin.

Carlo backed out, careful not to let the doors slam shut, and went towards the back of the boat, where he saw Elettra standing with her hands braced on the back railing, her face raised in the direction of the sun. The engine was still rumbling loudly, covering the sound of his approach, but when he came silently up behind her and put both of his hands on the hollows of her back just above her hips, she gave no sign of being surprised. Indeed, she leaned backwards slightly and into his body. He bent down and kissed the top of her head and buried his face in the explosion of curls. His eyes shut, he stood like that, rocking against her in a steady rhythm. He heard a low rumbling that had nothing to do with the motor and opened his eyes. Off to his left, the towers of the city, distantly visible that morning, had disappeared, blocked out by a low bank of clouds that had already enveloped Pellestrina and were now scuttling towards their boat.

'*Oh, Dio*,' he said, and at the shock in his voice she opened her eyes to see a dark wall tumbling towards them. Instinctively, he put his arms around her and pulled her back against his chest. He turned his head back towards the cabin: his uncle was still talking on the phone, eyes intent on the two of them and, beyond them, at the storm that approached with such savage speed.

Vittorio said something else, flipped the phone shut, and put it back into the pocket of his jacket. Stiff armed, he pushed the door open and shouted to Carlo to come into the cabin.

He moved away from Elettra and towards his uncle, and as he did, he felt the back of the boat rise up under his feet, as though some giant hand had lifted it from the water, helping him forward. He looked back and saw her, both hands firmly grasped to the railing.

He pulled open the door. 'What is it?'

Rather than answer, his uncle reached out both hands and grabbed him by the collar of his jacket, pulling his face down closer to his own. 'I told you she was trouble,' he said. Once, twice, he jerked savagely at Carlo's collar, and when the younger man tried to pull away, he yanked him even lower, closer. 'Her boss is there, in the bar. They know about Bottin and they know about the phone call.'

Utterly confused, Carlo demanded, 'Who knows? The Finanza? They've always known. Why do you think they threw me out?'

'No, not the Finanza, you fool,' Vittorio

shouted back at him, his voice raised against the wind that had begun to sweep from behind them, pushing the boat forward. 'The police. Her boss, that commissario; he had the tape with him. He played it in the bar, and that drunk Pavanello told him it was Bottin you talked to.' He released his hold on Carlo's collar and swatted him away with the back of his hand, shouting, 'They'd have to be idiots not to realize I killed them.'

Ever since Carlo had told his family why he'd been dismissed from the Finanza, he'd half feared and half known his uncle would take some sort of revenge, but Vittorio's bold-faced admission still shocked him. 'Don't say that,' he protested. 'I don't want to know.' Behind him, the cabin door banged open and shut repeatedly, and he felt rain on his shoulders.

Vittorio waved towards the back of the boat. 'What did you tell her?'

'Nothing,' Carlo shouted.

The wind and the pounding door erased some of Vittorio's words, but still the rage propelling them was enough to alarm Carlo. 'You knew where she worked. Her stupid cousin told everyone. I told you to stay away from her, but you knew better. What are we going to do about her now?'

The wind raged at them, sweeping all thought and memory up into a whirlwind and tearing them away from Carlo and out to sea, leaving him with only the thought of Elettra. He wheeled out of the cabin and fought his way to the back of the boat; he put his arms around a shivering Elettra as the skies erupted and a sheet of rain washed across them.

He staggered, freed one arm and grabbed at the railing. Unconscious of moving or of any decision to move, he tightened his left arm around her and half pulled, half steered her towards the cabin door. He shouldered it open, and together they crashed inside, then into the left side as a wave slammed into them from the right.

Another wave hit the boat, knocking Elettra against Vittorio, but he did no more than flick her aside with his elbow and turn back to the tiller, both hands locked to the wheel. Carlo looked through the windscreen; the wipers slapped uselessly against the sheets of water that washed across it. In the darkness that had descended on them, the three searchlights were helpless, and he could make out nothing except the rain and the white menace of waves and spray.

The noise pounded at them from every side, and suddenly the wind picked up volume, drowning out everything else. Carlo felt the small hairs at the back of his neck bristle, but he was aware of the sensation and aware of a cramp of fear even before he realized that the sudden increase in the sound of the wind was caused by the silence of the motor.

He saw, but could not hear, Vittorio ramming his thumb on to the starter, his other palm flat against the panel to feel the vibrations if the motor came to life again. Repeatedly he pressed, released, pressed, and only once did Carlo feel a faint rhythmic throb under his feet. But it was momentary and gone almost before he was aware of it. Again, he watched that blunt thumb press and release and press again, and then his feet felt the motor come alive, churning out a staggered beat below them.

Vittorio took his hand from the starter and put it back on the wheel. He rose on his toes for leverage and then brought all of his weight down to swing the wheel to the left. At one point, the wheel fought back and carried him half off the floor. Carlo pushed past a frozen Elettra and, placing both hands on one of the sprouting handles of the wheel, added his weight to his uncle's. The boat responded, and he felt their weight shift as it followed the command of the rudder, turning heavily to the left.

Carlo had no idea where they were or what his uncle intended to do. The young man gave no thought to the map, to Ca' Roman or to the Porto di Chioggia, an open slip of water that would pull them out to the Adriatic and into its deadly waves. He braced his feet on either side of the wheel and together they pulled the boat even farther to the left. Vittorio removed his right hand from the wheel and shoved the throttle full forward. Through his feet, Carlo felt the throbbing of the motor increase, but his awareness of the world outside the boat was so confused that he could detect no alteration in the boat's movements. Then, at the same instant he felt the motor die, the boat thundered to a stop, hurling him against one of the spokes of the tiller and his uncle on top of him. He looked up in time to see Elettra, who had been knocked against the wall by the original impact, ricochet backwards and through the cabin doors, out on to the deck. Then there was a shuddering crash, and the boat was suddenly still.

Carlo shoved his uncle aside and lifted himself to his feet. Aware of pain in his left side, he was concerned only to follow Elettra. Again, when he moved forward, he felt the pain, but he ignored it as he pushed through the doors of the cabin. Outside, he found crashes of thunder, the groans of roaring wind and rain. In the light that spilled out from the cabin, he saw Elettra kneeling on the deck, already pulling herself to her feet. A wave broke over the back of the boat and swept forward, slapping her down again and swirling her up the deck until she banged against Carlo's feet. He started to lean down to help her, but as he moved the pain caught inside him, and he froze in place, suddenly fearful for himself and, because of that, for her.

As he looked down at her, helpless, time stopped. Elettra raised herself to one knee and, glancing up, saw him. With her left hand, she pushed her fingers through her hair, trying to sweep the tangle from her face, but it was sodden with rain and sea water, and she could do no more than shift it to one side. He remembered how, once, he had watched her sleep, her face half covered by her hair in much the same way – and then the cabin doors exploded against his back as Vittorio burst on to the deck.

It happened so quickly that Carlo could not have stopped him even if he had not been frozen by the pain in his side and the fear of the greater pain he knew motion would bring. Vittorio swept down over Elettra, screaming at her, screaming words none of them could hear. He grabbed her tangled hair with his left hand, yanking her to one side, screaming down at her all the while. His right hand slipped inside his jacket and emerged, clasped around his gutting knife. He cocked his arm back across his body and, knuckles upwards, swiped at her, aiming for her face or her neck.

Carlo moved before he thought. He braced one hand against the railing on the side of the boat and kicked forward, his aim commanded only by instinct. His boot caught his uncle's forearm just as it crossed in front of his face, deflecting it upwards. The knife sliced through the sleeve of Vittorio's jacket, opening his arm to the wrist, and then cut through the hair he still held tight in his other hand, just grazing Elettra's scalp. The wind stole his scream, and the knife flew out of his hand to join it. From his other hand strands of Elettra's hair danced wildly in the wind.

Vittorio loosened his grip and the wind tore the hair away. He pulled his arm to his stomach, turned towards his nephew as though he meant to do him violence, but what he saw behind

Carlo made him turn to the front of the boat and run to the prow. He didn't hesitate an instant but leaped forward into the water, cradling his arm to himself as best he could. The wave broke across them, knocking Carlo first to the deck and then up against the listing side of the boat. Its retreat sucked him towards the back, but Elettra's body blocked him, and they ended in a tangled mass, half in and half out of the cabin doorway, bodies entwined in a grotesque parody of the past.

Again, instinct prevailed and he tried to get to his feet, succeeding only when Elettra knelt beside him and pried him from the deck. Speech rendered futile by noise, he grabbed her upper arm and started towards the prow, slowed by pain. Pushing, pulling, they hauled themselves to the pointed prow. He pushed her over, without a moment's thought. The searchlights provided enough light to allow him to see her sink, then come bobbing up in the water directly in front of him. He jumped after her, sinking into water that came above his head. When he surfaced, he screamed her name – and felt fingers grab at his hair and tug at him, though he had lost all sense, all thought, all direction. His arms floated limp at his side, and he found that he could not kick his feet, lacked the strength to do anything but float in the wake of whatever hand it was that pulled at him. Something hit against his feet, and he felt mild irritation at the sensation. He was comforted by weightlessness, which removed the pain in his side; he didn't want to have to swim or stand, when floating was so much easier, so painless.

But the hand pulled at him, and he was powerless to resist it. When his feet touched bottom for an instant, the pain took this as a sign that it was safe to return. Stabbing, jabbing, cutting, it filled his side, bending him over until his feet floated free and his face plunged into the water. But the hand, relentless, grabbed at his hair again, jerking him sideways and forward, away from the pleasant safety of the deep water, the ease and weightless comfort it offered. He allowed himself to be pulled a metre forward through the water and then another, and then suddenly he could go no farther. Quite reasonably, he thought, he reached to place his right hand on the fingers that still tugged at him. He patted them once, twice, and then in his most reasonable voice, he said, 'Thank you, but that's enough.' Like the tree in the uninhabited forest, his words went unheard, and then an enormous wave rolled across him.

25

Like a beached whale, Brunetti lay on the sand, unable to move. He'd swallowed a great deal of water, and fierce coughing had exhausted him. He lay in the rain as waves came and flirted with his feet and legs, as if to suggest he stop lying there on the sand and come in and have a proper swim. Their solicitations went unheeded. Occasionally, and entirely without conscious thought, he clawed and pushed himself forward a few centimetres, away from the frolicsome waves.

His panic diminished, then slowly left him as he lay there. The howling of the wind was no less fierce, the lash of the rain no less severe, but somehow the solidity beneath him, the safety of beach, sand, mother earth, lulled him into a sense of protected calm. His mind began to drift, and he found himself thinking that his jacket would have to be taken to the cleaners, was perhaps ruined entirely, and he minded that, for it was his best jacket, one he'd treated himself to when sent to Milan last year to testify, finally, in a court case concerning a murder that had been committed twelve years before. The thought passed through his mind that these were indeed strange thoughts to be entertaining in his present circumstances, and then he reflected upon his own ability to find these particular thoughts strange. How proud Paola, who always accused him of having a simple mind, would be when he told her of how very convoluted his thoughts had become, becalmed on a beach somewhere beyond Pellestrina. She'd mind about the jacket, too, he was sure; she'd always said it was the nicest one he had.

He lay prone in the rain and thought of his wife, and after a time that thought led him to pull one knee, and then the other, under him, and then it helped prod him to his feet. He looked around and saw nothing; his hearing was still dulled by the wind and rain. He turned in the direction from which he thought he must have come, searching for some sign of the boat or the single spotlight that had still been ablaze when he leaped from the deck, but darkness was everywhere.

He put his head back and yelled into the tempest, 'Montisi, Montisi!' When only the wind replied, he called again, 'Paolo, Paolo!' but still he heard no answer. He walked ahead a few steps, his hands stretched out in front of him like a blind man's calling as he went. After a few moments, his left hand hit against something: a flat surface rising up in front of him. This must be the wall of the abandoned fort of Ca' Roman, known to him only as a mark and a name on a map.

He moved closer until his chest touched the wall, then he spread his arms to explore outwards on both sides. Sticking close to the wall, he moved slowly to the right, turning to the side so that he could use both hands to feel ahead of him.

He heard a noise behind him and stopped, surprised, not by the noise itself so much as by the fact that he could hear it. He tried to empty his mind and listened afresh to the sound of the storm; after a time he grew certain that its sound was diminishing. Clearly, there, he heard what must be the crashing of a wave, the thunderous pelting of water on hard sand. As he listened, it seemed that the wind became still milder; as it decreased in intensity, he grew colder, though that might be nothing more than the passing of the dullness of shock. He untied the life jacket and let it fall to the ground.

He took a few more steps, reaching ahead of him, fingers delicate as a snail's antennae. Suddenly the surface disappeared beneath his left hand, and when he reached into the nothingness, he could feel the hard rectangularity surrounding a lintel or passageway. He outlined it, still unseeing, with the fingers of both hands and then placed a tentative foot into its centre, hunting for a step or stairway, either up or down.

A low step carried his foot down. Propping both hands on what seemed to be the sides of a narrow passageway, he went down one, two, three steps until he felt a wider area beneath his carefully exploring foot.

In the silence, cut off from the sound of the wind, his other senses sprang to life, and he was overwhelmed by the stink of urine and mould and he knew not what else. Inside, away from the buffeting wind, he should have grown warmer, but if anything, he now felt far colder than he had outside, as though the silence gave penetrating force to both cold and humidity.

He stood there, listening, focusing ahead of him on wherever this void would lead him, and backwards, up the steps and out into the diminishing storm. He moved to the right until he touched a wall, then turned and braced his back against it, comforted by stability. He stood like that for a long time until, glancing in what he thought was the direction of the opening, he saw light filtering in from the outside. He walked towards it, and when he stood in the glow it cast, he held his watch up to his face. Astonished to see that it was still only early evening, he moved closer to the now-illumined steps, drawn by the promise of light and by the silence that spilled down the steps.

He emerged into splendour: to the west, the sun made its languorous way towards the horizon, dipping behind the scattered clouds the passing storm had forgotten to sweep away and dappling the still waters of the *laguna* with their reflection. He turned to the east and, not far removed from the coast, saw the rear edge of the storm, thrashing its way towards what was left of Yugoslavia, as if eager to see what sort of new damage it could take there.

Brunetti was racked with a sudden chill as hunger, stress and the slow drop in temperature had their way with his body. He wrapped his arms around himself and moved forward. Again, he called Montisi's name, and again he heard nothing in response. From what he could see, the land around him was surrounded on three sides by water with a thin trail of narrow beach leading off to the north. His recent study of the map of the *laguna* told his memory that this must be the sanctuary of Ca' Roman, though whatever wildlife was meant to be protected here was nowhere in evidence, no doubt battered into flight or cover by the recent storm.

He turned and saw the ruined fort behind him. He went back to it: perhaps there were other doors or other entrances in which the pilot might have taken shelter. To the left of the doorway he'd used there was another one, leading up. He climbed up a single flight of stairs, hoping that the movement would bring some relief to his chilling body, but he found neither warmth nor Montisi. He went back outside and returned to where he had started, seeing nothing. Still farther along to the left, he found another door, also leading down.

At the entrance he called the pilot's name. A noise, perhaps a voice, answered him, and he went down the steps. Montisi sat against the wall just at the bottom, his head leaning back against it, his huddled body illuminated by the sun that cascaded down the steps. When he reached the older man, Brunetti could make out the paleness of his face, but he could see that the cut on his head had stopped bleeding. Montisi, too, had discarded his life jacket.

'Come on, Montisi,' he said, making himself sound hearty and in charge. 'Let's get out of here and back to Pellestrina.'

Montisi smiled agreement and started to get to his feet. Brunetti helped him up; once he was upright, the older man seemed fairly steady.

'How are you?' Brunetti asked.

'Got a terrible headache,' the pilot said, smiling, 'but at least I've still got a head to ache.' He freed himself from Brunetti's arm and started up the stairs. At the top, he turned and called back down, 'God, what a storm. Nothing like it since 1927.'

Because the shadow cast by Montisi's body fell down the stairway, blocking the light, Brunetti looked down at the first step to see where to set his foot. When he looked up, he saw that Montisi had sprouted a branch. Even before he registered the impossibility of this, the panic he'd felt during the storm leaped at him.

Men don't grow branches; pieces of wood do not grow out of the chests of men. Not unless they have been pushed in from the other side.

His mind was still processing this information when his body moved. It pushed aside reflection, cause–effect reasoning, and the ability to draw a conclusion, all those things which are said to define humanity. His body pounded up the stairs, he opened his mouth and emitted an animal roar of bare-fanged aggression. Montisi turned, very gently and slowly, like a groom about to kiss his bride, and fell down the steps towards Brunetti. He twisted as he fell, his weight so heavy that Brunetti had no hope of supporting him as he crashed past him. The piece of wood jutting from his chest, a thick sliver that could at one time have been an oar, or a sharp piece of tree limb, dragged across Brunetti's legs, snagging the wool of his trousers and leaving a red welt on his thighs.

Instinct registered that Montisi was beyond help and propelled Brunetti up the stairs and into the fading light of a tranquil spring evening. In front of him stood a short, barrel-chested man, one of the men he'd seen in Signora Follini's store, his hands raised in a wrestler's expectant grasp. He'd been momentarily stunned by Brunetti's shout and now by his sudden appearance, but now he recovered and moved towards Brunetti on wide-spread legs, his thick body compressed with menace. His left hand glowed red in the light of the setting sun.

Brunetti was unarmed. As an adult, words

and wit had always served him as sufficient weaponry, and he had seldom, since becoming a policeman, been called upon to defend himself. But he had been raised a Venetian, in a poor family, with a father given to violence and drink. He had learned early how to defend himself, not only against his father but against anyone who mocked him for his father's behaviour. Civilization dropped from him, and he kicked the man between the legs.

Spadini crumpled, collapsed to the ground with a howl, his hands helplessly clutching at himself. He lay there, moaning and sobbing, paralysed with pain. Brunetti ran down the steps and turned Montisi gently on to his back; the pilot looked back at him with surprised eyes. Brunetti flipped Montisi's jacket open and pulled his clasp knife from the right pocket of his uniform trousers, where he'd seen the pilot put it a hundred times, a thousand times, for more years than Chiara had been alive. Brunetti ran back up the stairs.

The man still lay on the ground; his moans had not decreased. Looking around him, Brunetti saw a plastic shopping bag lying on the ground; he picked it up and, using Montisi's knife, sliced it into strips. He yanked the man's hands away from his body and pulled them behind him. Roughly, wanting to hurt him, Brunetti tied his wrists together, then found another bag and repeated the process, careless of how tightly he drew the strips. He tested them by trying to pull the man's arms apart, but they held fast. He found a third bag, cut it into more strips, and tied the man's ankles together. Then, remembering something he'd once read in a report from Amnesty International, he threaded a strip between the wrists and the ankles and yanked the man's legs up until he was anchored in a backward curve that Brunetti hoped was even more painful than it looked.

More slowly this time, he went back down the steps and over to Montisi. Knowing that the bodies of murder victims must not be touched until the medical examiner has declared them dead, he nevertheless bent down over Montisi and pressed his eyes closed, keeping his fingers pressed against the lids for long seconds. When he took his hands away, the eyes remained shut. He searched the pockets of Montisi's jacket, then of his thermal vest, bloody now, until he found the pilot's *telefonino*.

He went back outside and dialled 112. The phone rang fifteen times before it was answered. Too tired to comment, he gave his name and rank and explained where he was. He gave a brief account of the situation and asked that either a launch or a helicopter be sent immediately.

'This is the Carabinieri, Commissario,' the young officer explained. 'Perhaps it would be better if you called your own commander with your request.'

The chill that had worked itself into Brunetti's bones washed into his voice. 'Officer, it is now 6.37. If your phone log doesn't show you placed a call for a launch or helicopter within the next two minutes, you will regret it.' As he spoke, he began to spin wild plans: to find out this man's name, to have Paola's father use his position to threaten his commander into dismissing him, tell the other pilots who had refused to help Montisi.

Before he got to the end of the list, the man answered, 'Yes, sir,' and hung up.

From memory, he dialled Vianello's number.

'Vianello,' he answered on the third ring.

'It's me, Lorenzo,' Brunetti said.

'What's wrong?'

'Montisi's dead. I'm at Ca' Roman, by the fort.' He waited for Vianello to say something, but the sergeant remained silent, waiting.

'I've got the man who did it. He's here.' The man lay at his feet, his face flushed crimson as he strained at the strips holding him in that painful, helpless curve. Brunetti looked down at him, and the man opened his mouth, either to protest or to implore.

Brunetti kicked him. He didn't aim for any particular place, not for his head and not for his face. He just lashed out with his right foot, and as chance had it, he caught the man on the top of his shoulder, just where it joined his neck. He groaned and went silent.

Brunetti turned his attention back to Vianello. 'I called and told them to send a launch or a helicopter.'

'Who'd you call?' Vianello asked.

'I dialled 112.'

'They're hopeless,' Vianello decreed. 'I'll call Massimo and get out there in half an hour. Where are you, exactly?'

'By the fort,' Brunetti said, not at all concerned to know who Massimo was or just what Vianello would do.

'I'll be there,' Vianello said and hung up.

Brunetti put the *telefonino* into the pocket of his jacket, forgetting to switch it off. Without so much as a glance at the man on the ground, he went and sat on an immense stone by the wall of the fort. He leaned back against the wall and stared off to the west, his face warmed by the fading rays of the sun. He took his hands from his armpits and held the palms out towards the sun, as a chilled man would towards a fire. He thought of removing his jacket but decided it would take too much effort to do so, even though he knew he'd be warmer if he could free himself of its sodden weight.

He waited for something to happen. Nothing much did. The man on the ground moaned and moved around but Brunetti bothered to look at him only occasionally and then only to assure himself that his ankles and hands were still securely tied. At one point, he found himself thinking that, if he were to pick up one of the stones that lay nearby and hit the man on the front of the head with it, he could claim the man had attacked him after killing Montisi and he'd died during the ensuing struggle. It troubled Brunetti to find himself thinking this, but it troubled him even more to realize he was dissuaded from action, at least in part, by his realization that the marks of the ligatures on the man's wrists and ankles would show what had really happened.

Slowly, taking the warmth of the day with it, the sun surrendered itself to the grey flatness of the coastline. To the north, the light faded, erasing the jagged ramparts and jutting spires of that horror, Marghera. He heard a fly buzz. Listening intently, he realized it was not a fly but the sound of a motor, sharp and high and approaching at great speed. A launch from the Questura? Vianello and the heroic Massimo? Brunetti had no idea which of his possible saviours it might be; it could just as easily be a passing taxi or some waterborne commuter hurrying home, now that the storm was over and peace restored. He thought for a moment of what a comfort it would be to see Vianello, tough and bear-like Vianello, and then he remembered that Vianello was Montisi's greatest friend on the force.

He had three children, Montisi: a doctor, a psychologist and an archaeologist, and it had all been done on the salary of a police pilot. Yet Montisi had always been the first to insist on paying for a round of coffees or drinks; police rumour had it that he and his wife helped support a young Bosnian woman who had studied archaeology with their youngest son and needed to pass only two more exams before graduation. Brunetti had no idea if this were true, and now he'd probably never know. It hardly mattered, though.

The buzzing grew closer, then stopped, and he heard a man's voice shout his name.

26

Brunetti pushed himself to his feet, feeling for the first time in his life a warning shot from the territory of age. So this was what it would be like, the aching hip, the long pull of muscles in the thighs, the unsteadiness of the ground under his feet, and the overwhelming realization that everything was simply too much trouble. He started towards the beach, heading in the general direction of the voice that had called his name. Once he stumbled when his right foot caught in a trailing plant, and another time he started back in fear when a bird shot up from under his feet, no doubt warning him away from her nest.

Protecting her young, protecting her young, and who to protect Montisi's children, even though they were no longer young? He heard a noise from the opposite direction and looked up, hoping to see Vianello, but it was Signorina Elettra. At least, a bedraggled young woman who looked very much like Signorina Elettra. One sleeve of her jacket was gone, and through a long tear in her slacks, he could see her calf. One foot was bare, a bloody scrape across the top of her instep. But it was her hair that most surprised him, for in a wide patch just above her right ear it was cut short, no more than a few centimetres from her head. It stuck out like the hair on the tops of the ears of baby jaguars and was little longer than that.

'Are you all right?' he asked.

She raised a hand towards Brunetti. 'Come and find him. Please.' She didn't wait for him to answer but turned and made off in the direction from which she must have come. He noticed that she favoured her left foot, the one without a shoe.

'*Signore*,' he heard Vianello say behind him.

Brunetti turned and saw him, dressed in jeans and a heavy woollen sweater. Over his arm he carried a second one. Behind him stood another man in civilian clothes, a hunting rifle in one hand: no doubt the Massimo that Vianello said would bring him out so quickly.

'There's a man over there by the fort, on the ground. Watch him,' Brunetti called to the man with the gun, then beckoned to Vianello and set off after Signorina Elettra.

The beach was littered with all sorts of junk,

the hundreds of things that get stirred up from the bottom of the *laguna* by every storm and left to rot until a tide or a new storm carries them back to their watery dump. He saw pieces of life buoys, countless plastic bottles, some with their tops screwed on tightly; there were large hunks of fishing net, shoes and boots, plastic cutlery, seemingly enough for an army. Each time he saw a piece of wood, a sliver of oar or branch, he turned his eyes away, looking for bottles or plastic cups.

When they came upon her, she was kneeling on the sand at the edge of the water. Lying in the shallow water just in front of her was a fishing boat. Its left side was stove in, and the water around it was covered with an expanding slick of black oil.

Hearing them approach, she looked up. 'I don't know what happened, but he's gone.'

Vianello walked over to her, draped the sweater around her shoulders, and offered her his hand to help her to her feet. She ignored him and pulled the sweater down from her shoulders, letting it drop on the sand

Vianello squatted down beside her. Fussily, he picked up the sweater and placed it back over her shoulders, tying the arms together under her chin. 'Come with us now,' he said and got to his feet, helping her to stand beside him.

He started to speak but stopped when he heard a noise from the direction of Pellestrina. The three of them, like chickens on a perch, turned their heads in the direction of the sharp keening that announced the arrival of the Carabinieri.

Elettra began to shiver uncontrollably.

They stood on the beach and waited while the Carabinieri launch approached. It swept up in a tight curve, and the pilot killed the motor and drifted to a stop a few metres offshore. Three flak-jacketed officers at the bow held shotguns aimed at the people on the beach. When the man at the wheel recognized Vianello and called out to the others to lower their guns, they did so, though with a certain reluctance.

'Two of you come and help her,' Brunetti called out, ignoring the fact that even his rank gave him no authority over these men. 'Take her back to the hospital.' The three officers looked to their pilot for instruction. He nodded. There was no landing stage, so they would have to jump into the surf and wade ashore. While they hesitated, Signorina Elettra turned to Brunetti and said, 'I can't go back without him.'

Before Brunetti could answer, Vianello turned to Elettra and picked her up bodily, one arm around her shoulder, the other under her knees. He walked into the water and waded out to the boat. Brunetti saw her start to protest, but her words, as well as Vianello's response, were cut off by the noise of his splashing. When Vianello reached the side of the boat, one of the Carabinieri knelt and reached over the side, taking Signorina Elettra from his arms.

He sat her upright and Brunetti saw Vianello reach into the boat and adjust the sweater over her shoulders, then the motor sprang into life again, and the boat started to move away. Vianello standing in the water and Brunetti on the beach both watched as it grew smaller, but Signorina Elettra did not turn back to them.

Vianello came back to the shore, and silently the two of them returned to Massimo and his prisoner. They found Vianello's friend sitting on the stone where Brunetti had waited earlier, his rifle lying across his knees. The bound man cried out when he saw them approach. 'Cut me loose!' He shouted it as an order. The men ignored him.

'Montisi's down there,' Brunetti said, indicating the doorway and the steps running down from it. It was harder to see down inside now that the light was abandoning the day.

'Massimo,' Vianello said, turning to his friend. 'Give me the flashlight.' From one of the many pockets of his hunting jacket, Massimo took a thin black flashlight and held it out to Vianello.

'Wait here,' Brunetti said to the man with the gun. They went down together, the light streaming out in front of them. As they descended the steps, Brunetti pleaded with something he didn't believe in to let them somehow find Montisi alive down there; wounded and stunned but alive. He had long ago abandoned his childhood habit of trying to cut a deal with whoever it was that might control these things, and so he merely asked for it to be true, offering nothing in return.

But Montisi, though certainly wounded, was

not alive, and never again would he be stunned by anything. His last earthly shock had been the sudden explosion of pain in his chest as he turned back towards Brunetti from the steps, making his joke about still having a head and marvelling at the power of the storm.

Vianello flashed the light across his friend's face for just a moment, then let his hand fall to his side. The light illuminated his shoes, a filthy patch of ground, and Montisi's left shoulder, just enough to show the jagged point of wood that protruded so inappropriately from his chest.

After a minute, Vianello went back to the stairway, careful to keep the light from shining on Montisi's face again. Brunetti followed him. At the top, they saw that Vianello's friend hadn't moved, nor had the rifle, nor had the hog-tied man.

'Please,' the bound man pleaded, all threat, all menace gone from his voice. 'Please.'

Vianello took a knife from the back pocket of his jeans, flicked it open, and knelt down over him. Idly, Brunetti wondered if the sergeant were going to cut the man's bonds or his throat and couldn't find it in himself to care much, either way. He watched as the hand holding the knife disappeared, blocked from sight by Vianello's body. The man's body twitched, and his legs swung forward, cut free of his wrists.

He lay still for a moment, gasping with the pain it caused him to move. Motionless, he watched Vianello through narrowed eyes. The sergeant pushed the blade closed with the palm of his right hand and reached around to slip the knife back into his pocket. The bound man chose that instant to strike. He pulled his knees towards his chest, gasping at the pain it caused his stretched muscles to do it, and struck out at Vianello with his bound feet, striking him just at the hip and knocking him sprawling.

He pulled his feet back, cocking them in order to kick Vianello again, but Massimo got to his feet as the man was still in motion and walked over to him, holding the rifle upside down. The bound man sensed the presence looming over him and relaxed, stretching his feet out in front of him, away from Vianello, who was struggling to his feet. 'All right, all right. I stopped,' Spadini said and smiled. Massimo, quite casually, brought the rifle up into the air and plunged it down, smashing the butt into Spadini's nose. Brunetti could hear it break, a wet, crunching sound, like the sound of stepping on a cockroach or a water beetle.

Spadini howled and rolled away in circles to escape the man with the rifle, his hands trapped behind his back. Calmly, Massimo set the butt of the gun into a tuft of sandy grass at his feet. After he'd wiped it back and forth a half-dozen times, he inspected the butt, finding it clean enough. Ignoring the sobs of the man whose shattered nose continued to leak blood on to the sand below his head, Massimo went back to the stone by the wall and sat down again.

He glanced at Brunetti. 'I used to go fishing with Montisi.'

No one said anything until a Carabinieri all-terrain vehicle arrived from Pellestrina and sped across the sand towards them, careless of the destruction it caused to the dunes or to the nesting birds who could not escape its wheels.

27

The Carabinieri who emerged from the jeep
showed little surprise at what they saw, and
when Brunetti finally explained things to them,
they seemed even less interested in his story.
One of them went down the stairs to the bunker;
when he came back, he was already talking on
his *telefonino*, calling for an ambulance to come
and pick up the body.

In the meantime, the other two had pushed
Spadini into the jeep, not bothering to untie his
hands and leaving him propped on the back seat
like an unsteady package. Neither Brunetti nor
Vianello was willing to leave Montisi's body
unattended, so they refused the offer to accom-
pany the others back to the Carabinieri post on
the Lido. As they watched, one of the

Carabinieri climbed into the back seat beside Spadini, then the other two got into the front and their jeep sped away.

Vianello's bulk no longer held out the promise of animal comfort to Brunetti, so he walked down to the edge of the water. Vianello let him go, choosing to stand to the left of the doorway leading down to the bunker. For a while, he watched the motionless Brunetti, himself watching the motionless city in the distance, visible again now that the storm had passed. Both of them were sodden and chilled but neither of them paid any particular attention to this until Massimo came back from his boat with a captain's jacket for Brunetti. He helped the Commissario remove his own jacket and held the other for him while he stuffed his arms into the sleeves. Brunetti's jacket remained on the ground. At the sound of a siren approaching from the north, Vianello turned his attention to that and abandoned his commander to his reflections.

Brunetti returned to the fort when he heard the ambulance pull up. Neither he nor Vianello went down the stairs to help the two attendants with the stretcher. When they emerged, their burden tilted awkwardly to enable them to manoeuvre it up the steps and through the narrow doorway, a blue cloth lay draped over it, its centre projecting like a narrow pyramid. The attendants went to the back of the ambulance and slid the stretcher through the doors. Before they closed them, Brunetti and Vianello climbed inside and pulled down the folding seats at either side. Silently, they rode back to Lido, and then back to Venice on a water ambulance with the equally silent Montisi.

At the Questura, Brunetti initiated the process of formally charging Spadini with the murder of Montisi. At best, and Brunetti knew this, the evidence linking him with the murders of the Bottins and of Signora Follini was no more than circumstantial: though he could be shown to have motive, no evidence had yet been found to link him directly with either crime. He would certainly have alibis, and they would certainly turn out to be, all of them, from fishermen, all of whom were guaranteed to swear that Spadini had been with them when the two men were murdered and when Signora Follini drowned.

Brunetti told the morgue attendants not to touch the wooden stake that had killed Montisi, and he ordered that a technician be sent to take fingerprints from it before it was removed from his body. It was unlikely that, this time, Spadini would find someone able to provide him an alibi.

His thoughts turned to Montisi's widow and to their three children, now fatherless. Men go about their business of killing one another, often in defence of their honour, that most meretricious of baubles, leaving women to pay the price. The thought of an other woman, Signorina Elettra, came into his mind, and he wondered what grief all of this would cost her.

Pushing this away, he got up from his desk and, hardly conscious of the thought of honour, went to speak to Montisi's widow.

Later, at home, he explained as much as he could to Paola. 'All she kept saying was that he had less than a year, that all he wanted to do was go fishing and enjoy his grandchildren.' The words clung to him, like the fiery robes that had destroyed Creon's daughter: no matter how he twisted and turned, trying to pull free of them, they stuck to him, burning.

Brunetti and Paola sat talking on the terrace, the children huddled like anchorites in their rooms, preparing for the year-end exams. To the west, the light was long gone away from all of them, leaving behind only sound and the memory of form and line.

'What will she do?' Paola asked

'Who? Anna?' he asked, thinking still of Montisi's widow.

'No. She has her family. Elettra.'

Startled by the question, he answered, 'I don't know. I hadn't thought.'

'Is he dead, the young man?' she asked.

'They're looking for him,' was the only answer Brunetti could give.

'Who?'

'The Guardia di Finanza sent two boats out, and we've got a launch looking for him.'

'And?' Paola asked, familiar with this sort of answer.

'I doubt it. Not after a storm like this.'

Paola could think of nothing to say to this and so asked, instead, 'And the uncle?'

Brunetti had spent the last hours considering this. 'I doubt we'll get anyone on Pellestrina to say they know anything about the murders there. Even with someone like Spadini, they still won't talk.'

'God, and we say it's Southerners who are crippled by ideas about *omertà*,' Paola exclaimed. When Brunetti didn't respond to this, she asked, 'What about Montisi?'

'There's no way he can get out of that. He'll get twenty years,' Brunetti said, thinking how little difference it seemed to make.

Neither of them spoke for a long time.

At last, turning her thoughts to life, Paola asked, 'Will Elettra get over it?'

'I don't know,' Brunetti demurred, then added, surprising himself, 'I don't really know her that well.'

Paola gave this a great deal of thought and finally answered, 'We never know them well, do we?'

'Who?'

'Real people.'

'What do you mean, "real people"?'

'As opposed to people in books,' Paola explained. 'They're the only ones we ever really know well, or know truly.' Again she gave him a moment to consider, then said, 'Maybe that's because they're the only ones about whom we get reliable information.' She glanced at him, then added, as she would to a class, just to see if they were following, 'Narrators never lie.'

'And my perception of you?' he asked, voice close to indignation, driven towards anger by the seeming irrelevance of this conversation or by the circumstances in which she'd chosen to begin it. 'Isn't that true?'

She smiled. 'As real as mine of you.'

His response was immediate. 'I don't like that answer.'

'That's neither here nor there, my dear.' They lapsed into silence. After a long time, she reached across to him and placed her hand on his arm. 'She'll be all right so long as she's still sure that her friends love her.'

It did not occur to Brunetti to question her use of the word 'love'.

'We do.'

'I know,' Paola said and went to check on the children.

ALSO AVAILABLE IN ARROW

A Noble Radiance

Donna Leon

In a small village at the foot of the Italian Dolomites, the gardens of a deserted farmhouse have lain untouched for decades. But the new owner, keen for renovations to begin, is summoned urgently to the house when his workmen disturb a macabre grave.

Wild animals have done their grisly work and the human corpse is badly decomposed. Then a valuable signet ring is found close by, providing the first vital clue. It leads Commissario Guido Brunetti right to the heart of aristocratic Venice, to a family still grieving for their abducted son . . .

'The marvel of this book is that almost every detail on every page forms part of a succession of clues, planted with exquisite precision, to unravelling the mystery of Roberto's death.'
Sunday Times

'Goes a long way to confirming Donna Leon's claim to have taken literary possession of Venice . . . *A Noble Radiance* finds her at the height of her power. It gives the reader a delightful foretaste of the summer holidays to come, but also offers much more than that.'
Independent on Sunday

'An intriguing mystery, with an alluring backdrop of a corrupt and aristocratic Venice.'
Evening Standard

arrow books

Friends in High Places

Donna Leon

When Commissario Guido Brunetti is visited by a young bureaucrat investigating the lack of official approval for the building of his apartment years earlier, his first reaction, like any other Venetian, is to think of whom he knows who might bring pressure to bear on the relevant government department. But when the bureaucrat rings Brunetti at work, clearly scared, and is then found dead after a fall from scaffolding; something is obviously going on that has implications greater than the fate of Brunetti's apartment . . .

'Leon tells the story as if she loves Venice as much as her detective does, warts and all. The plot and subplots unfold elegantly; beauty and the beast march hand in hand, and the result is rich entertainment.'
Sunday Times

'All Donna Leon's novels are excellent in their evocation of place, whilst in Brunetti she has created a character, who becomes more real in each book . . . However, *Friends in High Places* is by far the best and makes a quantum leap forward.'
Evening Standard

arrow books

ALSO AVAILABLE IN ARROW

Fatal Remedies

Donna Leon

It began with an early morning phone call. A sudden act of vandalism had just been committed in the chill Venetian dawn. But Commissario Guido Brunetti soon finds out that the perpetrator is no petty criminal. For the culprit waiting to be apprehended at the scene is none other than Paola Brunetti, his wife.

As Paola's actions provoke a crisis in the Brunetti household, Brunetti himself is under increasing pressure at work: a daring robbery with Mafia connections is then linked to a suspicious death and his superiors need quick results. As his professional and personal lives clash, Brunetti's own career is under threat – and the conspiracy which Paola risked everything to expose draws him inexorably to the brink . . .

'Donna Leon has established Commissario Guido Brunetti as one of the most engaging of fictional detectives . . . Brunetti is . . . back on track, sadder perhaps, but wiser and wittier than ever.'
Sunday Times

'A splendid series . . . with a backdrop of the city so vivid you can smell it.'
Sunday Telegraph

arrow books

Uniform Justice

Donna Leon

Neither Commissario Brunetti nor his wife Paola have ever had much sympathy for the Italian armed forces, so when a young cadet is found hanged, a presumed suicide, in Venice's elite military academy, Brunetti's emotions are complex: pity and sorrow for the death of a boy, close in age to his own son, and contempt and irritation for the arrogance and high-handedness of the boy's teachers and fellow-students.

The young man is the son of a doctor and former politician, a man of an impeccable integrity all too rare in Italian politics. But as Brunetti – and the indispensable Signorina Elettra – investigate further into the doctor's political career and his familiy circumstances, no-one seems willing to talk, as the military protects its own and civilians – even the boy's parents – keep their own counsel. Is this the natural reluctance of Italians to involve themselves with the authorities, or is Brunetti facing a conspiracy of silence?

'Brunetti . . . long ago joined the ranks of the classic fictional detectives.'
Evening Standard

'Complex and thought-provoking and lingers in the mind.'
Sunday Times

'Wonderfully familiar characters, a powerful sense of place and expert plotting . . . A page-turner with real psychological depth and a disturbing, quiet power.'
Guardian

'Read it in the dusk, with a grappa.'
Libby Purves in the *Good Book Guide*

arrow books

Blood From A Stone

Donna Leon

On a cold Venetian night shortly before Christmas, a street vendor is killed in Campo Santo Stefano. The closest witnesses to the event are the tourists who had been browsing the man's wares before his death – fake handbags of every designer label. The dead man had been working as a *vú cumprá*, one of the many Black Africans purveying goods out of hours, trading without work permits.

When Commissario Brunetti arrives on the scene, his response is that of everybody involved: why would anyone kill an illegal immigrant? They have few social connections and little money; in-fighting is the obvious answer. But once Brunetti begins to investigate this unfamiliar Venetian underworld, he discovers that matters of great value are at stake .

'Comfort reading of the highest order.' *TLS*

'[Leon's] passion for all things Venetian – churches, palaces, statues and especially the food – comes over loud and clear . . . No one writes about the grey areas of life better.' *Guardian*

'The thoughtful and charming [Brunetti] is on top form . . . His nicely balanced world . . . is cumulatively engrossing.'
Sunday Times

arrow books

Suffer the Little Children

Donna Leon

When Commissario Brunetti is summoned to the hospital bedside of a senior pediatrician whose skull has been fractured, he is confronted with more questions than answers. Three men – a Carabinieri captain and two privates from out of town – have burst into the doctor's apartment in the middle of the night, attacked him and taken away his eighteen-month old baby. What can have motivated such a violent assault by the police?

But then Brunetti begins to uncover a story of infertility, desperation, and an underworld in which babies can be bought for cash, at the same time as Inspector Vianello uncovers a money-making scam between pharmacists and doctors in the city. But one of the pharmacists is motivated by more than thoughts of gain – the power of knowledge and delusions of moral rectitude can be as destructive and powerful as love of money. And the uses of information about one's neighbours can lead to all kinds of corruption and all sorts of pain . . .

Praise for Donna Leon:

'*Through A Glass, Darkly*, like all her work, has the exuberance of a Puccini opera.' *Independent*

'A joy from start to finish.'
Evening Standard

THE POWER OF READING

Visit the Random House website and get connected with information on all our books and authors

EXTRACTS from our recently published books and selected backlist titles

COMPETITIONS AND PRIZE DRAWS Win signed books, audiobooks and more

AUTHOR EVENTS Find out which of our authors are on tour and where you can meet them

LATEST NEWS on bestsellers, awards and new publications

MINISITES with exclusive special features dedicated to our authors and their titles

READING GROUPS Reading guides, special features and all the information you need for your reading group

LISTEN to extracts from the latest audiobook publications

WATCH video clips of interviews and readings with our authors

RANDOM HOUSE INFORMATION including advice for writers, job vacancies and all your general queries answered

Come home to Random House
www.rbooks.co.uk